SO LONG AS YOU NEED ME

Twins are seldom really alike, although they may look alike. So it was with the Rushton twins. These two attractive nurses were poles apart by nature. One was serious, and in love with her job—the other gay, and always in trouble. This leads them to switch their jobs, with intriguing results.

You will find Magda an enchanting heroine, but the gay and fun-loving Copper will make an equally irresistible appeal.

SO LONG AS YOU NEED ME

Kay Winchester

Curley Publishing, Inc.
South Yarmouth, Ma.

Library of Congress Cataloging-in-Publication Data

Winchester, Kay.
  So long as you need me / Kay Winchester.
     p. cm.
  ISBN 0–7927–0094–5 (lg. print)
  1. Large type books.   I. Title.
[PR6073.I476S6   1989]   89–35614
823′.914—dc20   CIP

Published in Large Print by arrangement with the author

Printed in Great Britain

CHAPTER ONE

ACROSS the expanse of white and gold satin that was Sylvia Brand's eiderdown, the two women faced each other. The little nurse red-faced and confused, her brown eyes glinting with a mixture of embarrassment and anger. The other woman slightly amused, slightly annoyed, her pencilled eyebrows delicately raised in an unspoken question.

'When St. Joseph's undertake to send me a nurse called "Magda Rushton" I am rather put out to find that on arrival she turns out to be "Lily-Ann" Rushton, without any explanation.'

'Well . . . St. Joseph's don't know,' the nurse offered, her flushed face rapidly cooling, leaving a milky complexion that was lovely enough to need little make-up. Under her starched cap with its flowing tails, red hair, thick wavy red hair, peeped. Sylvia Brand wasn't sure that she approved of such a good-looking young nurse.

'I see. Am I supposed to pretend it hasn't happened, or am I entitled to know what caused the switch? I suppose it *is* a switch?'

'Oh, yes. Magda's my sister. Look, Mrs.

1

Brand, if I tell you what happened, promise you won't tell? We'll get into awful trouble, but you won't suffer at all by the change.'

'How do you know I won't?'

'Well, there isn't a lot to choose between our nursing, but whereas my patients get cheered up as well as nursed back to health, my sister Magda's a bit on the serious side,' the little nurse said, with an impudent grin.

Sylvia Brand's eyes narrowed. She didn't like surprises nor did she like the people she employed to do things without her consent. On the other hand, she loathed serious people, and this girl looked rather fun.

'Well, I'll think about it. Now you'd better talk fast, young woman, and make the story good.'

Lily-Ann smiled.

'Magda was detailed to come down here and she couldn't manage it. We get into awful trouble at the hospital if we flunk—I mean, if we don't keep the appointments given to us. So she asked me to come, on the grounds that she'd take the appointment given to me the next day. I said I would.'

'Why?' Sylvia Brand asked, coolly.

Lily-Ann bit her lip, then made up her mind suddenly and took the plunge.

'I'd heard from other nurses you'd had

before, that you were an awfully good sport,' she said, smiling wickedly from under absurdly long dark lashes.

Against her will, Sylvia Brand's small pretty face broke into a smile.

'Well! What a reputation to have! I suppose you were also told that I was awfully rich and not really ill, eh?'

The nurse looked prim.

'Certainly not,' she began, then chuckled. 'Are you going to report me, Mrs. Brand?'

'I don't know,' Sylvia Brand said, slowly. 'I never make rash promises, nor do I do things without expecting something in return. If I keep mum about this most unethical and really dreadful thing you two have done, will you hold yourself ready to do anything I ask in return?'

'Oh, rather!'

'By the way, what happens when you go back and they find out it isn't your sister who was on this job?'

'I don't suppose anyone will know. You see, we're twins. No one can tell us apart if I go about looking awfully solemn.'

'Oh!' Sylvia Brand frowned in concentration. 'Now that *is* interesting. By the way, it's two days since you arrived. That means your sister got her appointment, I suppose.

What did she get?'

'Oh, someone perfectly awful,' Lily-Ann grinned. 'One of the hospital governors. He had a car accident. He's bad enough without being a patient, but now he's got his leg trussed up to the ceiling—oh!'

She clapped her hand to her mouth. Her patient was sitting up, leaning on one elbow, an interested expression on her face, an amused pucker round her mouth.

'I suppose you mean Andrew Debenham?' she said, coolly.

'Oh,' wailed Lily-Ann, 'why don't I shut my mouth? I forgot he lived in this district! So you know him! Now I *have* done it.' She worriedly pushed her hair under her cap, and Mrs. Brand guessed that she was always trying to hide it, probably on account of its colour. 'I'm always blurting things out. I've got no tact.'

'So I see. Well, Lily-Ann, at least you'll amuse me while you're here. By the way, what do they call you at the hospital? I can't manage that awful name—how on earth did you get it?'

'Two aunts,' the nurse said, making a moué. 'My friends call me "Copper".'

'That'll do. Now bring me my make-up box and clear out. I think you and I are going to get on well together.'

Sylvia Brand's home lay in a hollow. A new, luxury-built house that her late husband had designed for her. Just a little vulgar in its taste, but the evidence of wealth lay everywhere.

Vigorously smearing cream into her face after Copper had gone, Sylvia remembered him again. Flashes of him came vividly, and this one came principally because Copper had mentioned Andrew Debenham. Andrew was everything that Sylvia's late husband had not been. Young—well, certainly not more than thirty-five—and very good-looking in a dark, taciturn way. You could rarely tell what he was thinking, and it was fun finding out. But poor Horace had been none of these things. He had been not so young, and rather boring. Terribly obvious, too. You knew what he was thinking all the time, and most of the time the poor man had been thinking of ways in which he could keep his pretty young wife interested and amused. Sylvia thought it might be interesting to see what sort of efforts Andrew Debenham might make to keep her amused, but so far the going had been slow. And now he had a young, red-headed nurse who was reputed to be exactly like her twin sister, and if that were so, then she was very good-looking indeed.

Sylvia thrust her make-up box away, and reached for the telephone. Debenham Mount was on a rise, and had been in Andrew's family for generations. Sylvia could see it, in wintertime, when the trees were bare, from her own bedroom window. It had nothing of bad taste about it. Old stones, some pretence of fine architecture mellowed by time, and covered with creepers. Inside, it was mainly oak. Mellow oak walls, floors and furniture. Too much oak, Sylvia considered, but there was plenty of time to change all that. But despite its age, it was modernised to the extent of electric light and the telephone.

She smiled as Hobbs answered. Cautiously, very cautiously, he said he would find out from the nurse if the master was well enough to take a telephone call. After a little while Andrew's voice came through.

'Well, well, who is it?'

Testy, more testy than usual, Sylvia thought, with raised brows. Perhaps his accident had indeed been a bad one. But then poor Andrew was hardly likely to take an excuse for a rest in bed, as she often did!

'Andrew, I won't stay a minute on the line,' she said, in her nicest voice. 'I just wanted to say "hallo" and to ask how you were.'

6

'If I told you in medical terms just what I'm suffering from, you'd be none the wiser. So I'll put it in plain language. My leg is knocked about. It's in plaster. It isn't pretty, and the pain's hellish. Good-bye.'

'No, wait, Andrew. Don't be a beast. I wanted to ask you what your nurse was like. Is she efficient?'

'All St. Joseph's nurses are efficient, and it was my bad luck that my own hospital was too full for even a bed for me to be wangled,' he said, bitterly.

'So that you wouldn't be pestered by telephone calls?' she queried, laughing. 'I'll be kind, and leave you alone. But when I'm well, I shall visit you—'

'When you're *what?*' he broke in.

She rang off, laughing. The fact that she had once had a hunting accident and still professed to feel occasional pain in her back deceived no one, least of all Andrew. But it was a badly wrenched ankle this time, and she hated the thought of Andrew laughing at her cry of "wolf". She knew he also despised wealthy women who hired his nurses when he had better use for them.

The last time, Andrew had threatened to have her examined at the hospital, and said she should change her doctor.

7

'My back really does bother me,' she had told him earnestly. 'My own doctor is only going on my accounts of pain, and I am in pain.'

'Rheumatism,' Andrew had said, curtly.

She wondered what he was like to have to look after, and tried to visualise his bedroom, that very masculine room which she had seen only once, when it had been refurnished, and Andrew's aunt had taken her to see it. Nice old Mrs. Debenham who managed his household so perfectly. Much better than a mother-in-law, Sylvia thought, with satisfaction.

But Andrew had infuriated even his nice old aunt, he had been so impossible. The little nurse had regarded her, outside his room, with wide, serious brown eyes, and said nothing.

'Do you often have patients like my nephew, my dear?' Mrs. Debenham had said.

'Often,' Magda assured her, gravely.

'Well, if that is the case, then I can only say that the nursing profession should be honoured much more than it is!'

'It can't be very nice to have such a mess made of your own beautiful bedroom, after having the bad luck to have an accident,' Magda said, soothingly.

'It's my nephew's own stupid fault,' the old

lady said, severely. 'He should have gone into some other hospital, since his own was full. But no, I'm afraid he always was very obstinate.'

During Magda's two free hours that evening, she had a telephone call from Copper, who had cycled into the village.

'How're you feeling, you ass?' Copper shouted.

'Oh, better. Much better, thanks. How's the job?'

'Easy, dead easy. She's only got a sprained ankle,' Copper giggled.

'*What?*'

'Oh, and she's supposed to have pains in her back, and the poor old doctor comes every day and solemnly goes over it. Her back, I mean. One of these days he'll tell her he can't find anything.'

'Why doesn't she have it X-rayed?'

'Search me! Magda, I'm in trouble.'

'Oh, no, not already, Copper?'

'Well, you know me. I started talking, and then, well, I let it out!'

'Let what out?'

'About the switch. Us.'

'Oh, no!'

Magda was more appalled than she sounded.

9

'Copper, you silly fool, don't you know who I got?'

'Yes. One of the hospital governors. I also put my foot in it there, too,' Copper said, and recounted the conversation.

'Oh, now we'll both get the sack,' Magda said, worriedly.

'No, I don't think so. She's a good sport, and I don't think she'll tell.'

'Is she?' Magda asked, doubtfully. From her long experience of nursing, she had found that few women patients were good sports, expecially where red-headed nurses were concerned. With that coloured hair, it seemed that one was regarded with suspicion right from the start, though Magda couldn't see why.

'And has she got money! Honestly, you ought to see her bedroom! Like something in a film! Truly. Hollywood drapes, all satin and frills. And a white carpet with yellow flowers! And her clothes. Oh, old girl, you missed something. But I don't think it's going to last long. It can't, can it? I mean, how long can you keep a nurse binding up an ankle, even if you have got a lot of money?'

'Just as long as you like,' Magda said, firmly. 'Besides, she might really have bad pains in her back. Now listen, Copper, do *try*,

10

darling. Try to keep out of trouble, just for a while, till I pull myself together. I've got a tonic, and I think the country air will do me good. And don't, for heaven's sake, let on about that!'

'I won't!' Copper promised, gaily, and rang off without specifying when she'd contact her twin again.

Magda put the receiver down, and worriedly shrugged herself into her uniform coat for her evening walk. Copper was a lovable scamp, but all the years since they left their home and took up nursing together, she had been constantly in trouble. Copper liked nursing, but life was a lark. She could take nothing terribly seriously.

Magda, on the other hand, loved nursing. It was everything. No patient, even the objectionable Andrew Debenham, was too irritating for Magda to give of her best, and willingly. As Andrew Debenham had already found out.

He had stared at her only that morning, and said: 'Many nurses would have thrown that bowl of water at me! The last time I had an accident, I had nine changes of nurses. They didn't like me.'

Magda smiled faintly, and went on washing him.

11

'They wouldn't stay!' he added, hopefully.

'Well, I shall stay,' she told him, firmly, 'just as long as ever you need me.'

It struck her that he was very like a tiresome schoolboy, conscious of his badness, and rather proud of it; disappointed when he found someone whom he couldn't impress with his badness. Cheated.

'Ah, you won't say that after you've been here a couple of weeks,' he said, with confidence.

He had a dark clever face. Thin, with a high forehead, and wavy black hair that he did his best to brush straight. Hair that was inclined to get turbulent when he was in bed, and unable to get to his brush set. His eyes were steel-blue and keen, and his lips, though thin and firm, had a tender quality about them. Almost as if he was trying to be tough, and didn't always manage to keep up the masquerade.

Magda liked the house and its masculine quality. It was a house that had been lived in and loved by generations of men; men in every sense of the word. Hard-living, hard-riding men. Men who loved horses and dogs, who could handle guns and raise prize cattle. The home farm was still largely presided over by Andrew, between his hospital board duties.

He was a countryman first, and everything else came afterwards.

There were country newspapers and magazines about, and farm catalogues. Guns and weapons on the walls; some modern, others historic. There was a smell of leather and old wood, and there was no modern gas or electric fires; the old open fireplaces yawned in the great rooms as they had for centuries. A house to love.

Magda thought with some amusement, how strangely it had turned out. Copper had been intended for this job. What havoc she would have made in this quiet, dignified place, Magda could only guess at. She herself, on the other hand, would have been miserable in the luxury home in which Copper had alighted. She didn't like too much frippery in a sick-room. Ten chances to one, this Mrs. Brand wouldn't like the windows flung wide, because all her draperies would blow about in the breeze. But Andrew Debenham loved fresh air as she herself did.

What was she to do about Copper, she asked herself? Sooner or later, there would be trouble with that twin sister of hers. Big trouble. There had already been rows at St. Joseph's. There was the time when Copper had insisted on going to that absurd fancy dress ball, and Magda had tried to impersonate her. Just to keep her out of trouble and to give her another chance. But although Copper could imitate Magda's serene, serious manner and quiet voice almost perfectly, Magda was no good whatever at being saucy and gay like Copper, and her impersonation flopped badly. Sister was furious, and Matron was cold. Only Magda's fine record saved her, and Copper was saved only through Magda's pleading for her. Magda had chased round and seen to her own patients, and done the few duties that Copper should have been there to do. Copper hadn't actually been supposed to be on ward duty at the time; just in.

There was never any peace. Perhaps it was this anxiety about Copper, and her own overwork, doing the duties very often for both of them, that had caused Magda's 'turns'. Those curious dizzy spells, and the sickening sense of not being well. She had applied everything she knew, and got the dispenser to mix her a stiff tonic. But nothing made any difference. Behind it all was the nagging anxiety of what would happen if she were to be taken ill, really ill. What would become of herself, or of Copper? Sure enough, Copper would get into bad trouble, and that would be the end for both of them. Neither of them could do anything else except nursing.

Magda liked these outdoor jobs. The hospital was very nice, but it wasn't always easy, working so close among a lot of other women. The probationers were difficult, and a lot of extra work fell on the old hands. And she didn't like the little undercurrents, the intrigues, that went on. Copper did. She thrived on it all, and thought it would be a very dull life without them.

Magda got through her first week fairly well, and was rewarded by old Mrs. Debenham's approval.

'I don't know what you're doing to my nephew, young woman, but you're certainly calming him down. I've never known him to be so amenable before!'

Magda hadn't thought he was at all amenable, but if that were his best, she had the gravest misgivings of what his worst could be like.

'He's in a lot of pain,' she ventured, gently.

'Rubbish!' the old lady said, robustly. 'You should have seen him when he hurt his back, mountain climbing in the Alps. He's crazy. He used to deliberately go to all the most dangerous spots, then he cursed the guides when he had his accident. He cursed his doctors, and insulted his nurses so badly that

15

there was quite a series of them, and one after another they packed up and went, either in indignation or tears. A disgraceful business. But he *was* in some pain at the time. Well, well, this leg may be bad,' she allowed, 'but no pain is bad enough to cause a grown man to behave in an illmannered fashion to his medical advisers and helpers.'

But the second week wasn't so uneventful. Andrew began to chafe against the calm existence which Magda imposed.

'Why don't you answer me back, or throw things, or stalk out of the room and leave me?' he asked, testily, one day. 'All this sweet patience and forbearance gets me! I loathe it. It—damn it, it isn't natural!'

'Why should I do that?' Magda asked, in surprise. 'I'm just here to help the doctor heal your leg. I don't mind what you're like. I may never see you again.'

'D'you know I'm on the Board?' he shouted.

'Yes sir.'

'Well, I could get you sacked!'

'For—being patient and forbearing?' It wasn't cheek, but a slightly puzzled question. He could cheerfully have choked her for it, and also for making him seem so much more ill-behaved than he knew he was being.

'I'm not sure I won't get you sacked!' he threatened. 'And now get out!'

She went quietly, gathering up her thermometer and fountain pen, and the chart. In no way ruffled by his ill humour or the injustice of his remarks. Only when the visitor came that afternoon, did Magda feel the first prick of resentment, because she saw how he could really be to a woman if he liked. At least, that was what she put the reason down to.

The visitor was a lovely creature, blonde and frail, helped in on two sticks by the chauffeur. A slender young woman in a pale summery flowered dress and shady hat, and long white kid gloves. Dressed for a garden-party, Magda thought in amusement, not for a visit to a sick-bed.

Only when she helped her into Andrew's room, and Andrew sat up in bed with a mixture of incredulity and amusement, did Magda realise who the visitor was.

'Sylvia Brand!' he shouted, and went into peals of hearty masculine laughter.

'Hallo, Andrew,' Mrs. Brand said, easily, and flicked a glance at Magda. A glance which seemed to say, 'Well, clear out . . . what are you waiting for?'

As Magda closed the door behind her, she heard Andrew say, in his strong, carrying voice: 'You fraud, what dragged you from your sick-bed? Oh, but it's good to see you. You look like something out of a Bond Street window. I'm fed-up with the rustle of starched uniform. You look good enough to eat!'

Magda wondered why Copper hadn't come with Mrs. Brand. In the ordinary way, the nurse would accompany the patient on her outings, if she couldn't walk, and undoubtedly Mrs. Brand's foot was still giving her trouble. It seemed rather soon to be about on it, Magda thought, with a frown. And what had happened to the pains in the back? Magda hoped that Copper hadn't been giving rein to her particular brand of humour, and made the patient wish to be inordinately quick in getting about again and so dispensing with her services. That had happened once before.

In the days that followed, Magda soon found out why Mrs. Brand had got about so soon. Mrs. Brand came visiting at Debenham Mount every day. She stayed to tea, and was—if not exactly insulting—at least, rather rude in a nice sort of way to Magda. Andrew Debenham didn't seem to notice anything. He frowned a little when Magda came near him, as though he felt she was fussing, but he seemed to enjoy Mrs. Brand's company to the full. There were other visitors, more as the days went by and Andrew Debenham's leg progressed. He was strong, the virile type, and Magda could see that his leg would heal more quickly than she had at first expected. The doctor had endorsed this opinion, and told her, with a smile, of some of the other accidents which his turbulent patient had had in the past.

'He kicks out of a sick bed pretty quickly,' the old man said, with a smile. 'He should think himself lucky that his state of health is so good.'

Old Mrs. Debenham showed her disapproval of her nephew's most frequent visitor in a curious way. While she took tea in his room with other people—mostly County people whom she knew and was friendly with herself—she always absented herself, with puckered lips, when Mrs. Brand came. Sylvia Brand noticed this, and came, with some amusement, one day, with a lot of other people. But Mrs. Debenham was equal to the occasion. She made her excuses gracefully on the grounds that she was not well, and after that, she stopped taking tea with her nephew.

And Copper stayed at the Brand house. She came over one day and spent her free hours with Magda.

'How d'you get on with the Ogre?' she grinned.

'If you're referring to Andrew Debenham,' Magda said, with a trace of anger in her usually serene little voice, 'I'm not. It's the first case in which I've been interested in a limb of the patient and loathed the sight of the patient himself—is that awful?'

'Horrible!' Copper mocked. 'What's wrong, then?'

Magda stared at her sister.

'Nothing very much. Not that I can tell anyone about, without sounding as if I was making a lot out of nothing!'

'He sounds decent enough to me. You get more free time than I do, and you're allowed to spend it in the rose-gardens! I get thrown out, and have to go to the village if I want to stretch my legs!'

'Oh, well, he likes me within ear-shot in case he wants me,' Magda said. 'I think it's his off-hand manner that angers me so much. And it's only when Mrs. Brand's there. At least, he's a lot worse when she's there with him. His aunt doesn't like her.'

'Did she tell you that?'

'No, but you can see she doesn't. She won't take tea with them.'

'Is that all? That's probably tact. The old dear probably thinks they're courting.'

'Are they?' Magda was startled.

'Well—Mrs. Brand thinks they are,' Copper gurgled. 'Magda . . . I'm giving up nursing!'

At first, Magda thought she hadn't heard aright.

Copper repeated it for her benefit, with a little more drama about it than was actually needed.

'Well, what are you going to do instead?' Magda asked, weakly, when the shock had subsided.

'I notice you're not telling me with consternation, what a loss the nursing world is about to sustain,' Copper said.

Magda bit her lip. She could hardly do that. Copper was just an ordinary nurse. She hadn't ever worked for a record such as Magda had. She just scraped through everything. It had been the same with her examinations. Magda knew in her heart that if she hadn't gone to such exertions to help Copper with her lectures and written work, she would have given nursing up before she had got through her training. It was her cheerfulness and willingness that had endeared her to everyone, not her skill. That all the patients

21

liked her, was no guarantee that those same patients felt safe in Copper's hands if they were very ill.

'I suppose you know best,' Magda said, doubtfully. 'It's to do with Mrs Brand, isn't it?'

'Now what made you say that!' Copper flushed, but quickly grinned, and took her sister's arm. 'Look, old girl, you know me. I'm sick of slaving for a pittance. I like living in a house like the Brand house, and when she offered me a job, permanent, mind you, as a sort of secretary-companion-maid—'

'—maid-of-all-work,' Magda amended, shrewdly.

'Now don't be mean or I won't tell you about it! Anyway she's giving me just three times what I get at the hospital, and even you can't say that isn't a consideration!'

'I wish I knew what was behind this,' Magda said, worriedly. 'You're not trained. You can't even write a letter for yourself, let alone anyone else. Be careful, for heaven's sake, Copper, before you give up your job at the hospital. Nursing is hard enough to get into, without wanting to leap out of it!'

'I shall get kicked out, if I don't give up myself,' Copper said, ruefully. 'Anyway, where's it going to get us?' she demanded, fiercely, after a short pause. 'Look at us. In our middle twenties. Oh, we're all right at the moment. We're good-looking and smart . . . when we're off duty, that is, and we've managed to leave those frightful uniforms behind—'

'Copper, I thought you were proud of your uniform!' Magda cried, shocked.

'You might be, but I'm not, and that's being honest, for once. I feel a frump in it, and we're seen in them for most of our lives, if you take all the best hours of the day and evening. But what's going to happen when we're thirty? Have you thought of that?'

'It's rather a goodish way off, isn't it?' Magda smiled. Copper had always been inclined to exaggerate, to dramatise herself.

'It's five years, if you must be reminded, and I don't want to go on being a frump. I want to wear nice clothes and give nice men an opportunity of seeing me. I don't want to be an old maid, good for nothing but nursing beastly catty women and being bossed about by other women like ourselves, dressed in this ghastly uniform and all puffed out with a bit of authority.'

'I think you're taking a very material view of it all,' Magda said, worriedly, reflecting that this was a part of her twin that she didn't

23

know very well. Characteristically she blamed herself for not finding out how Copper felt about it long ago. Perhaps she ought not to have plunged her into nursing in the first place, but got her into some other occupation with more amusement, if less security.

'Perhaps I am,' Copper said, irritably, 'but honestly, Magda, I haven't enjoyed these years. The hospital's fun and all that, but the work is pretty grim, and it's an awful bore trying to get through exams, and pretty rotten to know that it's only because of you that I've managed to get through. I haven't liked it. You can call me ungrateful if you like, but the fact is, I'm a bit tired of you propelling me along. I'd like to stand on my own feet for a change.'

Magda thought, with a queer little lump in her throat, that it was odd that Copper should feel like this, since no one had ever prevented her from standing on her own feet. It was her unwillingness to do so that had provoked Magda to help her at all.

'Well, it might turn out better than either of us can see,' she allowed, looking at Copper with new eyes. 'You may like working for Mrs. Brand very much. Anyway, it isn't as if you'd never had a boy-friend. If you'd always been unattached, I could understand it. But you're engaged to be married. You hadn't forgotten that, I suppose?'

Copper laughed.

'Almost,' she chuckled. 'Being engaged at seventeen is all very fine, but when it drags on eight years, it becomes a habit like eating and drinking.'

'That's only because Jim's abroad,' Magda comforted.

'Do you really feel that?' Copper demanded. 'If so, why are you always so worried about my future?'

'Well, only because I'm afraid you'll do something mad before Jim comes back to take care of you, and that I shan't be able to—'

'Before Jim comes back!' Copper echoed, with fine scorn. 'Do you really think he's ever coming back? Don't you think if he'd wanted to, he could have got back before this? Oh, I know he's got plenty of fine excuses, every time he writes, but honestly, I've forgotten what he looks like!'

'Copper!'

'Well, he's been away four years. He was a scarecrow when he went—oh, well, you know what I mean, with his long skinny limbs and those glasses of his. It's all very

25

fine for everyone to wag their heads and say he's got a brilliant future, but meantime I'm getting old and tired of waiting. Tired of waiting for him to find something to stagger the world and make a fortune out of it. First it was a mysterious drug to benefit mankind, and then it was an unknown orchid. Then he found a beetle that turned out a bigger pest than any known one, and now he's off after something else.'

'Well, give him a bit longer.' Magda urged, feeling the ground giving beneath her feet, arguing with this new Copper.

'No. It's too late. I've already written telling him I'm chucking nursing, and . . . chucking him, too,' Copper said, with finality.

CHAPTER TWO

COPPER settled into the Brand household gleefully. She liked luxury. She liked the smell of roses, and the sight of them in the great polished urns and ornamental jugs that stood about. She liked the delicate porcelain ornaments, the outrageous colour-schemes—such as the lime and black music room with its walls of mirrors, and the little writing-room with its ivory walls, its old rose carpet and the ivory and old rose striped upholstery—and the blatant show of wealth everywhere.

Copper had no taste. She couldn't have picked out a period piece if she'd tried, and the word 'ostentatious' meant absolutely nothing to her. She only knew that she was still young and energetic, and that in this house there was life.

There was a difference between the flowers here and those in hospital wards. But the greatest difference of all was the smell. No more would she smell that curious mixture of ether, disinfectant and floor polish that had been the background of her life for so long. Outside jobs were few, and didn't last long as a rule, and then, always, it was back to the hospital, where the only fun was what you made yourself, and the only excitement was the trouble you got into.

Mrs. Brand's servants were quiet and soft-footed. Her friends were noisy and *chic*. Copper liked the look of both. She also liked Max.

Max was Mrs. Brand's secretary. He had, it appeared, always been there. The 'always' constituted the time he had left college, until now, which was an indeterminate number of years. He would never tell Copper how old he was. Sometimes she thought he was only twenty-six. Sometimes she was sure he must be almost forty, a young forty. A thin, scholarly young man, with the quiet of the servants, and the assurance of a senior member of the family; the person who arranged everything on the social side, and took the brunt of Mrs. Brand's bad moods. It was Max who wrote smooth, healing letters when Mrs. Brand wanted to hurl explosive missives through the post, Max who kept Mrs. Brand's friends for her, and helped to restrain her from making enemies. It was Max, too, who saw to it that the staff weren't extravagant, as well as keeping an easy rein on his employer's own expenditure.

'Max, can I afford to give a reception?'

Sylvia Brand would ask plaintively, and he would guardedly tell her yes, a small one, or perhaps persuade her into giving instead one of those small exclusive parties of hers. Max saw to the investments, and had a flair for making money. Copper sometimes thought that it was Max's own establishment, so well did he run it for his employer.

The first day of Copper's working life in the small room off Max's, was disastrous. He took her away from his immaculate portable typewriter after he had seen her performance and told her not to touch it again. With speed and incredible neatness he typed off the few letters which Copper had been struggling with, and with tightened lips he went back to his own work, which appeared to Copper's outraged eyes to be the writing up of an engagement book.

'I may not be very bright,' she told him, as she scanned the letters on the blotter, awaiting her employer's signature, 'and I know that my shorthand is only the home-made kind which I taught myself for fun, but I do know that Mrs. Brand didn't dictate those letters or anything like them! This one, for instance, says, in essence, yes. Mrs. Brand dictated a very loud no, not on your life! She was furious about it!'

'Yes,' Max said, calmly, 'but Mrs. Brand doesn't always mean to send the letters she dictates. Besides, we can't offend the Archbishop's niece. I don't know why you were engaged for this job,' he said, turning round to Copper and staring at her in some distaste.

'Neither do I,' she said, frankly. 'I didn't know Mrs. Brand had a secretary already.'

'What else were you supposed to do?' he asked.

'I was supposed to be a companion.'

'Well, you'd better scoot off and be companionable, and let me get on with my work.'

Mrs. Brand, however, was having a dress fitting, and was already loathing the people in the room with her. She screamed to Copper to get out and stay out. There was some sort of recommendation that she 'do the flowers,' but they had already been done. Finally, she was called back to the work she really knew— nursing. One of the maids had badly cut her hand, and Copper went and attended to it.

At last Max found jobs for her, to keep her out of his way. There was the man-sized job of taking down each book in the library—the one room that was disused and alien in this frivolous house, but had been the cherished possession of Mrs. Brand's late husband—and thoroughly dusting it, mending

30

torn pages and covers where necessary, and listing them.

'Do you read?' Max asked Copper, watching her, in the sober dark brown frock which Mrs. Brand had insisted she wore, sitting on the top of the ladder frowning at an enormous tome.

She shook her head, laughing. Her hair made a flaming patch of light against the dark of the shelves and books, and her piquant little face was full of mischief.

'I thought not,' Max said, resignedly, and left her.

It was into this room—and its muddle that was consistent with the way in which Copper did a job—that Magda was shown, on a warm day in late July. She had been given the afternoon off, and in a cool cream dress with small brown flower-buds and leaves on it, and a cream straw hat in her hand, she decided to take a walk in the woods.

Max came in looking for his glasses, and snorted as he caught sight of her.

'Asking for trouble, young woman? You know Mrs. Brand won't permit that sort of attire!'

Magda watched him fumbling on the table among the papers and books, and waited until he had found what he was looking for. As he settled his glasses on his nose, he caught sight of her hat, and said, with faint displeasure:

'Oh, running out on the job. I thought you wouldn't manage it. Oh, well, cut along, before Mrs. Brand sees you!'

'I'm not Copper,' Magda said, and as she spoke, his face changed. There was a difference about their voices that couldn't be denied. Magda's was richer, deeper, and without that sound of bubbling nonsense which vaguely irritated Max, and made him feel older than he was. 'I'm her twin, Magda.'

'I see,' Max said, and invited her to sit down.

The chairs were all filled with dirty books and papers, so Magda smilingly declined.

'Is my sister supposed to be doing this?'

Max agreed that it was Copper's work.

'She's no good at anything practical,' Magda said, affectionately. 'I'm so sorry to intrude like this, but I have a letter for her. It was delivered to Debenham Mount.'

'I'll send for her,' Max offered.

He waited politely, but Copper didn't come. Finally, Magda decided to leave it with him. It had a Gold Coast stamp on it, and was addressed in an untidy masculine hand. Magda hoped that it meant that Jim was now coming home. Copper had been allowed to run

32

loose for too long. He'd lose her soon, if he didn't do something about it.

'I expect the sender got mixed up as to which of us was going to Debenham Mount,' she said, uncomfortably, aware of the little awkward silence with which Max received the information.

He nodded.

'Aren't you surprised to find that there are two of us?' she persisted.

'Should I be?'

'Well, I don't think it's generally known, and if you don't mind, I think I'd prefer that you didn't mention it. You see,' she broke off, frowning, 'I rather hoped to be able to run into my sister (she working here, I mean), without anyone seeing me. I just intended to give her this and go.'

'I'll give it to her,' he offered. 'Do you read?'

'Oh, yes. I love books. I almost envy Copper this job. I didn't know she was going to have the care of the library.'

Max winced, but didn't attempt to correct Magda. He chatted to her in a desultory way about books, and then she went. Copper materialised later and announced that she had had a wigging for undertaking the cleaning of the books without her employer's permission.

'It's a bit thick!' she protested. 'Whose orders am I supposed to take?'

'I'll put it right,' Max said, mechanically, giving her the letter which Magda had brought.

Copper took the letter eagerly. He watched her, frowning. They were so different, these two. So different, in fact, that even allowing for their likeness in features and colouring, they were poles apart. He had a passion for colouring in a woman, and had felt it a great pity that so much beauty was wasted in the scatterbrained Copper. Now that he had met Magda, he saw what richness there could be, when beauty was combined with a thoughtful nature.

'Oh, Jim!' Copper said, disgustedly, putting the letter unopened into her pocket. 'What would you do with a bloke who won't take "no" for an answer?'

'Your fiancé?' Max enquired, feeling that an answer was expected of him, and not quite knowing what to say.

'Not any more,' Copper said, firmly. 'I've broken it off. I like a man who knows what he wants, and doesn't take his whole life in getting it.'

'I see. Does your sister feel like that?'

'Magda? What did you think of her? She

had a nerve, coming here like that! Who'd have thought she'd have it in her?'

'She's ... very much like you,' Max offered, for the sake of answering the question. 'Does she feel as you do about men?'

'Oh, heavens, no. She's got ideals and all that.'

'And she found the man of her choice?'

Copper said, carelessly, looking round at the books with distaste: 'Old Magda? Oh, heavens, no. She's wedded to nursing. Magda Nightingale,' Copper said, laughing at her own joke.

For some reason, Max experienced satisfaction. He said no more to Copper about her sister's visit, and when the girl had gone back to the distasteful job of dusting the books, he quietly left her and went back to his desk to sit and stare into space and dream of a pair of quiet brown eyes that had tranquillity in their depths, and of a girl who could discuss with enthusiasm and knowledge the works of George Eliot and Leigh Hunt, and who knew the difference between Milton and Keats.

It was Mrs. Brand's buzzer which roused him. He flushed at his own thoughts, and told himself defensively that it wasn't every day that a fellow met a pretty girl with brains. He hoped he wouldn't be disillusioned, and find that she had as empty a head as her sister.

Mrs. Brand was in a pettish mood.

'Max, what's going on?' she demanded.

He raised politely enquiring brows.

'Max, don't be obtuse. Are you getting a pash on that girl?'

He blinked. 'Which one, Mrs. Brand?'

Sylvia Brand's fair face flamed.

'The one who's supposed to be helping you, of course! How many are there? Betty said she saw her all dressed up and going out.'

Max sighed.

'It seems there are two of them. This is the one from Debenham Mount. She had time off, and wanted to speak to her sister. Someone showed her into the library.'

'Oh-oh. So that's it.' Sylvia Brand's eyes glittered in the way she had when she was thinking quickly and trying to turn something to her own advantage. 'Tell me, Max, what's she look like in her own clothes? Pretty? Eh?'

'I hardly noticed,' he replied. 'I was busy, and I couldn't find my glasses.'

'She looks a frump in her nurse's uniform. I wish I'd seen her,' Sylvia Brand muttered. 'Did she say how Mr. Debenham is?'

Max replied that Magda had said very little, but merely left a letter for her sister.

'Did she go straight back to the Mount?'

Max placed his letters in front of her, insinuatingly, waiting with a poised pen for her signature. He was tired of the conversation.

'No, I don't think so. It was her afternoon out,' he said, indifferently.

'Send for the car. I don't want to sign those yet,' Sylvia said, suddenly jumping up. 'Send Betty up at once,' she ordered.

Max took his letters away, and experienced a prick of uneasiness. He had never understood why his employer should have kept the little nurse on in this ridiculous position in the house, and now that there appeared to be a sister, also a nurse, at Debenham Mount, there seemed to be some significance, important enough to tantalise him, and yet it eluded him. That she was jealous of attractive young women, he was well aware, but these nurses should soon be going back. Why bother about them?

Sylvia Brand drove over to the Mount that afternoon, determined to break down old Mrs. Debenham's reserve as much as to see how Andrew was. If the nurse had a whole afternoon off, it must be that he was getting much better, but if she looked as attractive as Copper did in her outdoor things, it wouldn't do for Andrew to see her.

Mrs. Debenham wasn't about, but Andrew was sitting on the terrace, enjoying the sunshine, with his leg, still in plaster, raised on to the cane foot-rest. He seemed pleased to see her, but not as delighted as on other occasions.

'Darling, are you still in pain?' Sylvia asked.

'You're a rotten sick visitor,' he grinned. 'Of course I'm in pain, and shall be, till the leg's out of plaster. But your trouble is you don't manage to sound really concerned.'

She smiled.

'You sound a lot better. Almost your old self, Andrew. How's your aunt?'

He frowned.

'Not too well. It seems her heart's a bit groggy. She's got to go easy.'

'Oh, poor old thing. Shall I nip up and see her?'

Andrew grinned again.

'Now, be honest, Sylvia. You don't like her and Aunt Laura isn't keen on you. What would you say if I told you to go up and see her?'

He laughed outright at her look of dismay.

'There you are, you see! Now be a good girl and stay here with me. You came here to see me, so don't deny it.'

38

'Andrew, you're a beast.'

'All right. Now, what have you been doing with yourself?'

'Thinking of you,' she said, softly.

'And quarrelling with your friends, browbeating your staff and pushing poor old Max around,' he guessed accurately.

'Well, if that's true, it's because I'm lonely. I miss you so, Andrew.'

He shied away from the look in her eyes.

'Rubbish! You've been on your own for years now, and you've enjoyed yourself thoroughly. You're an outrageous flirt and get a lot of fun out of keeping us poor men on a string.'

She let the point go.

'When will your leg be out of plaster, Andrew?'

'Oh, another week or so.'

'Have you still got a nurse around?'

'Yes,' he said, and his lips tightened.

'What's the matter? Don't you like her?'

He hesitated for the fraction of a second. Then he said, 'I never like my nurses, nor do I ever enjoy being laid up.'

'Where is she now, Andrew? I'm always scared she'll come bristling out, all starchy and efficient. She makes me feel such an incompetent fool.'

39

'I really don't know,' he said, indifferently. 'I told her it was time she had a rest, and to clear out and get some fresh air.'

She breathed a little freer. Obviously he hadn't seen Magda out of her uniform. She wished she could see what the girl looked like. It may well be that she looked dowdy and that her own anxiety about Andrew didn't matter. On the other hand, with that colouring, she might manage to look utterly lovely. But would Andrew even notice? She couldn't say, and the conviction that he felt something strongly about Magda—whether dislike, or something else, she couldn't decide—was enough to make her wish that he had no further need of a nurse.

'I don't think I'm going to visit you any more, Andrew. I shall wait till you're well, and can come and see me.'

'Why?' he asked, lazily.

'Because you're pampered. You have so many visitors and so much attention that I don't believe you notice me at all. If I didn't come you'd neither notice nor care.'

'You want me to say I'd be heartbroken if you didn't come?' he hazarded, crinkling up his eyes at her.

'Oh, Andrew! You beast! You're laughing at me!' she stormed, getting up.

40

'No, I'm not. You just amuse me. Sylvia, my dear, you and I have known each other so long. If I ever had the urge to be married, and decided on you, I'd just ask you outright, in a casual way. I certainly shouldn't bother to court you. One only does that with a stranger, someone one isn't sure of.'

'And you're sure of me?' she asked softly, her eyes narrowing slightly.

'I know you through and through,' he assured her. 'Going to stay for tea?'

'I don't think so,' she said, gathering up her things. 'I suppose as we know each other so well, it'd be silly if I had the urge to kiss you good-bye and hope you'd get better soon, Andrew?'

'I shouldn't,' he warned her, laughing again. 'I might be contagious!'

He watched her go down to the drive, and frowned. The same old Sylvia. She couldn't resist flirting, even with him. After all the years they had known each other.

From Sylvia, his thoughts turned to Magda, and his own irritation about her. It wasn't reasonable or just. He didn't understand himself. The girl was so good to him, so utterly right in her manner, and such a fine nurse. Nothing was too much trouble for her, and however he treated her, she still remained patient and pleasant.

He rang the bell, and Magda, crossing the hall at the time, answered it. She had only just returned, and hadn't got back into her uniform.

'Hallo, you're back early,' Andrew said. 'I told you to stay out till dinner.'

'I got rather tired of walking about in the heat,' she smiled, 'and I thought it would be rather nice to have my tea in my own room, instead of the tea-rooms in the village.'

He stared at her dress, and was suddenly conscious that he was staring.

'You look nice,' he said, abruptly.

She was too surprised to say anything, and before she could speak, he said, 'I'd like my tea. I suppose you wouldn't care to have yours with me?'

He watched her go to see about it, and wondered what had possessed him to make that gesture, after being so consistently nasty to her. Perhaps it was an attack of conscience, he told himself, grimly, and wondered what his aunt would say when she came down after her rest.

Magda sat limply in the cane chair, beside him, and sipped her tea. She felt more tired than she had admitted. There were times when, after a morning of running about and being scolded by her patient, she felt like sitting down and dissolving into a flood of weak tears. It was this weakness, this creeping weakness of late, that worried her so much. In her free time she rested. Instead of going into the village or writing letters or knitting, she lay on her bed, flat on her back, and let the waves of exhaustion flow over her. She slept in every spare minute, and she slept all night, but on waking, she often felt she hadn't had any sleep at all. And every day she felt just a little less energetic. . . .

'You look fagged out,' Andrew said, abruptly. 'I'm working you too hard. No consideration.'

'Oh, no,' she protested, overcome by his civility.

'Never mind. You'll be released soon. Another week or two. Then you'll be able to go back to the hospital. I expect you'll be glad to get back?'

The hospital. Magda found it almost impossible to repress a shudder. In that moment, she almost sympathised with Copper and her repugnance at returning, though she knew her own reasons were different. The rows and rows of beds, and the eternal foot-work, and the work that never seemed to end.

'I expect I shall be glad,' she found herself

43

saying, dutifully. She fancied he looked faintly disappointed. 'Oh, I've loved it here of course. I love this house, and everything but I knew it couldn't go on for ever.'

'You love this house?' he said, in a low voice, full of interest. So few women did. Even Sylvia, he knew, thought it antiquated, and had an itch to alter it all.

'Oh, yes. It's a man's house. It felt like— well, this may sound odd to you, but when I first came here, it felt like coming home.'

'*Home*,' he repeated, softly, a strange look in his eyes. He had never heard a woman refer to it as home before, either. He wondered what Sylvia would say about it, if he really asked her to marry him.

Sylvia Brand thought about that all the way home. She sat holding the handle at the side of the window, in a grip that almost pulled it down. Her eyes stared sombrely and unseeingly at the hedges, and the cottage gardens bright with July blossoms, and she reflected that Andrew was the most elusive man she had ever met, and incidentally the only man who hadn't courted her from the first moment he had seen her. That, she supposed, was Andrew's main charm. She wondered how she would have felt about him if, like all the others, he had pursued her and

44

pestered her to marry him. But that was so unlike Andrew that her imagination wouldn't stretch that far. She couldn't even make him angry about her. Not like he was about Copper's sister.

She fought down a tide of unfriendliness towards Magda, and despised herself for it. To her, it suggested fear, and she had never been afraid of any other woman. And yet the unfriendliness persisted to such an extent that she couldn't resist sending for Copper, when she arrived home, and questioning her about Magda's visit.

'I hope you didn't mind, Mrs. Brand. I didn't know she was coming, or I'd have stopped her.'

'Well, why would you have done that?' Sylvia murmured. 'I didn't mind. I just wondered why she came, that's all.'

'Just to bring the letter.'

'From your boy-friend, I suppose?'

Copper frowned. 'He was my fiancé, till I broke it off.'

'Oh. Why did you do that?'

Copper answered impatiently. 'Oh, I want things out of life. I'll be poor for ever if I marry Jim. Probably not even have a roof over my head. Just a crazy wanderer like him!'

'And you want wealth and comfort? Oh, I've noticed how happy you've been since you came to this house,' Sylvia said, with understanding in her voice.

'Well, I don't want to be poor,' Copper temporised. 'I've always been poor. We both have, Magda and I.'

'And Magda, what does she feel about men?'

'Oh, she doesn't care one way or the other. She loves her work.'

Sylvia raised polite brows. 'Do you really believe that?'

'Of course I do,' Copper said, hotly.

'Well, you know her better than I do, of course, but to me, it doesn't seem normal. A good-looking young woman not wanting a man of her own and her own home, and comfort.'

'Oh, Magda's normal all right,' Copper said.

'And what about your Jim?' Sylvia gently probed.

'It's an awful nuisance, but my letter seems to have had the effect of making him want to come rushing home in a hurry, a thing he'd never have done if I'd asked him to.'

'And he'll want to marry you at once. What will your sister think? Does she want you to

46

marry him?'

'Oh, yes, she's aching for it. She thinks it'll keep me out of mischief, and I don't blame her,' Copper laughed.

'It's funny,' Sylvia Brand mused.

'What is, Mrs. Brand?'

'You being the one who wanted luxury. Now, if you'd said Magda, I could have understood it.'

'Magda!' Incredulity was in Copper's voice.

'Well, of course, I suppose I shouldn't say this, but as you know, I've been over to Debenham Mount this afternoon, and I think your sister is going to be relieved of her duties rather sooner than we thought.'

'Why?' Copper gasped. 'Her patient isn't well yet!'

'No. Far from it. In fact, his leg's still in plaster. But I gathered (nothing was said, mind you), that she was annoying him. Oh, well, you can't blame a girl, a nurse of all people, for wanting to settle down with a wealthy husband—'

Copper's face flamed.

'Mrs. Brand, you're mistaken. You must have got the wrong impression. My sister isn't that kind—'

Mrs. Brand changed the subject quickly.

'Perhaps I have. She may be there for quite a long time. This letter of yours, I almost forgot what a Gold Coast stamp looks like. I used to collect, you know.'

Copper mechanically gave her the letter, while she tried to reconcile all Magda had said about Andrew, and wondered if Magda had got so tired of him that she was giving notice herself. But that was hardly likely, or possible. Perhaps she was ill?

Sylvia Brand professed interest in the stamp. 'This issue's different from the ones I had,' she said. 'Um, that's odd. Very odd.'

'What is, Mrs. Brand?'

'Nothing, only—you know, if I didn't know better, I'd say this envelope had been steamed open. Yes, it certainly looks like it. Here, you look.'

Copper took the envelope, but could see nothing suspicious. She had opened it in her usual manner, ripping the top with her thumb, and half tearing the envelope as she did so. But Mrs. Brand insisted.

'Who would have done it?' Copper asked, thinking perhaps of the servants at Debenham Mount, or perhaps someone at the little post office-cum-general store, and dismissing both as equally unlikely.

'Oh, I don't know. No, I must be mistaken,'

Sylvia Brand said, and let Copper go.

Copper dismissed the whole thing. She wasn't addicted to thinking very deeply, and considered her employer's friendly mood in every way as disconcerting as her many unfriendly ones.

Magda was the first to arrange a meeting between the sisters. It didn't occur till a week later, after she had had an odd and touching little note from Max.

'You left your gloves,' he lied. 'I'd like to meet you to return them.'

And when she had gravely written arranging a meeting to receive back a pair of gloves that had never left her possession, he brought a book of Elizabethan verse and some flowers, and took her for a bus-ride and tea in a small town she had never seen before. He was a delightful companion, with a quiet, level way of speaking, and a contagious interest in everything, from books to old buildings, the English countryside to the mountainous regions of Thibet where he had once spent an unusual holiday, all alone.

He was so unusual that Magda felt the urge to meet Copper and tell her about him. She wondered why Copper hadn't mentioned him before, and thought with a smile that her sister probably found him dull.

49

'What did you want me for?' Copper greeted her, rather crossly. She had been in further tiresome trouble with her employer, and it was the hot sticky weather that heralds a storm. She hadn't had time to change out of the hated brown frock, and she felt unprepossessing, while Magda looked cool and lovely in cream linen.

'Only to tell you about my budding romance,' Magda said, with a smile.

Against her will, Copper recalled Mrs. Brand's suggestion (and the many repeated hints since on the same subject) that Magda was pursuing her employer.

'What romance?' Copper asked, cautiously, falling into step beside her sister after the bus had turned a bend in a cloud of dust.

'Honestly, he's the most unlikely person you'd expect me to be interested in,' Magda said, with her quiet smile.

Copper stared ahead, and waited. For once, her tongue didn't run away with her. She felt frozen inside. Magda had so much. She was so good at her work, and so strong-minded and reliable. She never had the tendency to get into trouble, and needed no one to look after her. She had never even cared about wealth and luxury. And now she seemed to be getting everything.

'Oh, I forgot to ask about you and Jim,' Magda said, contrite at once. 'Was the letter nice? I suppose he's dashing home at once to get you well and safely married?'

Copper shot round at her.

'How did you know that?' she murmured.

'Know it?' Magda asked, bewildered. 'I didn't, silly. It was only guesswork. Is it true, then? Well it's just the thing that *would* happen with Jim, or any other man, come to that now isn't it?'

She grasped her sister's shoulders warmly and gave her a quick hug. 'Don't disappoint us both, chick. I do so want to see you married to him and safely out of mischief. At my age, it's time I had a bit of a rest from looking out for you.'

She tried to laugh, but it wasn't very convincing. Copper construed it as being a confirmation of Mrs. Brand's words, and fought against it, with every ounce of her energy. It was so odd that Mrs. Brand should happen on what appeared to be the truth. What else could it be but the truth?

But Magda was counting the days that she could still manage to keep on her feet and carry on her job—not on getting a wealthy husband like Andrew Debenham.

CHAPTER THREE

MRS. DEBENHAM seemed to have taken a great fancy to Magda. She invited Magda to bring her knitting into her sitting-room when she was not free to go out, and she arranged that Magda's free time should coincide with Max's. She didn't know that it was Max whom Magda was seeing, and she didn't ask. She found out that Magda would have preferred Wednesday off instead of Saturday, and against her nephew's will, had it altered.

Andrew had a curious attitude towards Magda. He liked his nurse to be around all the time, and was at once resentful of any free hours she might have to have.

'But you're not ill now, Andrew,' his aunt protested. 'You can't tie the young woman to your bedside.'

'I am ill,' he insisted, grinning at her in that way of his, that made it so difficult for her to be angry with him all the time. 'I'm ill in the sense that I'm not fit. I can't leap up and get things, and it's no use ringing for the servants. They don't know where anything is.'

'Magda's spoilt you, I'm afraid,' his aunt observed.

'At least I don't spoil her, as you do, calling her by her Christian name and having tea with her in your room,' he retorted.

'Well, I like the girl,' his aunt said, composedly. 'And I can't think why you don't.'

'Who says I don't?' he demanded.

'It's rather obvious, isn't it?' Mrs. Debenham asked, gently. 'You've treated her abominably ever since she's been here.'

He shifted restlessly.

'Well, it's because she puts up with so much,' he said, at last. 'All the others chucked everything and cleared out, but she just takes all my moods and foul tempers, and is perfectly well-mannered. She makes me feel a boor.'

'And so you are,' his aunt told him. 'But is that all, Andrew?'

'I think so,' he said, rather stiffly. Then he added: 'But surely I'm not treating her so badly lately? Hasn't anyone noticed?'

She smiled and shook her head.

'If Magda ever notices, she'll collapse with shock,' she told him, adding with a smile, 'and so shall I!'

But he was more tolerant in his manner to Magda. Perhaps because after that small conversation, his aunt was on the look-out for this so-called change of his, she saw it. He

53

wasn't so rude, and his voice was almost moderate at times, which said a lot for him, but there was also something in his manner towards the girl which puzzled the older woman. Something that teased her, which she couldn't put her finger on. As far as she could see, there was no reason for Andrew to be like this with Magda. The other nurses in past times may well have irritated or annoyed him, or not troubled to understand him or put up with all his little foibles, but Magda had been so very good with him. Too good, perhaps.

Once a week, Magda fell in with seeing Copper. That had been going on almost since they came there. Just for an hour. Sometimes Magda went no further than the gates of Debenham Mount, meeting Copper there. Sometimes she snatched a few extra minutes to walk down the lane, and meet her sister. It kept them in touch. It also allowed Copper the opportunity to blow off steam.

After their conversation recently, Copper hadn't been there. Copper allowed two weekly meetings to elapse without seeing Magda, and it was towards the end of July that Magda gave Max a note to give to her sister, asking her to come, as she wanted to talk to her.

Copper came, in what was almost a surly mood. It was a golden evening, warm and clear, thick with the buzz of insects, heady with the scent of the fields and the crops. Copper had on a new dress, provocative of cut, and much more suitable for town than country. Magda had slipped out in her nurse's uniform.

'What did you want?' Copper demanded, without preamble.

'Hallo,' Magda said, in her warm, friendly voice. 'I just wanted to see you again, and I wondered how it was you'd missed for two weeks.'

'Oh, well, I was busy,' Copper said, turning away to lean over a gate. On the other side of the gate was a field-path, the way which Copper had come as a short cut, from Mrs. Brand's. It lost itself at the very end in a blue haze, as some of the light went out of the day. But Copper wasn't thinking of the beauty ahead of her, but wondering how far Magda would go in thrashing this matter out. That was the trouble with Magda. She would never have any undercurrents or bad feeling. She made you come out into the open, and pretty usually she made you feel it was all your fault, and that you were acting rather meanly. Magda was so open and forthright herself,

55

and so above anything that suggested pettiness.

'Cleaning out the library?' Magda smiled.

'That isn't funny!' Copper said, almost snapping. 'It's old and dirty and full of spiders and I hate the job. I might just as well be cleaning out the wards.'

'Well, tell Max you don't like it. He'll find something else for you to do.'

Copper turned round and stared at her sister.

'Oh, Max . . . yes, how did it happen that you met him and gave him my note?'

'How did it happen?' Magda sounded puzzled. 'Well, I was seeing him, of course.'

'Max too?' Copper sounded outraged.

'What d'you mean . . . Max too? I don't see anyone else.'

Copper snorted, disbelievingly.

'Copper, I don't quite understand. I told you about Max, that day when you were so wild. The last time you met me here, remember? Of course, there's nothing in it, really. We're just friends, but it's nice to meet someone on my half day and go for a ride or a walk.'

'I bet there's nothing in it!' Copper said, vigorously, and with scorn. 'And as to telling me about him, that's a tall one, if you like!'

'But I did!' Magda protested, frowning. 'I can't just remember what I did say—I was feeling pretty rotten that day, but I'm better now—but to the best of my ability, I recall that I said I wanted to tell you about my budding romance.'

'I know,' Copper said. 'But you didn't mention Max.'

'Well, that was him, only it isn't a romance really, it was just my joke. And don't for heaven's sake repeat this to him and spoil it all, will you?'

'I've a jolly good mind to,' Copper said, slowly. 'Of all the mouldy ways of getting out of anything, that is the limit! You weren't referring to Max at all. You were talking about Andrew Debenham. Why bother to deny it?'

'Copper, what *is* the matter with you lately? I don't know what you're talking about. Andrew Debenham! What put him into your head, for heaven's sake?'

'Everyone's talking about it. It must be true,' Copper said, slowly.

'*Everyone?*' Magda frowned. 'I think you'd better explain just what it is you've heard.'

Copper, never very good at explaining clearly at best, was at a loss to know where to begin. Since Mrs. Brand's hints about her own observations, the letter which she suggested had been steamed open, and Andrew's own supposed annoyance at Magda's open pursuing, Copper had heard other things. Hints and whispers, among Mrs. Brand's staff and in the village itself. It didn't occur to her that this was not only not confirmation of Mrs. Brand's words, but simply a rumour started by Mrs. Brand herself. It also never occurred to her that in a small place like this, the smallest rumour about one of the important people living in the district, provided news, and grew as it went around.

She did her best with explaining to Magda, but merely made it sound like something that was really happening, not to one of the sisters, but to someone else, some stranger, who was being talked about, openly, and in hostile fashion, by everyone.

Magda's head was in a whirl.

'But why . . . *why* should everyone talk about me like that?' she gasped. 'It's all so absurd! Nothing's changed. I'm still just his nurse, and he still isn't even civil to me. At least,' she temporised, struggling for the immaculate truth, 'until just recently. I must say he is being nice to me sometimes. Well, what I mean by nice is—' she floundered thinking of the day he commanded that she take tea with him, and one or two other similar incidents.

'I know quite well what you mean,' Copper said, cuttingly. 'Good heavens, what a simpleton I've been. I've come to you with all my troubles, and taken your advice blindly. And all the time you've found me nothing but a darned nuisance, and gone out of your way to get me married off to Jim, so you wouldn't have to worry any more! Well, I won't do it! I don't want to be poor, wandering from place to place, while you're a rich man's wife, having all the luxury and ease I've always craved for! It's always been you . . . you were the one who had the brains, and how you showed off, doing my exams for me and pushing me through everything, so you could say that I wouldn't have done it but for you! You always got the highest score with everything, and all the praise from everyone at the hospital. You were always on top, and all the time you tricked me into thinking you were the best friend I had! The best friend . . . I like that!'

Magda stared unbelievingly, waiting for her sister's anger to die down. The scene wasn't unusual—Copper's temper had always been uncertain, but she was all sunshine afterwards. The subject of the scene, however, was very unusual. The twins had

59

never quarrelled before, nor found fault with each other.

'I don't think I understand, even now,' Magda murmured, while Copper fought to get her breath.

'You don't understand!' Copper said, scathingly. 'Don't make it worse than it is. If someone hadn't been more smart than me, and drawn my attention to the fact that that letter of mine had been steamed open—'

Magda said, slowly, 'Do you mean the letter I brought over to you? The one from Jim?'

'What other letter was there?' Copper retorted. 'And who else had access to it but you?'

Magda said, softly, 'You don't mean you're silly enough to think that *I* steamed open your letter?'

'Well, how else would you have known that Jim wanted to come haring back at once, after he got mine?'

Magda started to laugh, not in amusement, but in sheer relief.

'Oh, Copper, you ass, you dear old ass! Think—just for a minute, think! I didn't *know*. I was just guessing, and it seemed a pretty obvious bit of guesswork to me. Of course Jim (or any other man) would react like that. And of course, I wanted it to happen. I think it would be so good for you to be married, and belong to someone who can take care of you. As to all the other bitter things you've said, well, you know as well as I do, that they aren't true. Just exaggerations, because you're feeling sore about something. We'll forget all about them, forget you ever said them.'

'Oh, no, we won't!' Copper retorted, mutinously. 'It's still where it was. You want me to be tied to Jim, and poor, while you get a rich husband.'

'But I don't!' Magda protested.

'Yes, you do, or why would you have put up with Andrew Debenham for so long? I always thought it funny, especially as you were ill enough to make that an excuse for giving up the job and taking a rest for a bit. No, you want a rich husband. And you being you, you'll get one. You always do, you're so beastly efficient and capable about everything you tackle.'

'Do you begrudge me wealth, if such an unlikely thing happened?' Magda asked, wistfully. 'I wouldn't begrudge you the good things of life.'

'It isn't a question of begrudging,' Copper said, looking faintly ashamed. 'It's just that

. . . well, it's all so beastly unfair. We're twins, but we've never been level. You've always been just that much ahead of me. When Daddie was alive, you came first with him. You always treated me as a young sister. . . .'

'I looked after you,' Magda agreed, looking pained. 'I need not have, but I liked doing it, and you didn't seem exactly capable of looking after yourself.'

Copper drew a deep breath.

'You never gave me the chance,' she accused.

There was a silence between them. The darkness gathered around them. It was almost time for Magda to go back.

'Don't let's part bad friends,' she pleaded. 'There isn't time to straighten this all out now. Let's meet on my half-day. I won't go out with Max this week.'

'And that's another thing!' Copper flared. 'I might have had Max for a friend, but you took him away from me too. He despises me because I'm not crazy about books, but he would have got used to that if you hadn't come poking in and showing off with your superior knowledge!'

'Oh, Copper, stop it. Stop being an ass!' Magda begged. 'I'm just friends with Max, and if it's interfering with your chances, I'll stop seeing him, though I can't see what he can mean to you, when you've got Jim. As to Andrew Debenham, I can't help it if there is a rumour about us, it just isn't true. I'll prove it to you. I'll terminate my job here, and go away. Will you believe me then?'

Copper laughed derisively.

'I'll believe that when I see it,' she jeered, and without giving Magda the chance to say any more, she climbed the gate and set off at a swinging pace along the footpath.

Magda called her, intending to confirm their meeting on her half-day, but Copper didn't answer, nor did she look back.

Magda watched her sister's back merge into the surrounding gloom, and heard the last of her footsteps die away, until there was only the chirping of a cricket, and the last cheep of a bird in the hedge. A faint glow was over the trees behind her, where the moon was rising. A new moon, silver against the blue-grey backcloth of the July sky. A beautiful world, if you were happy enough to enjoy it.

Tears misted her eyes as all Copper's words pelted rough-shod through her brain. Bitter, searing words. Not words hastily conjured up in the heat of the moment, but words which painted a picture of a long-term smarting over

63

fancied injuries. How could they be friends again after that?

Magda told herself that the answer to that was pretty much the same as it had been in the past. Magda herself would be the one to make the first overtures of friendship and to follow it up, vigorously, until she had broken down Copper's sullenness. Magda would be the one to give way, as always.

When Copper was little, she had always been the jealous one. 'I want,' had been her war-cry, her childish theme-song. She had plundered for love of plundering, and when she wasn't successful, she had stormed and wailed and felt very ill-used.

She had been the first of the twins to get engaged, but even that didn't satisfy her. Jim hadn't turned out as she had expected, and now that Magda had a man-friend, Copper wanted him, on principle.

And yet, Magda thought, with a rueful smile, she couldn't be angry with Copper for long. She was just Copper, stormy lovable Copper, who somehow managed to melt down all your defences, and forget her nasty little barbs so soon afterwards.

During the next few days, it appeared that Andrew's leg was indeed making a rapid recovery. He was soon to have the plaster taken off. It seemed to Magda rather churlish to hastily give up the job now, when in such a little while she would be able to pack and go. The gesture had been as much for proving to Copper the truth of her words, but then, Magda argued to herself, if Copper wanted to believe anything—right or wrong—she would. Was it worth doing something like this, this flinging up a case just before it was finished, and spoiling a fine record, just to appease her sister, when there was no certainty that it would satisfy Copper at all?

She decided to write to Copper, urging her to spend the next half-day with her. Copper, however, wrote back angrily to say that she had no intention of wasting any more half-days with Magda, until she supplied the proof she had spoken of.

Max, on the other hand, telephoned to Magda and eagerly asked her to spend her next free time with him on a trip to the coast. Common sense told her that in her present state of health an afternoon by the sea in the healing companionship of Max would be far better for her than spending it locally, wrangling with Copper. Max won, and when she met him at the cross-roads a few days later, she felt a gladness in her heart for the solid friendship he was offering her.

He looked so nice, standing there, in his comfortable, rather shabby tweeds, a tweed cap keeping down the thin dark hair that looked tenderly ridiculous when it blew up in the wind. Magda liked him in that tweed cap. He looked so much the countryman, oddly so, when you thought how very much the townsman he looked, in Mrs. Brand's library.

They went by bus to St. Chad's Bay, and then walked out of the little town up on to the cliff-tops, where the rolling downs met the sea. It was a sparkling blue day, with little white puff clouds, and gulls wheeling, and the sand almost white in the heat.

'Oh, nice,' Magda breathed, flopping down on to her raincoat.

'You look nice,' Max offered. Her broderie anglais dress, fresh-starched and full-skirted, looked crisp and cool, and a jaunty white piqué beret sat on her glowing hair.

'What makes you two so utterly different, I wonder?' he mused, sitting carefully beside her, and dumping the picnic basket behind him for a back-rest. 'You know, if Copper isn't careful, she'll be thrown out soon.'

Magda looked startled.

'Why, Max?'

He shook his head.

'I used to like her, the way you like a cheeky

young sister, when she first came there. But now she's a bit, well, bad-tempered, and difficult to manage. Mrs. Brand doesn't as a rule stand for that sort of thing. I don't know why she's putting up with it.'

'Max, have you—' Magda began, and hesitated.

'Have I—what?' he smiled.

'I hardly know how to say this, but have you heard any rather silly rumours about me, and Andrew Debenham?'

He frowned.

'Oh, that? Well, that's the sort of rumour that does start in our establishment. I don't know. It seems a hotbed of rumours and always has been. I discount them all. They don't matter, anyway.'

'Don't they?' she asked, her brown eyes searching his.

'If you mean, do I think any the worse of you, the answer is a most definite no!'

She smiled, that lovely smile of hers that sent his pulses racing. A smile that lived in her eyes and fanned out over her face, lingering.

'Max, dear Max. You wouldn't think ill of anyone. I know that. No, I don't mean you. I mean other people. I shall be going from here when the case is finished, and I don't want people to remember me as the tiresome nurse person who made an ass of herself chasing Andrew Debenham. It's undignified, it's beastly. It's also . . . untrue.'

'I know that,' he said. 'I don't think this particular rumour will have any more lasting effect than any of the others. I should forget about it, if I were you.'

'I don't even like Andrew Debenham,' she persisted.

'Don't you?' he murmured, thinking that liking hadn't much to do with the deeper feeling, that was sometimes lightly written off as 'being under the skin.' Was Andrew Debenham under her skin? Or if he wasn't, might not this rumour set her thinking of him to such an extent that that would be the ultimate result? He wondered, and hoped that it wouldn't be so.

'Mrs. Brand has been more or less expecting to become the mistress of Debenham Mount for a long time,' he offered, in a matter-of-fact voice. 'That isn't gossiping,' he smiled, as the tide of colour rushed up her face. 'We all know it, and I think most of us would like to see it happen. Uniting the two houses, and all that, oh, and of course, it would mean a more settled feeling for the staff of both establishments. We all want peace.'

68

She smiled at that. Max was in a way very much like herself. Giving service all his life, if a different kind of service. And being so bound up with the people he served, and their interests.

He offered, 'Mrs Brand is giving a birthday party soon. It's going to be a pretty big affair,' and he told her about it.

From Max's viewpoint, it meant invitations, sorting out the unsuitables whom Mrs. Brand wanted, from the suitables he considered should be given preference to, even if she didn't personally like them. The people who would be good for her to mix with, and who would perhaps help her socially. The people whom Andrew Debenham would like to see her mixing with, as the future mistress of Debenham Mount.

Then there was the vast and intricate job of the catering, and arranging the house for guests, the ballroom, and the flowers; gilt chairs and tables; the buffet and the vast dinner-table. A few choice guests would be there to dinner, and the rest would come and stay for dancing and the buffet supper. Max was master of ceremonies, secretary, adviser and friend, and general factotum, mixed, Magda considered, and admired him for his tact and for his knowledge; the vast knowledge not only of things but of people, or their weaknesses and their good points, their social standing or their lack of it.

'You should have been a diplomat, Max,' she smiled.

'I don't think the Diplomatic Corps has as much to offer me as Mrs. Brand's household,' he said, whimsically.

'Max,' Magda said, struck by a sudden thought, 'you're not in love with her, are you?'

'Oh, no. No! But she does mean a great deal to me. How can I put it? Like a master and his dog, our relationship, I suppose,' and he laughed at himself. 'No, more than that. She was my first employer, and I studied her. Made her my career. I thought at first that if I could serve her (and I admit she's difficult) then I could serve anyone. Now she's got such a habit with me that I wouldn't like to leave. Though I may have to, if she becomes Mrs. Debenham. I can't see her still wanting my services then.'

'What will you do, in that event?' Magda asked.

'We'll wait till it comes,' he said, philosophically.

It was a lovely day, and held a lovely memory for Magda for a long time. He drew her out to talk about herself and Copper, and she found herself telling him, easily, and without much personal feeling, about their childhood, and the difficult days of their nursing training. Their friends and the places they had been to. And all the interesting things she remembered of hospital staff and patients and the people who visited the patients.

They talked, too, of books and music, and the places Max had seen abroad, travelling with Mrs. Brand's household. In his time off, he had seen the museums and the less popular sights, but on duty, he had seen all the splendour of a rich hostess entertaining, and the cosmopolitan people she liked to collect around her. Dinners with Indian princes. A mad safari in the jungle. The trip she insisted on making to the South Sea Islands. And all the time, she had done it the wealthy tourist's way, seeing only the things she was intended to see, while Max slipped off on his own when he could, and got the colour of the places and the people.

After that day at the sea, with its intimate little picnic meal and the bus-trip back in the soft twilight, it seemed to Magda that there were no more free times until the eventful birthday party which Mrs. Brand gave.

Mrs. Debenham collapsed with a heart

attack, which forestalled Magda's leaving. That was a shock. She felt she ought to have seen, with her professional eye, that Andrew's aunt was far from well, but she had been so obsessed with his bad moods, the trouble with Copper, and her own bad health, that she had had little interest in anything beyond those things.

'Magda, I want you to stay, my dear. You must look after me. Will you?' Mrs. Debenham pleaded.

Magda realised with yet another shock that it was more than likely that Andrew wanted to engage another nurse to look after his aunt, and that he wanted her to go as much as she herself wanted to get away.

Mrs. Debenham made it so very difficult to refuse, that she found herself weakly agreeing, and this in spite of her feeling the need for a rest so badly.

'I'm mad,' she kept telling herself. 'I ought to be firm and say no, and go while the going's good. I'll get too involved, too deep in it to ever get away,' and her panic rose.

But the old lady seemed rested when she agreed to stay, so Magda transferred her attentions from Andrew's bedroom to the pale blue and silver room overlooking the rose gardens. That gracious room that was so perfect a background for a gracious old lady.

'I didn't think that my nephew would go to the Brand party,' Mrs. Debenham ventured, on the evening before the event, as Magda poured out her medicine and prepared to spend the evening with her.

'Well, he's quite recovered now,' Magda said, non-committally. 'Why shouldn't he?'

'Because he doesn't really like the woman,' Mrs. Debenham said, crisply. 'He pretends he does. It's that curious sense of humour of his. I don't like it. I prefer people to be totally without humour so long as they are frank and open with me.'

Magda was inclined to agree. She often felt that her employer's sense of humour was the most disconcerting thing about him.

'And another thing, my nephew doesn't dance. He must also be well aware that that wretched woman means him to propose to her. I don't want her to come here and wrest this dear old house from me. Not that I don't want my nephew to marry. Far from it. With the right woman in his life to guide him and give him sons, I could die happy.'

'Who's talking of dying? I don't like my patients to mention the word,' Magda said, coolly.

'Don't be a bully, girl,' the old lady

73

chuckled. 'I mean what I say. I could die happily. But if my nephew found such a woman, I'd be surprised. He's mad. Not in the strict sense of the word, you understand, but in the way these tiresome moderns call crazy. Crazy. That just describes him.'

Again Magda had to agree.

The old lady sighed. 'Ah, well, we shall see the outcome of it all after to-morrow.'

Magda, who had been feeling brighter since the day by the sea, began to experience that wilting feeling again, and shut her mind resolutely to what it meant, and what would happen. Mrs. Debenham's case might well be a long one. The doctor seemed to think it unlikely that she would get really well again, but she might remain an invalid for a very long time. Years perhaps. Magda realised she would have to apply for leave, at some time. She couldn't have said why she didn't want to yet. Two of three weeks surely couldn't make very much difference to old Mrs. Debenham or to anyone else. Yet she put it off.

Just before Andrew went off in his long, sleek black car, to the Brand party, he came up to say good-bye to his aunt. The old lady was as excited as a girl because he looked so nice.

'I've told Magda that she's to take an hour

or two in this nice warm fresh air, but she won't agree. You tell her, Andrew.'

He said, curtly, to Magda, 'You must do as my aunt wishes, Nurse.'

'Tell her it would do her good, Andrew,' his aunt urged.

'Really, aunt,' he protested, 'I don't see how I can force Nurse to do what she doesn't feel inclined to. We must leave it to her, I think, but she must consider herself free to take a turn outside, and be within calling, of course.'

'What a pompous young devil he is, when he likes,' Mrs. Debenham sighed, when he had gone. 'I can't think why he's like it to you, and yet I think I know. Didn't he look nice in his tails? The tall men do, I always think.'

Magda smiled tenderly.

'He did look nice,' she agreed, sincerely.

Andrew was wondering himself why he was so savage with Magda, as he left his car and walked up the wide steps of Sylvia Brand's house. The thought of Magda's stricken face as he snapped at her, haunted him through the evening. Sylvia, in a peach velvet crinoline gown, her fair hair exquisitely dressed and her face so beautifully made up that she had almost achieved the glow of early and bewitching youth to-night, felt a secret pang

75

as she realised she was just failing to claim all his attention. She couldn't see how she was failing, and by such a very narrow margin, but she knew that it was so.

Only when she followed him into the library, a little way behind him, did she realise the truth. He stopped dead, as he saw Copper turn round from the shelves. She had been waiting there to speak to Max but Max was so busy, that he was likely to be some time, and Copper was idly staring at the less boring titles on the shelves.

One girl's dress was very like another's, to Andrew, unless it happened to be the startling kind which Sylvia Brand wore. So it was hardly surprising that he should think it was Magda standing there. How she had come to be here at the time hardly occurred to him at that moment. The fact that he had given her permission to leave his aunt's side for a walk in the garden, and that she had come as far as this, attracted no doubt by someone here, was the point looming so largely for him.

Copper stared, and her habitual grin was not in evidence. She knew, too, that she shouldn't really be down in the library while a party was on, and the fact that Mrs. Brand was coming up behind Andrew, didn't help matters.

'What on earth are you doing here, Nurse?' Andrew had demanded, on first sight of her.

Sylvia glanced quickly at his face and at Copper's. Copper gathered some papers and prepared to leave through the door to Max's study, without a word.

'What are *you* doing here, Andrew?' Sylvia asked, in a low teasing voice, and she gently guided Andrew back to the ballroom. She fought down her fury, while she talked gaily to him. Without attempting the impossible and making a secret of the fact that there were twins, she had so far managed to keep the information from him. That much she had ascertained to her satisfaction. But how much longer she could do so, now that that little fool Copper had managed to be where she wasn't supposed to be, it was difficult to say.

Sylvia Brand knew that it would take all her tact and her cleverness to make him either forget the incident or better still, to ask her to be his wife before he left the party that night.

CHAPTER FOUR

ANDREW followed Sylvia morosely back into the ballroom. The dance band was playing a dreamy waltz. A few couples had already taken the floor, and Sylvia commanded him to dance with her. Andrew wasn't to be trusted with a samba or a quickstep, but he managed a waltz nicely, and he looked distinguished on the floor. She watched herself in his arms in the mirrors, with satisfaction, and thought how splendid it would be if this scene were being enacted at Debenham Mount, with herself as mistress. Herself as hostess, with all the dreary shadows of that old place chased away, and a bit of gaiety introduced. It was an attractive dream, and she wasn't pleased when he broke into it, sharply.

'Who was that girl?' he demanded.

'What girl, Andrew?'

'Didn't you see anyone in the library just now?' he asked, frowning into her pretty face.

'No,' she lied, smoothly, after the slightest hesitation. 'Who did you think you saw?'

'You've seen my nurse, haven't you?'

'Of course, darling.'

He didn't seem to notice the endearment, or if he did, he accepted it as the casual endearment Sylvia and her friends bestowed on anyone without discrimination, a habit which vaguely irritated him.

'Well, I thought it was her.'

She laughed, lightly, astonished almost.

'Oh, Andrew! You're giving yourself the willies. You're well and about again, and you ought to forget all that now. Good gracious, the girl's back in hospital and probably being sent miles away on some other job—'

'She's at Debenham Mount, or should be at this moment, looking after my aunt,' he said, crisply.

The dance finished, and as he led her to her chair, her head was in a whirl. She had understood from Copper that her sister was not even staying to finish her case with Andrew. There seemed to have been a convenient row between the sisters, and Magda had sworn she was going to pack up. What on earth had happened to make her change her mind?

Andrew said, 'Would you like a cocktail?'

'No, I . . . I think I'd like to dance again, Andrew. This is another waltz, and you do them so divinely.'

He suffered himself to be led out on to the

floor again and Sylvia couldn't help wondering if he knew just how grim and unattainable he looked when he was dancing.

'Andrew, I didn't know your aunt was really ill,' she began, delicately leaving the subject of Magda to come up on a different approach.

'She's had heart trouble for some time, but it's got serious now. She's in bed.'

'And needs a nurse?'

He nodded.

'For how long?'

He shrugged.

'It might be a long time. Anyway, don't you worry about Aunt Laura on your birthday night. Are you having a nice birthday?'

'Andrew, when you get to my age, you don't have nice birthdays any more. Up till seventeen, yes. After that, they lose their magic, somehow. Didn't you find that out?'

'I don't think so,' he said, well aware that she had side-tracked him, but couldn't tell where it was going to lead to. 'Aunt Laura has always made them so nice for me. I've a lot of pleasant memories, thanks to her.'

'Whose idea was it that your nurse looked after her?' Sylvia Brand suddenly thrust at him.

'Aunt Laura's, I believe.'

'Um.'

'What does that mean, Sylvia?' he asked, suspiciously.

'Only that I thought your little nurse might have suggested it, wanting to stay in the house for a longer period.'

'As far as I know, she was dying to get out of it,' he said, acidly. 'I can't imagine anyone wanting to stay near me for long.'

'Did she tell you she was dying to go?'

'No, but—'

'Then what made you think she was?'

'Well, dash it all, Sylvia, I didn't make it very comfortable for her! I should have thought she'd have gone ages ago.'

'So should I,' Sylvia agreed, softly.

'What d'you mean by that?' he demanded.

'Oh, nothing, only I've seen you in action, my boy. I only know that if *I* were engaged as your nurse, and got treated as you treated her, I'd have gone the first day. I wouldn't have allowed myself to stay and get insulted like that. I've got too much pride. But she stayed, heavens, how long has she been there?'

'Oh, some weeks,' he said, indifferently. 'Still, I don't see why she shouldn't stay till the end of the case. When these nurses apply for outside jobs, they usually stay the course.'

'Yes, but what often puzzles me is, what makes them apply for outside jobs, anyway? You look at it from her point of view,' she said, allowing him to take her out into the coolness of the night for a breath of air. 'In hospital, *they* can share all the work, and share the difficult patients with the easy ones. On an outside job, they do all the dirty work alone, and are on call all the time.'

'Oh, she had plenty of time off,' he said.

'Did she? I wouldn't call it plenty. I've heard that some of these nurses pray for a male patient, a wealthy one at that, and preferably unattached. Having found one, of course I suppose it would be silly to abandon the job, just because it was difficult.'

'I don't think I get what all this is about,' he said, stiffly.

'Don't you? Don't be silly, Andrew. You're unattached, good-looking, rich, and in fact, the answer to a nurse's prayer. I'm willing to bet she went out of her way to be willing and helpful to you. To put up with all your mouldy moods, and in short to show you only the nicest side of her nature. I bet she thinks she's pretty good to look at herself—they're awfully conceited, these auburn-haired women.'

He was silent, smoking and staring out into

the night.

'And now she's got an extra lease of time at Debenham Mount, because fortunately she was asked (I think you said she was asked) to stay and look after your aunt. Watch out, Andrew—I'm warning you!'

She laughed lightly, and swiftly changed the subject before he could say anything more.

The terrace was wide and paved, and little rose bushes were in green-painted tubs, dotted here and there. A wide flight of shallow steps ran down to smooth turf and rock gardens, and the trees were lit with small coloured electric-light bulbs. Max had put the finishing touch to everything by floodlighting the small summer-houses of stone, scattered around the grounds, and also the little fountain.

'Thank you for your gift, Andrew,' she said, lifting up the small evening-bag shaped like a metal book, and handsomely fitted with mirrors and cosmetics, each in their own little pockets. 'Did you choose it yourself?'

'Don't ask questions,' he laughed.

She experienced a pang of disappointment, and a wild panic surged through her, in case he had asked that nurse of his to suggest something. She dismissed the thought, and decided that this was a man's choice. She knew it was expensive. The stone-encrusted exterior was beautifully worked, and probably composed of precious stones. It was always the real thing with Andrew. But she would have preferred something a little more personal. Pearls or a pendant, or even better, one of the family trinkets. That, at least, would have meant something but this extravagant bit of nonsense might just as well have been given to any of his women friends.

She dare not try and lead him any more towards the subject so dear to her, and she could only hope that her little hints about Magda would have the effect of his changing his aunt's nurse, and sending the girl away. Then, and only then, could she hope to get rid of Copper. She had been so sure, when they had quarrelled, that Magda would have packed up and gone. She had the feeling that Copper was surprised at her staying on, too.

It wasn't until the next day that Sylvia Brand learned of Magda's friendship with Max. She didn't know whether to find pleasure in that discovery, or to be furious. Up till then, Max had been her possession. She had been so sure that he filled his waking thoughts with service for her. He had never been attracted to friendships with other women, all

84

the years she had known him, and when she had thrust Copper on him she had been amused at his look of horror, mingled with contempt. He had written Copper off as a beautiful nitwit, and, although the girl had done her best to start a flirtation with him, Max simply hadn't bitten.

But that Magda had quietly led him into a friendship with her, frightened Sylvia Brand. The girl must be a menace. She didn't bother to dress up or even make up, and seemed to have little to say for herself, and would put up with anything, it seemed. And yet she attracted these men where her glamorous sister failed.

Sylvia played with the idea of having Magda over, and talking to her. Suggesting to her that the whole neighbourhood was talking about her and Andrew. But somehow she felt that more subtle tactics would have to be used. This girl was no fool. She probably knew that her strongest entry was through old Mrs. Debenham, and there Sylvia had failed dismally. She had tried, recognising that the old lady could be a powerful ally, but, from the first, they had hated each other. It was no use. Sylvia considered the old lady a tiresome old dragon, and the old lady saw through Sylvia and put up an effective barrage to protect her nephew and the house.

Funny, how they all seemed so attached to that wretched old mausoleum. It was the same when Andrew's parents were alive—not only the family but the servants were all devoted to it, and looked with horror on anyone who suggested that it wanted brightening up. And now Copper was saying that her sister felt like that about the Mount, too.

Magda felt it even more strongly the next morning when she was called to Andrew's study. She had never been in there before, and had a swift impression of the smell of old leather and tobacco, a book-lined room with rich old rugs on the polished boards, and furniture polished so that it caught the yellow and red gleam of brass and bronze in its fine surface. The sunshine streamed through the small leads of the windows at each end, and a few old weapons were arranged with love and care over the red brick fireplace.

Andrew fitted into that background so well. Like Max, he looked most at home in old and favourite tweeds, and this morning he was cleaning an ancient meerschaum pipe with a great deal of care, instead of his usual short briar.

He glanced curiously at her, then motioned her to sit down facing him. She looked fresh and clean in her pale green uniform with its crackling white starched apron, its frilly cuffs, and the high piled folds of linen with their flapping tails which Magda referred to with great dignity as her cap, and which Copper had always called with ribald laughter, 'the Bird of Paradise'. Copper's cap had always had limp ends, and had been a source of great trouble to her. Magda's looked as it was intended to look, snowy and crisp and rather impressive.

'When I said you could go out last night, I only meant for a brief turn in the grounds, you know,' Andrew Debenham began.

Magda gravely agreed with him.

He waited, but she didn't offer any information as to where she had been.

'Are you—pretty comfortable here?' he asked.

'Oh, yes, very,' she assured him.

'You didn't mind being asked to stay on and look after my aunt?'

She hesitated. She would have dearly loved to say that she had been intending to go before he was really well, both on account of her own need of a rest, and because she found it uncongenial, but somehow it seemed, at this stage, unconvincing. He would ask immediately what had made her change her mind.

Whichever way she looked at it, she could say nothing whatever on that subject without involving Copper. The thought of telling this man that she had a twin sister who had been a nurse at her hospital, who had given up nursing to work for Mrs. Brand after having been Mrs. Brand's nurse, and who moreover was detailed to come and look after him instead of herself—all seemed to spell disaster. Not for Copper so much, since she had lightheartedly jettisoned nursing, but for herself and her own future. After all, Copper had Jim, but she herself would probably have to go on nursing for ever. Besides, would Andrew Debenham have the patience to listen to all that? Might he not be inclined to flare up into a temper before he had heard half of it, and get quite the wrong impression? And might not that wrong impression do harm to Copper after all?

She half-smiled to herself. It always came back to that question: would it, now or ultimately, hurt Copper?

'No, I didn't mind being asked to stay and look after Mrs. Debenham,' she answered.

'Easy patient, eh? Not like me!'

She wriggled uncomfortably. She could hardly agree with him, since that sounded like cheek. But if she had been honest, she would have said that it was such a relief to nurse his aunt after him that it was almost like a holiday anyway.

Etiquette, however, wouldn't permit of such honesty.

'Oh, you weren't so bad, Mr. Debenham,' she said, with a faint smile.

Anyone that described his behaviour, while in bed, as 'not bad,' was grossly exaggerating, he considered, and wondered after all, as other people had before, whether there was not something of truth in what Sylvia Brand had said.

'Tell me, isn't outside work very hard?' he probed.

'Oh, if it is, sir, it's very interesting.'

'Which do you like best. Male patients, or women patients?'

'Well,' Magda said, trying to be fair and yet not offend him, 'Women patients are usually more trying, though your aunt is an exception. I really don't mind which, though.'

'Are you always going to keep outside appointments? You have a choice, I believe?'

'Yes. Well, I think so. It's very interesting, being in different places, and it's so peaceful after the noise and bustle of the hospital. And this old house. I love it so.'

'Yes, you said so before,' he said, dryly.

'But surely, it retards the possibility of your following a private life of your own? Or do you intend to stay in nursing for the rest of your days?'

Magda was puzzled. She didn't see where all this was leading to, and wondered if he, too, had heard the rumour which Copper was so sure had gone the rounds of the district.

She flushed faintly.

'I don't think I understand,' she said. 'Aren't you satisfied with my services, sir?'

'I think you're an excellent nurse,' he said, carefully. 'I don't, however, wish to hold you here for what might be a very long job, without your fully understanding the position. If a change must be made, it would be better for a change of nurses now, before my aunt gets really used to you.'

Magda thought of her own health, and played with the idea of giving up now. But to do that would be tantamount to admitting to herself that she was unfit to carry on. There was a nagging fear all the time, that if she did that, she might give way and be ill for too long, longer than she could afford. On the other hand, if she could manage to keep on, the psychological angle might help her. She had always been a great believer in insisting that she was well, and therefore keeping well.

'May I think it over?' she said, at last.

'Of course,' he said.

She got up, and as he rose, he said, brusquely. 'By the way, returning to the subject I mentioned when you first came down—while you're under this roof, consider yourself under as much discipline as if you were at the hospital. If I say you may take a turn in the grounds, I don't mean that you're free to go as far as the Brand house for the evening.'

Her eyes widened with surprise.

'When I saw you in the library,' he went on, 'you didn't answer me when I spoke to you. You no doubt felt as I did, that it was neither the time nor the place for explanations. I imagine you were well aware that you had no business to be there, and that Mrs. Brand herself didn't know of it?'

Magda's face cleared. Copper again! So the little idiot had let herself be seen, and by Andrew Debenham, of all people. What was the use of trying to keep the fact that they were twins, secret, if she were going to be so careless?

'Did you go over there to see someone?' he insisted.

'Well, I hardly thought it could do any harm,' Magda stammered, wondering what on earth she could say to evade involving

Copper, and yet stick to the truth herself.

'Who is it you know in the Brand household, then?' he frowned, well aware that it was none of his business, and yet curious to know. As far as he knew the only likely male there was Max, the secretary.

Magda herself unwittingly confirmed this.

'I know Mrs. Brand's secretary,' she offered.

'I see.' He was angry with himself. He felt undignified that he should stoop to all this questioning. It was, after all, none of his business. He was also furious because he knew that he had been hoping she would say she'd made friends with some woman on Mrs. Brand's staff. If the rumour was true about Magda—as indeed her own answers to his questions seemed to confirm—it was doubly infuriating that she should at the same time be carrying on a friendship with a male employee of Mrs. Brand's household.

'Well, that's all,' Andrew said, curtly.

He watched her go, and something in the quiet set of her back, and her walk, and the proud way she held that glowing red head under its snowy linen, reproached him. He felt he had been mean, when all the time he had wanted to be friendly with her. He was conscious that he had enjoyed the few minutes of friendship that they had had lately, since he had stopped snapping at her, and he was conscious, too, of having lost something. He began to wish that she would suddenly decide to go, to leave the house at once, so that he could forget her.

And what then? He knew that the way he had been going on pointed to only one thing. He would have to marry Sylvia Brand. It was expected of him. He didn't want that. He objected to it most violently, as he objected violently to being jockeyed into any position when it seemed that Fate was against him, and people looked to him to do as Fate drove him to.

When he went up to see his aunt that morning, she, too, he found, wasn't pleased with him.

'Andrew, what have you been doing to my Magda?' she demanded, and he saw she was looking distressed.

'I? Doing to her?' he gasped.

'Well, you sent for her this morning, and kept her a long time in the study. What was going on all that time?'

'Oh, I just wanted to sound her about one or two things,' he evaded.

'Well, what things?'

93

'Don't you worry about that, Aunt Laura. You concentrate on getting well,' he said, smiling tenderly at her.

She eyed him suspiciously. Her nephew was rarely tender, and when he was, it either meant that he was feeling contrite about something, or that he wasn't even conscious of the way he seemed.

'How can I get well if you upset my little nurse? I like her, and I want her to be happy in this house. I'm well aware that she may have to stay for some time, so don't try to sidetrack me by saying it doesn't matter because she won't be here long.'

'Well, she may not, at that. She may not want to stay here so long. It's a pretty dead hole, anyway.'

'You don't think so!' she accused.

'No, but from her point of view, it might well be.'

'She doesn't think so, either,' his aunt said, quietly, 'and I won't have her upset.'

'Well, what have I done to upset her?' he growled.

'That's what I'd like to know. She was crying.'

He didn't know why that should give him a shock, but it did. He somehow didn't like the thought of Magda crying, and tried to jolly himself out of feeling anything at all about her by reminding himself that she was just the nurse, and that if he were concerned about anyone at all, it ought to be Sylvia Brand.

'Perhaps she's got private troubles,' he offered.

'I don't think so,' his aunt said, slowly.

'Has she said anything about it?' he asked.

'No, and I didn't press her to tell me,' Mrs. Debenham said with some asperity. 'I know she's got a friend she meets once a week, but I wouldn't ask her about it. It's her business, not ours.'

'It's Max,' he said, curtly.

'Oh. Did she tell you?'

'I asked her.'

'Well, then, Andrew, you had no business to. Max is a nice fellow, and an ideal companion for the girl, while she's here, and I'm glad. But we've no business to pry. Now please leave her alone, and don't upset her again.'

'I just wondered who put the idea into her head about staying on to look after you. That's all.'

'I did,' she said. 'And what about it?'

'Well, since she's friends with this Max fellow, she might run off and marry him, and then where would you be?'

'If you think that, Andrew, then you're a great deal more stupid than even I thought you were! In the first place, Max isn't a marrying man, and in the second place, even if he did decide to marry Magda and she was willing do you suppose she's the sort of girl to run off in the middle of a case and get married, because I don't! Nor would she neglect her case because of foolish thoughts about her love affair! Really, Andrew, considering you're a governor on the hospital board, I do think you show a surprising lack of sense at times!'

When Magda's half-day came round, she stayed in. Mrs. Debenham discovered this when the afternoon had half gone, and she heard Magda's voice on the staircase. She sent for her and asked her why she was not out.

'Oh, I don't know, I just didn't feel like it. It's hot. I didn't disturb you, did I, Mrs. Debenham?'

'No, my dear, but what about your young man?'

'What young man?' she asked, flushing.

'Now Magda, don't think I want to pry, but I thought it quite likely that it was a young man you were meeting each Wednesday. You needn't tell me if you don't want to.'

Magda avoided the old lady's eye.

'I have got a friend,' she admitted, 'but he's only a friend, and it isn't important. I thought I'd stay in with a book.'

'Won't he be disappointed?'

'I hadn't thought of it. I don't suppose so. He's pretty busy.'

'What else is troubling you, my dear? It's too nice a day for a pretty young girl to want to be staying in.'

'I don't like the district,' Magda said, unwillingly.

'But I thought you loved it!'

'Oh, the countryside and all that,' she said, 'but it's the people.'

'What about them?'

Magda shifted uneasily. She hadn't wanted to say this, and hadn't thought that Mrs. Debenham would take it up so strongly if she didn't make use of her half-day.

'Sit down, Magda. You've been looking rather peaky lately, I've thought. I began to think that my nephew had been wearing you down, while you were nursing him. But now it occurs to me that you're secretly worried about something. Is it so?'

'Yes,' Magda admitted.

'Hadn't you better confide in me, my dear?'

'I can't entirely, without involving others,'

Magda said. 'It's just that the people gossip a lot, and just lately I've heard that they're gossiping about . . . me. It isn't nice to be going along and see two people break off their conversation and look at you, and all the time you're wondering if it's you they were discussing.'

'But what is there for anyone to discuss about you that you don't like, Magda?'

'Well, I didn't think there was anything, but it seems that people have managed to make up something, in the way they do. I can't make anyone see it isn't true, and I didn't even try. It seemed so silly. But people seem to believe the gossip they hear, and you can't shake them.'

There was a tendency, these days, Magda noticed, for tears to be too near the surface. Almost a weakness, she supposed, due to her run-down state. She was angry with herself about it, but there was little she could do.

At this moment, when she most wanted to keep calm, she felt that overpowering sense of helplessness stealing over her, and bit her lips fiercely. Mrs. Debenham stared in horror at the girl, and wondered what on earth the scandalmongers of the neighbourhood had managed to cook up about Magda, who was in her opinion, the nicest young woman she had happened on for a long, long time.

She talked to her for a while, in general terms, about not taking any notice of people and their love of gossip, but certainly not to give in to it to the extent of not going out. She didn't press for more details, though she was well aware that Magda had told her absolutely nothing about it, beyond the fact that there was gossip. She hoped that after a while, the girl would feel like coming to her and voluntarily confiding in her. She wondered if her nephew had heard of the gossip or whether he had been instrumental in starting it, by his way of treating the girl in the first place. She didn't know, but her innate breeding and her own good manners forced her to disapprove strongly of his attitude all along, and led her to speak to him about it often, though with no visible effect. Bad manners to subordinates, in Mrs. Debenham's view, were as much an offence as being unacceptable to society through some vice. Bad manners in her code, were, indeed, a vice.

She watched Magda carefully for the next day or two. It was early autumn now. The weather was still good enough for any summer's day, but the year was advancing, and Magda had been in the house long enough to have almost become part of it. The staff accepted her, and had been nice to her, Mrs. Debenham noticed, but during the last week or two there had been a change, almost imperceptible, but now noticeable. She thought it might be because she was watching for it, after what Magda had said about the gossip. Nevertheless, it occurred to her that the staff were not quite so polite to Magda, and that the very faintest tinge of interest was in their eyes when they looked at her.

One day she spoke of it to Andrew.

'Have you heard any gossip about Magda, Andrew?' she had asked, idly.

To her surprise, he had flushed, and then whitened, but all she had got out of him was not a vigorous denial, but a show of boredom about the neighbourhood, its rumours, and his aunt's nurse herself. It struck her as being a little unconvincing.

And then Mrs. Debenham forgot Magda's troubles for a while, because of her own. She had another attack, and for days was very ill indeed. When she pulled out of it, and became a little brighter, she sent for Andrew and told him to sit by her bed where she could see him.

'Andrew,' she said, in the new faint voice that alarmed him so much, 'I'm going to pry.'

'Fire away, Aunt Laura,' he said, cheerfully. 'It's so unlike you that I think I can put up with it for once.'

'I want to ask you about Mrs. Brand.'

He stiffened, but still smiling a little, he said:

'What about her?'

'I've been thinking, my dear. She and I don't hit it off. You know that well enough. But if you like her as much as I now begin to suspect that you do, well, don't let my feelings influence you.'

'What's all this for, Auntie?' he gasped.

'I'm an old woman,' she said, and waved away, with a pale, almost transparent hand, his protests. 'And I haven't the rallying power that I had when I was younger. I don't think I can stand these attacks very much longer. But the old have a way of clinging to life. It's very good, after all. And if I should hang on a long time, I fear it will have the effect of putting off any . . . any plans, shall we say, that you might have been making.'

'If you mean, am I going to marry Sylvia?'

'That was just what I did mean, Andrew, but before you say yes or no, I wanted to suggest that I might perhaps be moved to a nursing-home. So that I didn't impede your plans, d'you see. It's a nuisance with an invalid in the house, and after all, the Mount isn't mine. It's yours, my dear, and you'll want your bride to be in complete charge of it.'

'I thought you'd always loathed the idea of Sylvia being my wife?'

'I'd never cared for the idea of her taking my place here,' his aunt corrected him mildly, 'but I've never said a word about your wife, my dear. No, on the whole, I think my plan is a good one. That is, if you could arrange for me to take Magda with me. I'd want Magda to look after me, you know.'

'Magda?' he stared. 'You're very attached to her, aren't you, Aunt Laura?'

'I am. She's a dear girl.'

'It's funny. You're not usually taken in by people,' he mused.

'You think Magda's taking us in?' she asked, shrewdly.

He hesitated, and then got up. Abruptly he pushed his chair back, and said, 'I do think this is a dashed silly conversation, Aunt Laura. You jolly well stay there until you're better. As to my marriage, that's your idea, not mine.'

He left her without another word, and she didn't know whether to be satisfied or to feel that she had lost the battle on all points.

Magda put the final touch to it all.

'Now that you're better again,' she said carefully, that evening, 'would you mind very much if I handed over to someone else?'

Mrs. Debenham hadn't been expecting this, and was so alarmed that Magda hurriedly said that of course if she didn't like the idea, then she would stay on.

'But what makes you want to leave me, my dear?' Mrs. Debenham asked, agitatedly.

'Oh, it's nothing,' Magda said, confused.

'Is it all this gossip you spoke of?'

'Oh, that, and other things. I feel I ought perhaps to be moving on to some other place.'

Mrs. Debenham thought quickly, and was shocked to find how tired it made her.

'Magda, you must know, as a nurse, how much longer I've got. Couldn't you find it in your heart to stay with me for that little while?'

Magda's eyes filled, to her own horror.

'Oh, I'm so sorry. I didn't mean to upset you. It's just that I feel . . . well, such a failure!'

'But why? Why? You're the best and only nurse I want!'

'Well, something must be wrong with me,' Magda said, slowly. 'Or your nephew wouldn't act the way he is.' She hesitated, then said, slowly, 'He's just as cold and distant to me again as when I first came.'

CHAPTER FIVE

As the autumn advanced, Magda fell back on Max and his friendship a good deal. There were not so many trips about the district, it is true, for he was very busy, and his leisure hours were curtailed. The weather began to be tricky, and they never ventured far without raincoats and thick scarves. But they explored the immediate neighbourhood, and visited teashops and cinemas in the nearest town. It was all very simple entertainment, and all very pleasant.

Magda, looking very nice in a brown beret and belted topcoat, with a hand-knit woollen scarf of warm autumn yellows and russets, made for Max a satisfying companion. She was a good listener, and there was a tranquility in those dark brown eyes of hers that was contagious. Max felt all the tension easing out of himself when he was with her; that tension which crept over him almost unnoticed, through the effort of keeping on his toes in his service to Sylvia Brand.

And yet he liked serving Sylvia. He couldn't analyse his feelings about it, but she offered him an exciting—if fatiguing life. He knew that he had a power over her, in the sense that he could guide her expenditure, shape her pleasures, and be such a necessity to her that the mere thought of his leaving her frightened her.

He knew that she was possessive where he was concerned, and that, too, gave him a sense of power. He knew, too, that she lived in more or less constant fear of his getting married, and that amused him. He had never yet found a woman who would give him the sense of need for a wife. Life, so far, was all that he asked. An interesting, even exciting job, in a world which would normally be far out of his reach.

But Magda's coming into his life had raised the tiniest prick of doubt. He found himself thinking of her when she wasn't with him, and remembering the peach-blossom quality of her skin, and the loveliness of her smile. The beautiful unhurried movements of her limbs, and the calm efficiency of her. He found himself watching Copper, comparing her with her sister, wondering that twins could be so different in some ways, so alike in others. From a distance it was almost possible to believe that Copper was Magda, when she was standing still. Even if you knew them both, you were fooled for a moment, for both—besides having the same colouring— had the same curious proud lift of the chin, the same way of slightly lifting the shoulders and hands, expressive of surprise, and the same easy, graceful way of standing.

But when they started to move, it was difficult to be mistaken. Copper was dynamic. Her over-abundance of energy expressed itself in her movements, and in her voice, and in the quick grin, the dancing eyes and the lilting, excited laughter.

Copper was heady, if you liked that type, but there was a slow magic about Magda that wasn't at first apparent, and which crept over you without your at first being aware.

Was he falling in love with Magda? That was a question he asked himself, nervously assuring himself that he wasn't. He didn't want to be in love with anyone, but the friendship she offered was a thing to be grateful for, and to enjoy to the full. Yet he was conscious of not being quite fair. What did she want out of life? If she only asked to be a nurse, then that nice friendship of theirs could no doubt go on—that is, if Sylvia Brand didn't interfere too much. He was only too well aware that all this extra work she was finding for him, on the afternoons he happened to be going out with Magda, was not really necessary. He wasn't quite certain of Copper's attitude towards his friendship with Magda, either.

One day towards late September, on a bus together, Max slewed round to look at Magda, and to enjoy the uprush of her beautiful smile before he spoke.

'Happy?' he asked her.

She raised her brows, those lovely brows of reddish brown, delicately etched like the wings of some oriental bird.

'Yes. Yes, I believe I am. At least, when I'm out with you, Max.'

His heart lurched. He somehow passionately didn't want her to be in love with him, so that he could feel free to sort out his own feelings about her first. Conscious of his gross selfishness, he said:

'Why only when you're out with me? Does that mean you like your leisure time so much, or that you like the places we go to so much, or that you like being with a dreary old stick like me, Magda?'

She thought over the point, then raised her eyes to his, fearlessly, honestly.

'I'm not in love with you, Max, if that's what you mean.'

He ought to have felt relieved, but he wasn't. He couldn't tell just how he felt in that moment, and he found himself laughing a little.

'Did I say something funny, Max?'

'No. No, my dear. It's just—well, I don't know. You're so different to any other woman I've met, and I think the essential difference lies most in your honesty. You know, few women are quite so honest, and it rather pulls one up with a jerk.'

'Oh, does it?'

She wondered if he had already found out that her dear Copper wasn't quite as honest—no, that wasn't the word—quite as crystal-clear in her conception of telling the truth. Copper couldn't see quite straight. The truth for her, had always been what she had wanted it to be. Magda had pandered to this, because it was just one of Copper's funny little ways. But would a man think that? What did Jim know of that, and of all Copper's other little foibles? Did he know, and did he love her, in spite of them? She didn't know, and had never been able to find the answer.

'It does indeed. Magda, how long are you going to be at Debenham Mount?'

'I don't know, Max. It depends on Mrs. Debenham, I suppose, unless Mr. Debenham decides he doesn't want me around, and that a change of nurse would be better.'

Max looked startled.

'Why should he do that?'

'Oh, well, he's on the board of governors, and he's quite free to choose another nurse.'

'That didn't answer the question, Magda.'

'He and I don't seem to get on very well,' she said, with difficulty, averting her face.

'I see. Well, if you can't get on with him, my dear, I don't know who can.'

'Mrs. Brand seems to,' Magda said, smiling.

Max shrugged that away.

'Oh, well, Mrs. Brand! Why not? She's likely to be engaged to him. I meant, subordinates, like you and me.'

Subordinates. Yes, that was all she was, Magda thought, and was surprised that she had forgotten it for the moment. Yet despite all the discipline of the hospital, one never felt it there quite so much. It was, she supposed, being in the swim. They were all subordinates, and no one thought anything of it. Yet here, she had been made rather a pet of, she supposed, by Mrs. Debenham, and been called by her Christian name, and at first the staff had been very nice to her, and made her feel that she was someone rather special.

Andrew Debenham, however, altered all that. He altered it in an unfair way, too. One moment treating her so badly that she wanted to run away and never see him again, and the next moment being apparently friendly enough with her to ask her to take tea with him.

'Well, I shall stay as long as I can,' she said, grimly, 'because of his aunt. She's a dear.'

'When will she be well again, d'you suppose?'

Magda looked up at him.

'Don't you know? It's her heart. She won't ever be really well again.'

'Oh. Well, after this case is over, then what, Magda?'

'I shall go back to the hospital, I suppose. To be given another case, or go back to the wards.'

She nearly added, 'It depends on how I feel as regards my health,' but she didn't. Physical health meant so much to her, that to be below par was a thing to be ashamed of.

'And is that all you want out of life? To go on nursing?'

'It's all that life has offered me, so far,' she replied, carefully. 'If life had anything else, anything better, to put up, I'd consider it,' she laughed.

'Such as?'

'Oh, Max! Stop it! This horrid questionnaire! How would you like it if I turned it on you?'

'I suppose I'd answer in pretty much the same way, you know. I'd consider any better offer that might present itself.'

'And in the meantime, you're not going out of your way to look for something else,' she guessed, correctly.

It was this conversation which was turning over in Magda's mind that same evening, as she sat by the fire in Mrs. Debenham's big bedroom. Max was such a good companion, until you came up against that self-sufficiency in him, and then it had the curious effect of making you feel very lost and alone. Max would never be lost and alone. It wasn't in him.

Magda realised that while she could hardly say, being a woman, 'Of course I'll consider the right man if he came along,' because she was talking to a man, Max on the other hand might very well have said that he had never thought of marriage before, but that he hoped it would happen to him if he found the right woman. It seemed that he would never marry, because he simply didn't want marriage. He was so happy alone, in service.

Mrs. Debenham lay staring at the girl

through half-closed lids. They had had tea together, a dainty tea-set on the invalid table, with the silver tea-service, and the fine lace tray-cloth and serviettes. A tea which cook had prepared with loving care to tempt her mistress, with the tiny angel cakes and crisp biscuits, the fingers of toast and the little rolls of butter. And that fine blend of tea which Mrs. Debenham loved so much. She liked Magda to take tea with her, and to hear the funny, heart-breaking little stories of tea in the hospital, and the things the patients said, and the things they liked.

But it seemed to her to-day that Magda's manner was a trifle forced. The girl wasn't as happy as she appeared to be on the surface.

'Magda, I'm not asleep,' she said, suddenly.

Magda jumped, and hastily took up her knitting again.

'Don't pretend, my dear. You haven't done a stitch yet. You're worried about something. Is it still that stupid rumour you insist is around?'

'No. Oh, no, I've forgotten that.'

'You never told me what it was. Are you sure you wouldn't care to confide in an old woman?'

'I don't like repeating gossip,' Magda said, slowly. 'To hear it said in one's own words almost confirms the truth of it . . . and it isn't true. It isn't true.'

'I'm sure it isn't, whatever it is. Magda, that young friend of yours. Do you still see him?'

'Yes. We still go out once a week.'

'Is it—likely to be serious?'

Magda hesitated.

'It's only Max, you know. We're just friends.'

Mrs. Debenham relaxed a little. She had been hoping that Magda would tell her who her friend was, without her having to ask. It made everything else so much easier, and also confirmed her feeling that the girl was transparently honest.

'Then who is the man you're in love with?'

Magda flung up her head, caught out for a moment, the swift tide rushing up her fair skin.

'There isn't—' she began, then broke off, biting her lip. Suddenly she felt that she couldn't say with any certainty that there wasn't a special someone. And yet if this were being in love, this torment of wondering if someone was going to be nice, or perfectly beastly, and to know all the time that you were only looked on by him as a subordinate—if this were being in love, then she didn't want it. It was the most horrible situation to be in, that she could imagine.

'Never mind, my dear,' Mrs. Debenham said, chuckling a little. 'I was just teasing you. Don't look so confused. But seriously, if you aren't in love with Max, and there's no one else, and you aren't bothering unduly about the gossip you mentioned, then your trouble must be some other thing.'

Magda didn't answer, but stared into the fire. There was an aching urge to talk to someone about it, but to talk to Andrew's own aunt would surely be quite the wrong thing to do.

Mrs. Debenham said, gently, 'My dear, is it that you want to go away from here so much, and that you feel I'm keeping you here against your will?'

'Oh, no, no! I told you I wanted to go, but when I found how much it upset you, the thought of a change, then I naturally put it right out of my thoughts,' Magda said, wildly. 'Look, we're both getting agitated, and it's all nothing, really nothing. You must try and sleep, and if you find your nurse daydreaming a bit by the fire, well, it's just that it's a specially nice fire to day-dream by, and . . . and I've had such a nice afternoon out, it's fun to come home to a fire.'

114

'To come home,' the old lady repeated. 'So that's how you look at the Mount!'

'Oh, yes,' Magda breathed.

'I never thought I'd hear another young person refer to this old place as "home". My nephew Andrew is the one exception, and he's passionately fond of it. I sometimes fancy that he expends every ounce of the best of his nature on this house, and doesn't leave enough over for the human beings around him. You mustn't let him worry you, Magda, dear.'

'I'm nursing you now, aren't I?' Magda smiled.

'Tell me, did you have a happy home background?'

The question was put smilingly, and Magda, plumping up the old lady's pillows and straightening the bed before she resumed her fireside seat, almost fell into the trap of disclosing the fact that there were two of them, and revealing the secret that they were twins. It wasn't going to be easy, she reflected, as she took her time in answering the question.

'I had no mother. Just my father,' she said, at last.

'And what was his profession?'

Magda smiled tenderly.

'He did nothing much, and I don't suppose you could say he had a profession. He painted a bit, and played the piano a bit, and tutored a bit, and—whatever he felt like doing at the time, that would bring in a bit of money.'

'My dear!' Poor Mrs. Debenham was shocked. 'Hardly a suitable background for the bringing up of a young daughter!'

That, Magda thought sadly, was just what the trouble had been. There were two of them. It wouldn't have been so bad if there had just been one of them, for then his only sister wouldn't have minded taking the one child. But twins, and red-headed twins, had been the last straw. She had flatly refused.

'He was a wonderful person,' Magda said, dreaming into the fire. Pictures of herself and her father, sitting absorbed over books or music, flashed before her eyes, and the wild Copper—off on some mad scheme of her own—was never to be found when lessons were on foot.

'He used to say,' Magda continued, 'that Life had just so much to give each of us. If you made up your mind to work and make a fortune, despite Fate, then you were just batting your head against a brick wall, for if it wasn't there for you, you wouldn't get it despite your labours. And if it was in store for you, it

116

would come, even if you just sat down and waited for it.'

'A dangerous doctrine, my dear,' the old lady observed. 'What did you do?'

Again a difficult question to answer. Without revealing that Copper existed, how could she say anything about the anxiety she had gone through, wondering how to apply the little store of money her father had left, supplemented by what she had got for selling his paints, his music and the piano, and his other treasures she would so dearly have loved to keep? How could she reveal the months and years of anxiety, keeping Copper's nose to the grindstone, getting her through her exams as well as her own, until at last they were both qualified, and Magda could be reasonably sure that their small store of money wouldn't be thrown away?

'Oh, well,' she temporised, 'I chose what I considered the most solid profession, nursing. It seemed the only thing to do.'

'And you're following your father's advice, heh? Waiting for the plums of life to fall into your lap?'

Magda flushed painfully.

'I've never asked for anything more than peace,' she said, quietly, thinking that with Copper still on her hands, peace was the one thing that had so far been denied her. 'Is that a lot to ask?'

'No—o,' Mrs. Debenham said, hesitantly. 'Not a lot to ask, but a rather strange thing to ask, especially by so attractive a young woman. Of course, if that's all you want, I should have thought you'd find it here, of all places. But you haven't, have you?' she finished, shrewdly.

'I shan't find it anywhere,' Magda said, frowning into the fire, and sounding—without realising it—rather hopeless. She meant that while Copper was unmarried there would be no peace, and she had no guarantee that there would be peace if Copper did marry, whether she married Jim or some other man. Despite all Copper's brave talk about standing on her own feet, the habit of running to Magda to get her out of trouble, was too deeply ingrained for her to abandon now. Copper was, Magda felt, on her hands for ever.

'I'm so tired,' she found herself whispering.

The old lady didn't hear. She was pursuing a thread of thought of her own, and to this end, she suddenly said:

'My nephew Andrew had an unfortunate love affair once.'

Just like that. A bolt out of the blue. Magda

118

was startled in spite of herself. It was not so much that the old lady thought she was (or had been) crossed in love, that startled Magda, as the information that Andrew had been in love, or been capable of being in love. He was such a difficult person at best, and one couldn't call his friendship with Sylvia Brand being in love, surely?

'She was a very lovely creature,' Mrs. Debenham went on. 'Red-haired,' she added, with a casualness that deceived no one.

'What happened?' Magda asked, feeling that some sort of co-operation was required of her.

'I don't think I know quite,' Andrew's aunt murmured. 'She used to be here quite a lot. A gay person, with sparkling blue eyes, and a voice that almost sang. She used to make me feel younger, and she used to make me remember what it was like to be young. Now that's quite an accomplishment with anyone like me,' she finished, smiling at Magda.

'Did she . . . love your nephew?' Magda asked, trying to imagine him in love and loved in return, and failing. Puzzled, too, because the effort made her heart race, as it would by touching electric wires. The sort of feeling you got if you knew that what you were going to do was dangerous, yet being pushed imperatively towards it by some unseen force. The thought of Andrew's face, close to her own, his eyes intense and demanding, struck at her, and she pushed the imaginative picture away.

'I don't know if she loved him,' Mrs. Debenham allowed. 'She loved life, and I rather think it gave the illusion of her loving everyone. She was so . . . so utterly lovely and alive. I remember her running in from the garden, laughing, her arms full of white flowers, and she wore a blue dress, full and flounced. I remember her running down the terrace steps one night when there was a party. She was in white, laughing as always, and with little winking jewels at her throat and in her ears. I don't remember her wearing anything severe or prosaic, at all,' the old lady said, musingly. 'I think there is a tendency about some people to be remembered as pictures in a book, although I know of course that she didn't wear party clothes all the time.'

'And then?' Magda prompted, interested in spite of herself.

'And then she didn't come any more, and I saw her engagement to someone else announced in the papers, and Andrew went away without a word. It seemed to me rather like a sick animal going into hiding.'

'You mean she jilted him?'

'Possibly. It could hardly have been anything else.'

'But he's got over it now?'

'I don't know,' Mrs. Debenham said again.

She stared into the fire, while Magda tried to imagine what it would be like to be remembered in those lovely clothes, with an apparently leisured life where you could dash about laughing and carrying flowers.

'Does everyone in the district know about that? Magda asked, suddenly.

'Oh, yes,' Mrs. Debenham said.

'Even Mrs. Brand?'

The eyes of both women met.

'Particularly Mrs. Brand, I imagine,' Mrs. Debenham said, dryly.

Magda did some quick thinking. It might well be that she feared that Andrew would fall in love with Magda simply because her hair was red, and that it would remind him of that other affair, although to Magda it seemed a silly idea. She reasoned that if she had been in love with a man with dark hair, it didn't follow that she would fall in love again with someone with the same colouring. But Sylvia Brand evidently wasn't too sure of Andrew Debenham. After all, if she had known him

121

all that time . . . how long, Magda found herself clamouring?

'Mrs. Brand has been a widow for some time, hasn't she?' she heard herself say.

'For five years,' Mrs. Debenham said.

'And when was your nephew—when did his fiancée—?'

'He was jilted ten years ago,' Mrs. Debenham said, crisply.

'Oh, I see,' Magda thought.

How galling those first five years must have been for Sylvia Brand. And what had she been doing for the last five years? Trying to make Andrew forget that old affair? Or trying to break the shell of bachelorhood that had hardened around him?

If she had been all that time trying to get him to ask her to marry him, Magda decided, no wonder she was worried when another redhead came suddenly to live in his house. Not that she need have any fears that Andrew Debenham would marry one of the nurses at his hospital, Magda shrewdly saw, but that the sight of a redhead every day would bring back those memories of his first love, and show Mrs. Brand up in a poor comparison.

'Poor Mrs. Brand,' she found herself saying, thinking that she herself was a fool not to have so far seen that Mrs. Brand had started the rumours about herself and Andrew, for that purpose only. A frightened woman.

'Yes, I, too, feel sorry for her,' Andrew's aunt said. 'For whoever my nephew marries—whether Sylvia Brand or anyone else—no one will supersede in his thoughts the girl he was to have married so long ago.'

Their eyes met, and Magda took it as a warning, though it hurt her that Mrs. Debenham should think that she needed a warning. Was it possible that the old lady thought that Magda's anxieties simply meant that she was secretly in love with Andrew Debenham? And that perhaps his difficult bearing towards her was making her unhappy because of that?

Magda felt her cheeks burning with embarrassment. Why did everyone think she wanted Andrew Debenham to be attracted to her, when she hadn't even sorted out her own feelings towards him yet?

The answer to it all made her even more wretched. All this had been started by Sylvia Brand, who would stop at no lengths to get Andrew herself, even to keeping Copper in her house in some fictitious employment. It was painfully obvious, even to Magda, that nice as old Mrs. Debenham was, she, too, had somehow got to hear of the rumour, and against her will, believed it.

CHAPTER SIX

MAGDA's reaction to that little talk with Mrs. Debenham was to go out of her way to avoid Andrew.

This wasn't too difficult for a time, for as he was swiftly regaining the old use of his leg, he took up all his old duties again. Farming, riding, and the business of the tenants of the Debenham lands, took up so much of his time, that he was scarcely at the Mount during the day, and when at dinner there were friends. Sometimes he went to Town on the hospital business, but always, after dinner at night, there was the eternal bridge.

Magda, who didn't play cards, thought what a dreary existence it must have been, and wondered if this were one of the facets of Andrew which had driven that first girl away. There was a fat old judge, and the Dean, a retired stockbroker and a planter invalided home from the East, who formed the nucleus of Andrew's bridge evenings. They and their wives, and one or two elderly spinsters whom Mrs. Debenham knew, formed an almost constant card-playing crowd. Mrs. Debenham missed them, and pined to be up and about again.

'Don't you play bridge, my dear?' she asked Magda wistfully.

When Magda denied even the slightest knowledge of cards, she fancied Mrs. Debenham looked disappointed in her. She was rather amused, and asked, on the spur of the moment, if Andrew had any other pursuits.

Mrs. Debenham seemed rather at a loss to know how to answer that one.

'Well,' she said, at last, 'you mustn't let him know that I told you, but he used to be very fond of music. He played well, you know. The piano, and the organ. Sometimes he played the organ in church, for pleasure, you understand.'

'Your nephew did that?' Magda gasped.

Somehow the thought of his playing any musical instrument struck her as being completely alien to him.

'It was all so tied up with the young woman who jilted him,' his aunt explained. 'He used to be a very gay person in those days. The house seemed to be full of music and life and young people. But you must on no account let him know I told you.'

'Wouldn't he like it?'

'He would be furious, my dear. Andrew seems to have shut his old self up inside him

126

since that sad event. It was as if his old self died. He took up bridge soon after, and it sometimes seems to me that he set about making himself into a different person. Different in his pursuits and tastes, different in his outlook altogether. Only when he's on the home farm does he seem the same.'

'Oh, yes, I'm apt to forget that he's a farmer,' Magda said.

'He's a very good stock-breeder and progressive dairy farmer,' his aunt said, stoutly.

Magda smiled, and decided that she wouldn't like the home farm very much. It sounded like one of those very super efficient places, where the cows were milked by machinery and nothing was picturesque but painfully clean. She supposed that as a nurse she ought to appreciate that. But somehow the ideal farm was, to her, a place where everything was still done by hand, and beauty wasn't sacrificed to stream-lining.

She didn't say this to Mrs. Debenham, however, for fear of offending her, but the home farm was the one place in the district which Magda steadily avoided.

But then, as the days wore on, she began to avoid most places. The gossip didn't die down. Magda supposed that so long as Mrs. Brand was still dis-engaged, people would still speculate on who would get Andrew Debenham in the end—the scheming Mrs. Brand, or his pretty nurse. Magda crossly wished that people would mind their own business and leave her alone.

One day in October, she had to go to the village, to get some stamps and some wool for Mrs. Debenham. She didn't go there often, and was asking herself whether it was really the tired feeling that was almost always with her now, or whether it was really courage that she was lacking.

So engrossed was she in her own thoughts, that she almost passed Copper without recognising her.

Copper exclaimed sharply, and Magda looked up.

'Hallo, Copper,' she said, smiling faintly, and wondering what reception she would get after all this time. She had not seen her sister since that day when she had said she would give up her job because of the rumour about herself and Andrew Debenham.

Copper frowned.

'Good heavens, Magda, are you ill?'

'Ill?'

'Yes, you look awful! Just look at yourself in this window.'

Magda turned, dazed, and stared at herself

128

in the mirror at the back of the little milliner's shop window. It was true. She looked perfectly ghastly. There were dark circles under her eyes, and her face—usually delicately tinted, and rather tanned—was white. The whiteness that suggests faintness or chronic anaemia.

'I didn't know—I didn't realise—' Magda stammered looking helplessly at Copper.

Copper still had that vital look which Magda remembered so well, and in addition she was beautifully sunburnt, and it suited her. She looked well, and was nicely dressed, but not particularly happy.

'I'm thinking of chucking the job,' she said, pulling a face. 'If I'd known it was just going to be keeping dreary old books clean, well, I might as well have been a housemaid.'

'But you get plenty of freedom, don't you?' Magda asked.

Copper shrugged.

'Who wants freedom in a place like this?'

'I thought you said it would be such fun?' Magda pointed out, with justice. It seemed hard that after all her effort to get Copper into the nursing profession, and to keep her there, that she should throw it all up, and then get tired so soon of the new job she had jumped into.

'Oh, well, I could be wrong, I suppose,' Copper said, ungraciously. 'Anyway, never mind about me. What about you? If I were you, I'd take that rest I seem to remember you mentioning, and which I didn't really believe you meant!'

'I couldn't go, Copper. Mrs. Debenham was taken ill.'

'Are there no other nurses in the world?' Copper mocked.

Magda decided sadly that Copper didn't really want to be friends again after all, and probably wouldn't have stopped to speak to her, if Magda hadn't looked so ill.

'I asked her to get someone else, and I've asked her since,' Magda explained patiently, 'but she's old and one can't be unkind.'

Copper grinned mockingly, and although she didn't mention Andrew, Magda had the uncomfortable feeling that her sister believed the rumour just as fervently as everyone else did.

'Do you hear from Jim?' she ventured.

Copper scowled.

'Let's leave my love-life out of it, if you don't mind. Anyway, I'd better be getting along.'

Magda bought the wool but forgot the stamps, so upset was she about that meeting with her sister, and the revelation of just how ill she had become without noticing it.

She felt wobbly about the legs and made slow progress in getting back, and wondered how much longer she could go on.

Nurses weren't supposed to get ill. When they were off colour, they went to the dispensary and got it put right, plus a few hours off for rest. Few of them were ever in anything but tiptop health, and if one did get really ill and had to be away, it usually happened that the girl had a family to fall back on, in the meantime. Magda had no one. . . .

She told herself fiercely to stop it. She would be getting the jitters and be unable to carry on at all. She made herself walk with a firm step into Mrs. Debenham's bedroom, and talk with a cheerful note in her voice. But the effort it cost her, scared her.

'Ah, my dear,' Mrs. Debenham said, 'that's better. That's much better. I do believe that walk in the fresh air has done you a lot of good.'

'It was pleasant,' Magda forced herself to agree.

'You must go more often. Don't think that I don't notice how little you get out these days. You're beginning to look quite pale lately, and we can't have that.'

131

Magda poured tea, and Mrs. Debenham said, casually, and with a guileless air that almost took Magda unawares and made her spill the tea, 'Have you ever been really ill, Magda?'

Magda said, 'No, I haven't.'

'I often wonder if nurses ever get ill, and if so, how they manage. Is there a nurse's rest home?'

Magda gave her her tea, and said, firmly, with her nice smile, 'Now let's have no more of this talk about illness. It isn't at all the thing. I've never been ill, I'm not going to be ill, and you don't have to worry about me at all.'

'I only asked, my dear, because you said you have no home, and I wondered what would become of you until you were really well again.'

'But I'm not ill!' Magda insisted, and wondered if Mrs. Debenham noticed the tiny break in her voice that she couldn't prevent, and the way her hands shook.

The next day was a day of hard, brilliant sunshine, that made the bare trees look more conspicuous against the carpet of gold leaves beneath them. Autumn here was going to be unforgettable, Magda told herself, as she drew back the curtains, and prepared to get her patient ready for the day.

'Will you do a small errand for me to-day, Magda?' Mrs. Debenham asked.

Magda's heart sank. Another trip to the village, she supposed, or worse still, another of those letters to be delivered to the Manor.

'Yes, of course,' she smiled.

'I want you to take a message for me, to the home farm. Don't hurry back. I expect they'll want to show you round.'

Magda's face mirrored her feelings, how startled she felt. Would Andrew be there?

Mrs. Debenham continued, mildly, 'My nephew is away all to-day, otherwise I wouldn't bother you with this.'

Magda said, faintly, 'Of course I'll go, in that case.'

'The tenants are called Chandler, and they're very nice people. If they ask you to stay to tea, do so, my dear. You'll like it.'

Magda made up her mind to get the trip over as soon as possible and to get away, in case Andrew came back earlier than was expected. But once she had seen the farm, she altered her mind.

It lay in a hollow. An old, mellowed, untidy house, with sprawling gables and a roof of old tiles. A crimson creeper covered most of the place, and the windows peeped out like little

133

eyes under bushy eyebrows. A duck-pond, with ducks, and willows dripping into the water, and a huddle of ricks in a nearby stack-yard, rather squashed the picture Magda had built up of stream-lined, even-spaced buildings and a general air of efficiency. Sleepy animals made noises, and a dog peered out of a kennel and made an effort to bark at her as she stood, taking it all in.

A picture farm, on an autumn day of crimson and gold. Why hadn't someone told her before how beautiful it was? How was it no one had recommended her to come here?

Mrs. Chandler was an enormous woman, the comfortably fat type who is always smiling, always cheerful, and good company to be with. She beamed on Magda, then caught sight of her flaming hair as the girl pulled her beret off.

'From the Mount, eh? Oh, my dear, you fair gave me a turn. Reminded me of Miss Elizabeth, after all these years.'

She hastily recovered herself after a glance at someone behind her, and Magda turned to find the farmer standing there. A hefty, solemn man, who, Magda afterwards discovered, had a tremendous respect for Andrew, both as a farmer and as a man.

After he had gone out again, Magda said,

134

dropping into one of the old-fashioned horse-hair covered chairs with a patchwork antimacassar on its back, 'Mr. Chandler didn't like you mentioning Elizabeth, did he?'

Mrs. Chandler smiled. 'Well, the men, m'dear, they do so hate us to gossip, but there, where would we be without a bit to talk over and remember like?'

'Yes. I know about Elizabeth, anyway,' Magda mused, though she had never heard the name mentioned before. 'Did you like her?'

'Eh, well, she was such a gay thing, and so pretty. Just the same colouring, too, and it made me think for a minute—well, now, that's silly, seeing as she married and went out East, and they do say she died out there of fever, though I somehow can't bring myself to believe that. Made for life and laughter, that girl was, and never was anyone so surprised as myself when she went and did that dreadful thing, turning down our Mr. Andrew for some other fella.'

'Perhaps she wanted to go abroad to live?' Magda hazarded.

'Perhaps she wanted more money to spend I shouldn't wonder, though heaven knows our gentleman isn't a poor man. But there, I shouldn't be talking this way about her, and

135

don't you go getting any ideas about what I'm meaning, miss, because there wasn't any bad feelings towards our Miss Elizabeth, nor ever will be, whatever she did. She was like that. Everybody loved her, and would have, whatever she'd done.'

Everybody loved her. What had this girl really been like, this girl who did such heartless things, and yet who so held the love of everyone, and one man in particular, that they spoke so about her, so long afterwards, and he himself went so far as to change his habits, his very life, almost, to try and put her out of his mind? Elizabeth. A caressable name.

Magda suddenly felt she wanted to see a picture of Elizabeth, to hear Andrew say her name, to imagine the two of them together. To see Andrew sitting at the great grand piano, playing to her, while she stood in a picturesque attitude nearby.

However Magda thought about it, she couldn't imagine that girl as anything but theatrical and heartless. Nothing rang true about her. You couldn't just always look like a pretty picture, and yet gain everyone's affection for you. You couldn't be so good and lovable as they seemed to think, and yet jilt a man and mortally wound him, just for the

136

sake of a wealthier husband and a life out East.

Magda didn't stay to tea that day, but she went again, and yet again. She met the Chandlers' old parents, two sweet white-haired old creatures, who were shrewd as well as charming. If the family had heard the gossip about herself and Andrew, they gave no sign, yet it was unlikely that it had passed them by, since Mrs. Chandler was so interested in everything and everyone.

On the second day she took tea with them, Magda was sitting in the old wheel-backed chair by the fire. Old Mrs. Chandler was sitting placidly knitting opposite, and the old man was cleaning his pipe in the window.

Mrs. Chandler was hustling to and fro, getting tea, and keeping up a running conversation with her old mother-in-law and Magda, as she went in and out, but Magda said little. It was a day when she felt absolutely drenched with fatigue. Mrs. Debenham had told her to take four hours off, and to stay away longer if she liked. The old lady was allowed to get up for a while each day now, and her maid was adequate during Magda's free hours. Magda wondered if Mrs. Debenham had schemed to get her to go to the farm in the first instance, because she guessed at the girl's poor health and lack of fresh air.

'I was just saying to Gran here, you don't look like a nurse, Magda,' Mrs. Chandler said, cheerfully. 'I always thought nurses were all skin and bone, and hustle and bustle, but just look at you sitting there like as if you never did a day's turn in your life. Yet I do bet you bustle about right quick when you're on duty or it wouldn't have done for our Mr. Andrew!'

There was a general laugh, and Magda smiled faintly. It wouldn't have done at the hospital, either, she told herself.

She didn't even feel like the same person today. By way of cheering herself up, she had taken down her severe hairstyle, and let it drop to her shoulders, in thick rich red curls where she tied it back loosely with a brown ribbon. It gave a softness to her face, a more rounded look, and she fancied she looked less ill. She wore her one good dress, too. A deep, rich blue wool, which was warmer than her uniform, and had a gay air despite its plain cut. To wear an afternoon frock and black court shoes was in itself a holiday, she thought, smiling into the fire, and compared it humorously with what constituted a holiday for the glamorous Elizabeth, who now seemed never far from her thoughts.

She became aware of a little silence. It couldn't have been there more than a minute. The voices and the laughter had gone, and surprised, she turned round from the fire.

Andrew stood in the door, his height blocking the view and dwarfing the low room. He stared at her with a sort of hungry look, a yearning in his eyes that wrung her heart. It went almost at once, perhaps as she turned round from the fire, but his lips had moved. He had started to say something. Something that sounded like: 'Eliz—'

The others began talking immediately, and he answered them, saying perfunctorily that he had called in about the heifer, and that fetched Mrs. Chandler's husband at once and the two men vanished together. But Magda sat there paralysed. He hadn't spoken to her. Once the spell had been broken, he had dismissed her as if he had forgotten she was there.

'Why, don't sit there garping, miss,' old Mrs. Chandler laughed. 'You look as if you'd seen a ghost.'

'I think we both did,' she murmured, almost inaudibly.

Magda went early, unable to stay at the farm after Andrew's visit. It had spoiled something in an intangible way. She wished she could find the answer to why his presence had such an upsetting effect on her. Common sense told her it was because her name had been linked to his and was common gossip, but beneath that conviction was a lurking doubt, a doubt she did her best to quell.

Andrew Debenham was walking up the drive as she got back. He fell into step beside her.

'I didn't know you visited the farm,' he said, coldly.

'I went there on a message for your aunt, and they asked me to tea. I've been once or twice since.'

'I see. What d'you think of it?'

She could hardly believe that any thoughts of hers on the subject would interest him, but she struggled to answer the question, politely and truthfully.

'I didn't want to see it at first. I thought of it as an extremely modern place. When I found it was so . . . utterly lovely, and . . . how shall I say? Untouched? Yes, I think that's the word. Well, I just fell in love with it.'

She spoke so sincerely that he was pleased in spite of himself, and a flush of pleasure broke over his face.

'Have you been shown around?'

Magda admitted that she had, but she felt

there were other things she'd have to see yet.

'You'd better let the owner take you over the place. Come to-morrow.'

Magda looked up in surprise.

'You mean . . . you'll show me over the farm?'

He nodded, then said, half to himself, 'Your eyes are brown—I keep expecting them to be blue.'

Her surprise brought him back to himself, and he was at once furious. He nodded curtly to her and left her.

She wondered whether there was any way of getting out of that visit to the farm, but decided that there wasn't. She saw Andrew once or twice later, in the house, and he seemed to have forgotten what he said to her, forgotten, too, his anger when he realised that he was voicing his thoughts, and his nod and smile were almost friendly, for him.

He came into his aunt's room, too, while Magda was there. Sensitive, as always, to her nephew's moods, Mrs. Debenham said:

'Andrew, dear, you seem happier to-day. Has something pleasant occurred?'

'Of course it has. You've been up for a little while. Isn't that important?' he smiled, and his voice was softer than usual. 'You old scoundrel, pretending to be frightfully ill,

141

when all you wanted was a good long rest and looking after. Had us all properly scared, didn't you?'

She considered the point.

'No, dear, not scared,' she said, at last. 'But perhaps I made you all aware that nothing—neither age, nor health, nor even memories—can stay the same.'

He looked at her sharply, but she had reached for her knitting, and had apparently forgotten all about her last remark.

He left her soon afterwards, and turning to Magda, the old lady said, 'Oh, dear, my nephew is so quick to take offence these days. I wish I could do something for him, poor boy.'

Magda said, in a stifled voice, 'I wonder what his particular hell is like—living with a ghost.'

The old lady looked sharply up at her.

'You're very sensitive, Magda. Or is it that you're living in a hell of your own, and you know what it's like?'

Magda let that slide, but said, instead:

'That girl—his one-time fiancée—is she still alive?'

'Why do you ask, Magda?'

'Oh, I just wondered. If there was any likelihood of her coming back. Your nephew seeing her, I mean. You see, I should think that if you saw someone you'd been remembering for a long time, they might have grown so different that they'd automatically ease the desperate longing for the remembered person, the picture they represented.'

'Yes, I see your point, my dear, but I hardly think that's likely,' Mrs. Debenham said, and closed the subject.

Magda didn't go to the farm the next day, however. It was actually a fortnight before that visit happened. It surprised her that Andrew didn't forget. The weather intervened, and the rain beat down, and left deep white mists, and boggy ground. She hoped that somehow the visit would get lost in the press of work all around them. Andrew had troubles at the farm, attendant on the weather and the season, and Magda had her hands full with Mrs. Debenham, who had a slight relapse, and had to go back to bed again.

And yet all those two weeks, Andrew managed to convey to Magda that for some reason or other he was determined to keep on friendly terms with her. Whenever he had an opportunity, it seemed, he would stop and speak to her, if only to ask how his aunt was or to remark on the weather's not easing up enough for walking for pleasure, and he smiled, too. Not the singularly sweet smile she had seen him give sometimes to Mrs. Brand, or to his aunt, or anyone else to whom he was being consciously nice, but a rather sad, diffident little smile, as if he himself weren't entirely sure of its reception.

Mrs. Debenham said one day to Magda, 'My dear, be honest with me. You aren't really well, are you?'

Everything in her urged her to confide in the old lady, who, she sensed, would be her friend if she'd let her. But she could hardly make such a confidence without involving Copper, and all the difficult years.

'Yes, I'm all right, really, I am. Just a bit tired. I haven't been away for my annual holiday, you see.'

'Then you must take it, my dear, of course you must! Why didn't you say so before? Why didn't you tell me that that was the reason you wished to be released when I first became ill?'

'But it wasn't, it wasn't!' Magda said, wildly, then recovered her usual calm with an effort. 'I didn't want a holiday then. As a matter of fact, I didn't want to take it until the winter,' she lied, gallantly. 'I was saving for winter sports, you see.'

Mrs. Debenham unwillingly accepted that. 'I see,' she said, but didn't look wholly convinced. 'When did you last take a holiday?'

Again a difficult question. When had she last been away? Magda almost laughed wildly at the thought of herself having a holiday or anything else while Copper was around. Copper had had her leave cancelled because of some scrape, and finally Magda had managed to work it so that Copper could take Magda's leave, later, as the hospital was short-staffed at the time and couldn't spare them both. The year before that, Copper hadn't saved up enough to go away, so Magda had lent her her own savings. Copper had been so slow in paying back (and had indeed not managed to pay it all back yet, and Magda had written it off as a bad debt) that Magda herself hadn't had enough money to go away, so she had spent her leave staying with a one-time patient, in London.

And so it went on. Swiftly counting up how many years since she had had a proper holiday, a seaside holiday, Magda was shocked to find that it was five. Five years ago since she had really been away and had a good time! And those five years had been hard, gruelling even.

'Oh, well, I go away every year, of course,'

she said, with an effort, and again Mrs. Debenham accepted it, unwillingly as before.

'Well, I don't like the look of you, and I do feel that if it isn't a holiday you need, at least you should take a rest. Ah, well, I'm a silly old woman, I suppose, cutting off my own nose to spite my face. If my own nurse doesn't know how she feels, what am I being a stupid interfering old busybody for?' and she smiled nicely at the girl to signify dismissal.

That conversation worried her, and she really considered saying no when Andrew came in one morning, in riding breeches and shabby jacket, and announced that it was an excellent day for their tour over the farm.

'But I can hardly leave your aunt at this moment!' she protested, feebly.

'I'll go and see how she is,' he said, and installed one of the maids with his aunt for the afternoon.

If she had felt any trepidation on spending an afternoon with him, after all the curtness and the rudeness she had had from him in the past, she soon realised that she need not have worried. It was not that he put on any mantle of charm for her, or went out of his way to be nice. It was just that here he was a different person. Probably the person he used to be, before he shut himself up in the ice-box he kept for protecting himself against a curious world. Here, on the farm, his heart lay. She listened to him talking to Chandler, and to the farm workers, and saw the respect on their faces. He was no longer the hospital governor, the bridge enthusiast, the playboy dancing with Sylvia Brand. He was the farmer, and a good farmer, too, Magda sensed.

She didn't know anything about farming, and had a confused impression of breeds of cattle, kinds of poultry, conditions of soil and quality of grain. Sugar-beets and cattle-feeds, arable and grazing land, the names and worth of modern tractors and appliances against the old and tried tools, all these were not so much subjects to her as words bandied about, on that strange and disturbing afternoon.

Andrew's voice and the voices of the people with whom they stopped to speak, the low soughing of the wind in the pine-trees on the ridge that seemed to climb steadily above them the further they went, and the curious bang-banging of her heart despite the leisurely pace they employed, all became a fierce jumble, until she felt like a child about to cry from sheer need of a rest.

At last, Andrew said, 'Well, that's about all on the farm, but there's a view I'd like you to see. It's superb. I don't think there's anything like it in the whole county.'

She didn't answer, and was afraid he would press her for one. She couldn't get her breath. Typically, because of her profession, she tried to see herself as someone else, and to try and assess the symptoms. But it didn't work like that. With anyone else, she could see the symptoms from outside; with herself she only knew how she felt, and that wasn't a clear picture, because of all her arguments that she wasn't really ill, and her consequent belief that she was imagining half the things she had been feeling.

'Don't worry about your letter—we can post that on the way down,' he said, and she realised with a shock that she was still carrying the letter from Jim, that had arrived before she came out. It had been her intention to somehow drop it in to the Brand House, re-addressed to Copper, and to get away without anyone seeing her.

'It—isn't to post,' she said, in a stifled voice. 'It came—from someone abroad.'

He looked strangely at her, and said, after a short pause, 'Oh, I see.' Then, it was obvious, he forgot the matter.

He hurried her up a last steep slope.

'We have to take it quickly, to get the effect,' he said, and he seemed boyish all at once. Boyish, and intensely likeable.

She made the required effort, and hurried. A pain shot under her left arm, and stayed there, dull, persistent.

And then she almost forgot the pain, and the mist that attempted to blur everything, in the sheer beauty of the scene before her. The trees fell away in a wide arc to right and left, and the ground fell in a sheer cliff at their feet. Out and below lay a patchwork quilt of farmlands and trees; light and dark green, grey-blue, and all the shades of brown from a burnt ochre, tan, down to pale yellow. Threaded in between was a silver snake-like band, the river.

'Oh, it's ... it's so beautiful,' Magda gasped.

'You like it,' Andrew said, and sounded pleased.

'It's ... beautiful,' she said again, thinking, not so much of the scene, but of a heady quality of excitement that possessed her. She was here, at the top and the edge of the world, with this stranger—this satisfying stranger whose name was Andrew Debenham, but who was someone new and not the person she had nursed and suffered incredible rudeness from. This was a person it was good to be with. A person who offered her something, something that meant she would never be lonely or bewildered or unhappy any more.

'It's . . . quite misty, isn't it?' she heard herself say. There was a roar, too, like the roar of water going over a weir, and there was a numb feeling creeping up her legs.

'No, it isn't misty!' she heard him say, sharply. Then his voice, from a long way off, shouted: 'Here, Magda! Look out! Magda!' and a feeling of darkness, and falling. Then the falling sensation stopped, and she felt safe, as strong arms were about her.

CHAPTER SEVEN

MAGDA had never fainted before, though she had seen many other people faint, and knew just what to do for them. The thing to do, the professional thing, was to somehow manage to duck one's head between the legs. But this was impossible, for she was being held in a vice-like grip, and was leaning against a rough tweedy surface. Struggling to look upwards, she found a dark, lean face close to her own, and a pair of intense masculine eyes boring into hers.

There was a faint tang of Andrew's tobacco near her, and the fresh clean smell of his shaving-soap. She fancied, for a second, that his smooth, cool cheek had been against hers.

'You nearly went over the edge,' he said, in a matter-of-fact tone, but his voice was uncommonly gentle, thick, almost with emotion.

She struggled to get out of his grasp, then relinquished the effort and leaned back against him. She felt very ill, and the feeling was new and unpleasant.

'The height,' she muttered. 'Head went swimmy.'

He pushed her beret off. The rim had made a tight red mark over her forehead. He smoothed it with a gentle hand, and touched her hair.

'I've found the chink in your armour, Magda,' he said, softly.

'What?' she asked, in bewilderment, trying to collect her thoughts, and remember what she must do, in this strange, new situation, that had somehow got sadly out of hand. Was it really she, Magda Rushton—*Nurse* Magda Rushton—standing here in her patient's arms? The very thing the neighbourhood had been waiting for?

Colour began to creep back into her cheeks, and not entirely through returning health, but rather through embarrassment. Shame, almost.

'You were so efficient, so wretchedly efficient, that you made me feel like a tiresome schoolboy, being put in his place. No man likes that.'

'Oh, I didn't!' she protested, trying to break away, but still ineffectually.

'And now,' he smiled tenderly, 'now I find that that was just an act, put on for the sake of your job. Underneath you're a woman, a very feminine woman, who can't stand heights. I rather like that. At least you'll be dependent

152

on someone else for one thing.'

'I—I really don't know what's the matter with me,' she began furiously. 'I've never fainted before in my life. I feel dreadful about it.'

'Well, feeling better now? If so, we'd better get away from here. It can't be very pleasant for you.'

He let her get away from his arms, but slipped an arm through hers and began to walk her away.

'It's strange, isn't it?' he said, still in that new, low voice that came so oddly from him. Impossible to believe that this was the same man who had spoken harshly to her, curtly, rudely, not so very long ago. A man who appeared not to be able to stand the sight of her.

'Strange, and rather pleasant,' he continued, 'to find it should turn out like this. You've been in my house for months, now, and it's as though I've never really seen you until this moment. As if you've been hammering at my consciousness until at last you found a way in yourself. Against my will. And now you've achieved that, it feels as if I'd known you all my life.'

Panic surged through her. Sooner or later he'd remember the rumour, the rumour which Sylvia Brand had herself circulated, for surely he must have heard it? She would have seen to that! And he would feel trapped, and believe it to be true. He wouldn't look on it all so kindly, but feel angry and duped.

Magda closed her eyes, and tried to think clearly.

'It's an illusion,' she said, at last. 'They happen, in situations like this. I should never have come. Have you got my beret, Mr. Debenham?'

The use of his surname brought him back sharply. He looked down at her in surprise, and silently passed her the little brown cap, smiling ruefully as he realised he had been holding it so tightly in his hand.

'Don't be so formal, Magda,' he said, gently. 'You and I have just stood on the edge of something rather terrible, and we came through together. Doesn't that mean something?'

Savagely she fought back the wild longing to agree with him. It would be so wonderful to have this new Andrew for a friend, and experience this exquisite new relationship growing into something warmer, deeper, day by day. But instinct warned her against it, and she fought the temptation with every ounce of her returning strength.

'Yes, oh yes, of course it does, Mr.

Debenham. You saved my life, and I'll be grateful to you for it, for always. You know I will! But I'm still your aunt's nurse, still on the nursing staff of your hospital. Nothing has changed, really. You were just kind enough to show me your farm. That's all.'

He whitened, and she saw that she had hurt him. He looked as if she had struck him.

'I see.'

They walked in silence, slowly, Magda setting the pace, combating the tired feeling she was beginning to recognise as a familiar day-by-day thing, every step of the way.

Suddenly she realised that she had lost Copper's letter. She stopped, looking wildly about her.

'Oh, my letter! Did you see what happened to it?' she cried.

'Oh, yes, you had it at the top, didn't you?' He looked oddly at her again. 'It hadn't been opened, had it? Hadn't you stopped to read it?'

'It only just came as I came out,' she said. 'Oh, I must find it. Jim writes so seldom.'

'Jim? And who is Jim? A relation?' he asked.

Magda began walking back, and glanced sideways at him. A way had been presented to her to stop all this. A way that she didn't like,

155

but it had to be done.

'Jim's a—an old friend. He's out in Africa. Somewhere. I haven't seen him for ages. You—you didn't think I was unattached, did you?'

He laughed. A rather bitter little laugh. 'Funny, but I took it for granted that you were. That was idiotic of me, of course. Why should you remain unattached, an attractive young woman like you? I don't suppose your Jim has ever seen you in your uniform, making your poor patients toe the line.'

'No,' she agreed, wincing. 'He's never seen me like that.'

'When is he coming home?'

'I don't know. I expect he said that in the letter.' She thought of Copper and how furious she'd be if the letter had been lost, although she was professing not to care about Jim any more. Telling Copper about it would be difficult, too, without disclosing whom she had been with at the time the letter was lost, and what had happened to cause it to be lost. 'Oh, I do so hope I didn't drop it over the edge.'

'Don't worry,' Andrew said, crisply. 'If that has happened, I'll get it for you. I can't have you lose something that means so much to you.'

'Oh, but I didn't mean that I wanted—'

'Don't worry. I shall come to no harm, if that's what you're thinking. I've climbed mountains,' he grimly reminded her.

'Yes, but I don't want you to break your leg again,' she breathed, and hoped he hadn't heard her.

The letter had gone over the edge, but lay precariously balanced on the root of a stunted tree. Magda turned away as he went over the edge, and found she was clenching her fists so tightly that her nails bit into the soft palms. After what seemed ages, he was back again beside her, dusting himself down, and saying cheerfully:

'Well, here it is. Better put it away somewhere safe till you can get at it to read its precious contents.'

She held her hand out for it, and what she had feared now happened. He was reading the name on it.

'Miss Copper Rushton.'

His smile was lop-sided, and again there was that heart-breaking yearning in his eyes as he looked at her glowing hair again. 'So that's what they call you. Copper. How well it suits you. Or is it just your Jim who calls you that?'

'Just Jim,' Magda heard herself saying,

faintly.

He nodded.

'And when does the lucky Jim date from?'

Magda said, holding on to herself to keep her voice steady, 'Jim's an old family friend. He first thought about getting engaged eight years ago.'

Half-truths, Magda said to herself disgustedly. Half the truth, white lies, black lies, what did it matter what you called it? It was deception, pure and simple, and she loathed herself for it, but it had to be done. It was the only way.

'I was a fool, wasn't I, not to find out first if there was a Jim in evidence?' he said, lightly, but she could feel the deep hurt searing through him.

'Oh, please, don't feel like that,' she begged. 'You weren't to know. In fact, I don't see how you could have expected anything else, with that memory haunting you. It was the most foul bad luck that I had hair this colour. It must have reminded you of her all the time.'

He stopped dead and swung her round to face him.

'Just what d'you mean by that?'

'Well, perhaps I oughtn't to have mentioned it, but I was referring to the person you

158

used to know.'

She wanted to say, 'Elizabeth. That's whom I mean. A ghost who's beginning to take a real shape and haunt me as well,' but it was impossible to say more than she had done, with that hard, cold look creeping back into his face.

'Who told you about her?' he demanded.

She shrugged impressively.

'Everyone seems to be remembering, and though they don't say much, they say enough.'

He flushed darkly.

'Why can't people hold their tongues? All talking about me again, just as they did then! How I loathe gossip!'

'It can hardly be worse for you than for me!' she flashed. It seemed as if he were blaming her for the gossip and that seemed hardly fair.

'For you! How do you come into it?'

'Is it possible that you haven't heard the rumour about me, Mr. Debenham?'

She saw by his face that he had, and that up till now he had forgotten it.

'Do you suppose I want people to have more to go on than just a rumour?'

'If that's the case, I wonder you consented to come with me to-day,' he said, caustically.

'There wasn't much chance of backing out,' she found herself saying ruefully. 'Not without seeming rude. Oh, I don't mean to say that I didn't enjoy it—'

'Please don't trouble to be polite,' he begged, frigidly. 'Just thank your lucky stars for your Jim, that's all! You ought to be able to explode any rumours pretty successfully, with a letter like that to flash around. Even our gossipmongers will be impressed with a stamp like that, and an authentic masculine handwriting!'

'Don't! Oh, don't be beastly again,' Magda said, in a choked voice. 'If only you could be reasonably pleasant with me, as you have been to-day. You don't know how awful it is to work for someone who is—'

'Who is what?'

'I shouldn't say this to my employer, I know, but you have treated me so badly that I've felt worse than in the most wretched of my probationer days. I didn't like some of the higher-ups on the staff then—all probationers feel like that—but heavens above, there was some reason for it. I must have been a pest—most probationers are at first—stupid and bewildered and rather resentful of the new life. But now, well, there just wasn't any reason for your behaviour to me. I can't help but say it, Mr. Debenham, but you've been unjust.'

If she hadn't been feeling so upset and ill, she wouldn't have burst out like that. The minute she had said it, she knew she had done the most unwise thing. A man of Andrew Debenham's type could take that sort of censure less than the average man. His jaw set in the old unfriendly line, and he glared savagely down at the farm below them.

'I think, Miss Rushton, that a change of nurses for my aunt might be a good plan. I take it you agree with me?'

'Agree! I couldn't agree more!' Magda burst out. 'In fact, I've already made two attempts to move on, but your aunt doesn't seem to want that. She gets so dreadfully upset at the thought of it.'

'I'll see if I can alter her mind for her,' he said, grimly, and Magda knew that if he set about it, it was as good as done.

She delivered her letter to Copper, and made her way slowly back. Andrew had called again at the farm after he left her, she knew, and she wondered if he had yet gone back to the house.

She didn't see him any more that day, and Mrs. Debenham said nothing about him. Instead, she was all quick and excited talk about the fact that they would soon be preparing for Christmas.

'Christmas?' Magda stared blankly. 'But this is only the autumn.'

'A mere nine weeks to Christmas, Magda,' Mrs. Debenham said, blithely, 'and the way we entertain here at Christmas, it isn't too long in which to prepare. Oh, you'll see a real Christmas here, my girl, a Christmas you'll remember for the rest of your life. I love Christmas.'

Magda smiled faintly. It was very doubtful if she would spend Christmas anywhere else but at the hospital. On impulse, she sat down and talked about Christmas, and tried to draw the old lady out about what they would do here. But she wasn't to be drawn.

'No, it's a secret. It's rather nice to know that there'll be a stranger here, who'll see the Debenham Christmas for the first time. Most of our friends and neighbours are familiar with it, but they still love it. Oh, but don't you just adore the business of making the puddings and the cake? Cook makes an enormous cake loaded with brandy. It's so rich, you only want a very small piece, but it melts in the mouth. We were very lucky to get her. She worked on the Continent for a long time, and her cooking is an art. I always think male cooks are the best, but I must make an exception in her case.'

'What sort of Christmas do the Chandlers have?' Magda wanted to know.

'Oh, a very nice affair. A typical farm Christmas. The Chandlers are good people, nice tenants. Conscientious.'

Magda let the old lady talk, reminiscing of old neighbours who had died or moved away, and new ones who had fitted in so well. She saw the district as a place full of delightful people, people she had known and trusted for so long. Magda saw only the lower level, the staff of the big houses, and the people in the village, the people who gossiped about her and Andrew, and as such, were her enemies.

'What,' she asked the old lady, suddenly, 'was Christmas like at the Mount when Elizabeth was here?'

'Ah, yes, Elizabeth.' Mrs. Debenham's voice took on a new note. 'She came out of my box of memories like fragrantly perfumed handkerchiefs. Do you know what I mean, my dear? Every memory immaculate.'

'Even when she went away, and left your nephew so unhappy?'

'I didn't see her go, and I don't know whose fault it was,' Mrs. Debenham said, slowly. 'I only know that she brought back the grace

163

and beauty of my own young days, and combined it with a modern outlook that in no way offended. That, Magda, is a rare combination.'

Magda sadly agreed.

'I recall her on that last Christmas she was here. She wore pale lavender silk, and looked wonderful. And she sang. You haven't seen our music-room, have you, Magda? No, of course you haven't. Andrew had it locked up when she went away. We have various musical instruments, a very fine Bechstein grand, and an organ. Andrew is very proud of that organ. He played it while she sang. I remember her singing "Silent Night". Now I always think that that is a difficult song to sing. You can sing it well, and you can sing it pleasantly. But it takes a woman like Elizabeth to make it unforgettable. I hope I never hear it again, since she isn't here to sing it.'

Magda felt cold. An inner cold, as if the ghost of that girl were touching her heart, reminding her that she had stayed too long in this house, and that no one else had a right to try and take her place.

A maid came in with Mrs. Debenham's hot milk. Usually Magda brought it, but she had been talking so long to Mrs. Debenham, and it had gone slightly past the time. As the girl opened the door, a sound swept in on them. Organ music.

The maid looked frightened, and her eyes met her mistress's.

'Heavens, what's that?' ejaculated Mrs. Debenham.

'It's the master, madam. He's opened up the music-room and I saw him go and sit at the organ.'

Magda remembered for a long time the strange sensation she experienced at that moment. The three of them staring at each other, while the notes of the organ infiltrated and possessed the still room. The maid, after the briefest of pauses, put the tray down by Magda to give to her patient, and went out. As she quietly closed the door, blotting out most of the sound of the music, the spell was broken.

Mrs. Debenham heaved a little gusty sigh.

'What a funny thing. What a very funny thing!' she repeated. 'I never thought my nephew would do that.'

'Why not, Mrs. Debenham? Perhaps he feels he has mourned long enough.'

'Mourned? You speak as if Elizabeth were dead.'

Magda was surprised.

'Well, isn't she? How funny. I thought I

heard that she had died.'

'I never heard that,' Mrs. Debenham said, slowly. 'Tell me, you were with Andrew today. What happened, Magda?'

Magda whitened.

'What do you mean, Mrs. Debenham?'

'I wondered if anything was said, or anything happened, to make him do this very odd thing.'

'Oh. No, I don't think so,' Magda said, feeling sick of the need to mask her real feelings, and only tell half the truth all the time. There was nothing that had happened, as far as she could see, to make him fling open the music-room and play those mad cadences on the organ. Quite the contrary, in fact. But she would have given a lot to confide in Andrew's aunt, and tell her of all her fears and anxieties.

'He did say,' Magda said, as an afterthought, 'that he felt that in everyone's interests a change of nurses for you would be advisable. I agreed with him. You know I feel like that.'

The old lady looked steadily at Magda for a time, and Magda wondered if she had upset her again. But it was necessary to tell her that herself, if Mrs. Debenham was not to feel that she had been keeping something back. For

Andrew, Magda knew, had meant what he said, and would certainly approach his aunt about it.

'You don't mean to tell me what led up to that, Magda, I take it?'

'Your nephew will tell you,' Magda said.

'You know, I have a curious way of liking to hear both sides of the story,' Mrs. Debenham smiled. 'Now, Magda!'

Magda felt trapped.

'Well, you know how it has been since I came here. Somehow I manage to antagonise your nephew. I don't know how, but I do. We have never even been normally pleasant with each other, and you know, a male patient usually strikes up a friendship, however superficial, with his nurse, particularly when it's private work. There's such a degree of intimacy, and so much time spent together willy-nilly, that it does help things along, even if you both know you'll forget all about each other afterwards. I'm afraid that never happened where your nephew was concerned. He just hates me.'

'Is that entirely true, my dear?'

'Well, I think so. I know there have been flashes, since he's been about again, flashes of pleasantness, I suppose one might call them, but they vanish so quickly. And then it's the

167

same as before. Well, I think it would be better if I went, don't you?'

'Magda, child, answer me truthfully. Are you in love with my Andrew?'

It caught Magda by surprise, and on the raw. She flushed, and flung up her head, her dark eyes flashing.

'In love?' she gasped.

Mrs. Debenham read the wrong meaning into that ejaculation, and saw only what she wanted to see.

'Well, well, I'm very glad to hear it. I wouldn't like you to be in love with him. He'd break your heart, as his own was broken. And I've a feeling strong inside me that he'll marry that tiresome Mrs. Brand in the end. Oh, dear, how I do dislike that woman! And I know I shouldn't. It really isn't any business of mine. I shall be gone soon, but it grieves me to see this dear old place about to pass into her hands. It grieves me so much!'

A slow tear ran down the old lady's face, and Magda impulsively took her hands.

'Might he not always remain a bachelor?' she reminded Mrs. Debenham gently.

'But that would be worse, for then who would the estate go to? He must marry. He ought to, and have children. Oh, dear, why did Elizabeth leave him? There is something so gay and adorable about a redhead. You're not very gay, are you, my dear?' She patted Magda's hand. 'The only serious redhead I know!'

'I've never had much opportunity for gaiety,' Magda told her. 'But I think I could be, if I had the chance!'

'Has life been so very hard, my dear?'

Magda opened her lips to tell the old lady a bit about her past, but closed them again as Copper's name involuntarily rose to them. It was virtually impossible to talk much about herself without Copper coming into it.

'Oh, well, no harder than for most, I suppose,' she said, with a wry smile. 'I'm just sorry for myself—and that won't do.'

When Magda left the old lady, she was far from satisfied about the whole thing, and wondered how Mrs. Debenham would really react to her nephew's talk, and if, indeed, he would do as he had threatened to do after all, and speak to his aunt about Magda's going, knowing as he did that she didn't want to lose the girl.

But Andrew drove himself hard, and although he himself didn't want Magda to leave his house, he had said he would do it. He spoke to his aunt that evening, after Magda had left her alone.

'You must have someone else, Aunt Laura,' he said, without preamble. 'Nurse Rushton must go. It's time.'

'But why, Andrew?'

'You don't seem surprised that I should suggest that you have a change of nurses?' he asked suspiciously.

'No my dear. She told me about it herself this afternoon.'

'She told you—?' He was startled, and swung round to face his aunt. 'Did she tell you—just what did she tell you, Aunt Laura?'

'Very little, Andrew, dear. I confess I'd like to know what brought the subject up.'

He relaxed, and his aunt watched him closely.

'Oh, nothing. Nothing new. We just hate the sight of each other.'

'She doesn't hate you,' Mrs. Debenham said.

'No. Perhaps "hate" was the wrong word. She just despises me for a fool,' he said, bitterly.

'Nor that either, Andrew.'

'Did she tell you she's engaged to a fellow out in Africa?' he jeered. 'No, I thought not. That only came out because of a letter she had.'

'No, Andrew, I can't believe that. She

would have told me. Besides, she doesn't wear a ring. She isn't very happy, either, and I think she would be if she had a happy love affair. No, dear, you've misunderstood.'

'She's been engaged for eight years,' he insisted. 'You ask her for yourself. No, better still, don't bring it up at all. That letter's caused enough trouble,' he muttered, half to himself. To his aunt, he said, again, 'Let her go, Aunt Laura. Let her go at once.'

'No, my dear, I can't do that. Not on such a flimsy reason. Besides, she wanted to go herself, and I wouldn't let her. It would be unreasonable and unjust if I asked her to go now, because of a whim of yours.'

'So it was true, then?' He sounded surprised.

'That she asked to go herself? Of course. Did you doubt it?'

He shook his head, as though there were many things he didn't understand.

'Aunt Laura, you remember you said you wouldn't stand in my way, if I wanted to marry Sylvia?'

Her heart sank.

'Well, dear?'

'Well, I believe I'm going to take you up on that. No, it isn't that I want you to go away or anything. Not that part of it at all. But the part where you said in effect that you—well, that you two girls wouldn't fly at each other if you had anything to do with it.'

His aunt snorted.

'I said no such thing, Andrew, and you know it. If you insist on marrying Mrs. Brand, well, that's your own affair. But my dear, let me go out of this house before you marry her. That's all I ask.'

'But I don't want to turn you out!' he protested.

'You won't be, Andrew. You'll be doing me—you'll be doing us both—a favour, and I believe you're well aware of it. We can't stand each other, Sylvia Brand and I. And it's no good mincing matters.'

'She's tried to make friends with you,' he ventured. His aunt pulled a face.

'She's tried to do many things,' she said, obscurely, and would say no more.

'What about Nurse Rushton? Will you tell her to go?' he said, getting up at last.

'No, I will not, Andrew, and as she's my nurse at the moment, you really mustn't interfere. I won't have it. Why, it's shameful of you to worry me like this, a sick woman!'

'The other day you were saying you weren't sick and you'd soon be up and about again,' he laughed. 'Which is it? I think you alter your state to suit yourself.'

She looked queerly at him.

'I wish I could do that, my dear,' she said,
gently.

CHAPTER EIGHT

OCTOBER drew to a close with fogs and frosts, and Magda sometimes felt that she would never be free to leave this haunted place. It was strange, loving the house as she did, and yet to feel a nameless dread about staying there. She told herself that she was being fanciful, believing that Elizabeth still moved in and out of the great sombre rooms, and as her health grew no better, she began to accept the fact that a person who is far from well and driving herself to work each day despite her feelings, was bound to have sick fancies.

'Are you superstitious?' she asked Mrs. Debenham one day, as the old lady laughed at her efforts to put a spider out of the window without killing it.

'Good gracious, no child!' the old lady said, robustly. 'As a girl, I of course went through the usual Hallowe'en nonsense, to find out who was my lover, but nothing else ever worried me.'

'Never threw salt over your shoulder or refused to walk under a ladder?' Magda laughed.

'Never!' averred Mrs. Debenham.

'And never believed that ghosts do walk?' Magda said softly.

'Ah, well, that isn't being superstitious, is it?' Mrs. Debenham said, in a different tone. 'That's a different thing.'

'You do believe in ghosts?' Magda asked in surprise.

'I didn't say that, or put it quite like that. But I do feel that the goodness that was in those who died, never dies with them. Andrew's grandfather, for instance, was a very good man. He had an awful temper but he learned to control it. And I sometimes think that his spirit walks and helps Andrew. My nephew never knew that other Debenham, but I often see him pull himself up almost as though someone put his hand on Andrew's shoulder. I'm almost persuaded that I can see old Marcus Debenham standing there.'

'Tell me some more about your nephew's ancestors,' Magda said.

'What d'you want to know? The things they did, or what they were like themselves?'

'It's all tied up together, isn't it?' Magda smiled.

'Well, they were essentially outdoor people. They rode, and understood farming and were lovers of sport. The women did no

175

fine needlework nor did they sit around with music and fancy ways. But they knew how to run a house like this, and they were a power in the county.'

Magda dropped her eyes.

'I see.'

'Elizabeth would have taken her place among them quite easily. For all her pretty airs, she was a hard rider, and although Andrew felt at the time that she was making a mistake going out East, I think she had the constitution to stand up to the climate.'

Part of Magda's picture of Elizabeth became a little blurred.

'Is there a picture of her anywhere? I would so like to see it,' Magda said.

'Why, yes. There's a life-size portrait of her in the music-room,' Mrs. Debenham said. 'If, as I understand, my nephew has opened the music-room again, I see no reason why you shouldn't go and have a look.'

'You think I'm crazy, don't you, wanting to see what she really looks like?'

'No, my dear. It's natural curiosity. I've talked enough about her, heaven knows. Go now, and tell me what you think of her. Oh, never mind if my nephew does come in! Tell him I gave you permission, if he's difficult!'

Magda decided she wouldn't give Andrew a

chance to catch her, as she hurried down to the great room where the organ was. She'd just have one peep, and then escape.

But the music-room was such a wonderful apartment that she forgot the time, and wandered round, looking at everything, and where she touched, she touched reverently.

This was a room that obviously hadn't changed in generations, except for the addition of the grand piano. There was a spinet against a far wall, and a piece of priceless tapestry. Quaint carved seats stood about, and there was a harp and a lute with ribbons hanging from it. At one end, dominating the scene, was the organ, its great pipes touching the painted ceiling. At the other, the portrait of Elizabeth. . . .

Oddly enough, Magda had expected the portrait to depict a girl in a pretty frock, with flowers somewhere in it, and a picture hat. A traditional pretty-pretty theme. But it wasn't that at all. The girl in the picture was in riding clothes, and sat her great horse as easily as a man. There were dogs in the picture, too, and other riders in the distance.

Magda experienced shock. The picture had a curious sense of power about it. The horse was powerful and so were the dogs. The girl sat in a forceful manner, as though intent only on getting somewhere, fast. It seemed to Magda that a rider had been checked by the man making the portrait, and asked to pause and smile. The gaiety, the serenity, seemed to Magda to be superficial. A cloak to be put on when anyone was about. The blue eyes, she felt, could be calculating, penetrating, ruthless, but they smiled, and the smile hid everything else until you looked behind it, almost like drawing aside a heavy and beautiful curtain. The mouth, the beautiful chiselled mouth, smiled too, but there was a hint of leashed cruelty about it. Magda didn't find it so difficult to believe that this girl could jilt Andrew and go off with a richer man for a more exciting life, now that she had seen the portrait.

Because she had been so exacting in her examination of the canvas, she had forgotten the time. She turned and almost ran into Andrew himself. There was an inscrutable expression on his face.

'Well?' he snapped.

'Your aunt said I could—' Magda began.

'I know that. I've already seen her. She told me where I could find you.'

'You're not angry that I came here?'

He shrugged.

'You're here now, so what does it matter?'

178

She turned to go, feeling helpless as always, before the flail of his anger.

'I asked you what you thought of it,' he said.

'The portrait?'

'Of course.'

'She's . . . very beautiful,' Magda said, carefully.

'Anything else?'

'And very accomplished, I imagine.'

'Is that all?'

'No,' Magda said gently. 'She's all that people say she is, I'm sure.'

His face twitched, his eyes searched her face, boring into her eyes.

'And what do the gossips say she is?'

'Do you really want me to tell you? Won't it be painful to you to discuss it further?'

'What do they say?' he insisted.

Magda sighed. He was so very difficult, always.

'They say,' she said, softly, 'that she was gay and beautiful and . . . oh, they run out of words, but they give me the impression that when she went across their path she left a lovely colourful picture, a memory to treasure. They forgive her anything, because they loved her. She meant that much to them.'

He nodded, smiling bitterly, and what he said came as a shock to Magda.

'The fools! The poor fools!' he said, softly.

Magda said, recovering a little, 'It isn't any concern of mine, Mr. Debenham, but your aunt is one of those people. She treasures a memory. Don't take it from her, whatever bitter feelings you may have.'

'Bitter? Who said I was bitter?'

'I'm sorry. Perhaps I misunderstood. Please don't tell her I mentioned it, but your aunt particularly remembers your ex-fiancée singing.'

'I know. I've heard it all before. "Silent Night".'

She didn't understand him. She considered he would have decently covered his grief, not pretended to disparage the memory. Or was he pretending, after all?

'Do you like music?' he demanded.

'Like?' She shook her head. 'That isn't the word. Music is one of the few things I really care about.'

'I think you mean that!' He sounded surprised. 'What would you like?' he went on, sitting down at the grand piano.

'Oh—' Magda breathed, 'at this moment, I think some fragments of Mendelssohn. . . .'

He played well, very well, but there was a

savagery about him that hurt her and she suspected he was hurting himself, deliberately, playing for the little nurse, when all the time it ought to have been Elizabeth.

After he had finished, he said, with bitter satisfaction, and an unconscious cruelty, 'When I play that again, I shall not necessarily remember you. If *she* had asked me to play it, I'd never be able to hear it again without thinking of her ... she would have become the fragments, or rather, they would have become *her*. . . .'

Into the little silence, Magda spoke. Her sweet voice gently chided him.

'You must forgive her personality. It isn't a crime to swamp everyone else. I'm a colourless person, despite my hair. I pass by, and no one misses me.'

She quietly left him, and he was horrified to find that contrary to her words, she left him in his music-room with a sense of loss. Although he had not been able to chase her out of the house yet, he knew with certainty that she would be going soon, though if he had known how soon he would have been chilled. He wanted her to go, so that he could show himself that her going meant nothing to him. Yet half of him was afraid of the day that must come.

Mrs. Debenham's doctor was at the house a great deal these days. She was far from well and each day etched a deeper line into her old face. She didn't speak with the vigour that had begun to creep back into her voice, and this, Magda had noticed, had happened since that last relapse. They had all thought that the old lady would be one of those heart cases that partially recover and with care are able to get about again and lead a more or less normal life. Magda wanted to see her getting about the old house again, and taking little walks in the rose gardens. All that, she now began to see, was just a dream. It was doubtful, the doctor intimated to her, if Mrs. Debenham would ever get up again. She hadn't, it appeared, a very strong constitution, although everyone had somehow got a contrary impression.

Andrew was told, and Magda saw that it bit deeply. Whatever feelings he had for anyone else, his aunt was obviously very dear to him. He began to stay in the house more, a fact which unnerved Magda more than she had believed it could.

One day Mrs. Debenham said to him, 'Andrew, dear, don't neglect your duties and your pleasures because of me. Bring Mrs. Brand over if you want to. I'm a selfish old woman. Don't pander to me and let me stand in your way.'

He smiled faintly.

'I believe you want to see Sylvia again,' he teased.

'Heaven forbid!' Mrs. Debenham said, with a pale reflection of her old vigorous denial. 'But I shan't be rude to her if you want her to come and see me.'

And so Sylvia Brand began to come to Debenham Mount again. Sylvia in her new autumn things made Magda feel decidedly shabby. Sylvia wore superbly-cut tweeds and dashing soft suits. She had at least three fur coats, one a daring ocelot, but the one Magda loved most was a soft dark fur, rather like mink, worked in a wide circular yoke with a swinging back and great exaggerated sleeves, gathered into tiny fur cuffs at her small wrists.

Although she knew that blue was Elizabeth's main colour, Sylvia Brand was daring enough to wear it a great deal. Magda thought it unwise of her, and noticed how Andrew frowned when she came in any shade of blue. Particularly a soft pale blue velour cap she wore, plumed with pale blue and pale mauve feathers that curled round her cheek. A lovely thing, which set off her pretty fair face and made her look most desirable.

She began to be nicer to Magda, too, and that went well with Andrew, as he, too, had dropped being curt with Magda in public. Since Mrs. Brand started visiting Mrs. Debenham, Magda could hardly escape from her sight altogether, and had to be in the room at least part of the time. She hated it. She hated Sylvia Brand's light, rather insolent smile, that raked Magda's uniform, from the top of her head to the toe of her sensible black leather shoes. A look which said, 'My dear, do you know just how frumpish you look in that awful get-up?'

It was on one of the days when Sylvia Brand had been to tea in Mrs. Debenham's bedroom, that Magda almost fainted again. This time there was no hiding it. She clung to the bedpost for support, and could only thank her stars that Andrew wasn't in the room.

Mrs. Debenham had taken up her interrupted knitting, and settled back with a sigh of relief when the visitors had at last gone. Magda hoped she hadn't noticed her own bad turn, but the old lady had. She had paused in her work, and was quietly watching Magda from her bed.

'What is it, my dear?' she asked, when Magda moved at last and went to the window.

'Oh, nothing. Nothing,' Magda said, trying to laugh.

'I've felt for some time that you weren't yourself.' Mrs. Debenham said, 'and I've made many openings for you to confide in me.'

'It's just that I'm tired. As I said before, when we talked of holidays.'

'No. It's more than that. I wonder if you're going to have appendicitis?'

'Oh, no!' Magda swung round, at once alarmed. 'No, of course I'm not,' she broke off, laughing. 'I'm not sick or in pain. Just tired, that's all.'

'Well, I think you must see a doctor. See mine, when he comes again.'

Magda went swiftly to her side.

'Please, Mrs. Debenham, don't press me to see a doctor. I don't want to. Honestly. Just let me go away and take a rest. That's all I want. I'll be all right.'

'No, my dear. I must have my way about it this time. You'll go away and not look after yourself and for the rest of my days I shall worry about what becomes of you, if I don't personally see that you are medically examined.'

Mrs. Debenham spoke to her own doctor about Magda and persuaded him to see the girl.

Magda's heart sank, and a trapped feeling settled on her. She had been fighting off this day, unconsciously, for the last five or six months. Yet she had known that inevitably it must come.

After she had been examined, the doctor said, 'Why didn't you see someone about yourself before, Nurse?'

She explained, and he looked annoyed.

'You might have run a risk with your patient. You're not in a fit state to be nursing.'

'Doctor, I've tried, I've *begged*, to be allowed to go away and give up the case. I didn't want to take on nursing Mrs. Debenham, but she's so sweet and she wanted me to, and I really didn't like to refuse her. I hoped that her illness would have been of short duration and that when she was better I could have still gone away in time.'

Mrs. Debenham was shocked when she heard his report.

'The girl has no business to be working at all!' he snapped. 'She's in a bad way.'

'What's wrong with her?' Mrs. Debenham asked.

'She's worn out,' he said, bluntly. 'I imagine she's had some sort of personal trouble, as well as a great deal too much hard work. Tired heart. Same old story. I've no patience with these young people who know the danger signals and won't rest when they know they should.'

'I'm personally interested in her,' Mrs. Debenham said. 'What do you advise that she should do?'

He shrugged.

'A long rest and care, by the sea, preferably. There's no other cure.'

'Oh, dear. Well, I'll speak to her about it,' she said.

Magda was appalled by it all. The only thing about it all was that Andrew would be pleased, and so would Copper. Now she could go away and not bother either of them again.

She wondered what would happen to her now. There was a rest home for the nurses when they had been in their own hospital for operations, but her own affair looked as if it was going to take a long time. They made no provision for cases of long duration.

She thought of all the people she had known in the past, where she might perhaps go and stay, but there was no one she knew well enough to impose on them as an invalid resting. The only relatives she had were either very old people, living in towns, or had lost touch with her.

She felt the need to talk it over with someone, someone close to her. She ruled out Max, for just lately she had allowed their friendship to slow down, and she noticed that he hadn't gone out of his way to see why she had refused to go out with him. Perhaps he was as busy as he had said. Perhaps it was that Mrs. Brand had found out that she was seeing Max, and had stopped him from having so much free time. He had almost hinted as much when she had seen him last. He didn't seem to mind that his employer was jealous or possessive. It almost seemed to amuse him. That was a slant on his character that puzzled Magda. She liked men to be free, not tied to a woman employer to such an extent that their private lives were governed as well as their working lives.

No, Magda thought sadly, the only person in whom she could confide was Copper. Copper, who loathed responsibility, and shrank from the sight of ill-health in her close friends and associates, as something distasteful and as a threat against her own personal liberty.

She wrote a note to Copper and asked her to spend an hour or two with her as she had something important to talk over. She didn't expect Copper would consent to any such plan, and was surprised when Copper telephoned her to ask her where she should meet her.

They went to the nearest town and had tea in a small café called the Bun House. A quaint place composed of two tall old houses knocked into one, where a teashop was on the ground floor and the first floor catered for lunches. The waitresses were cheerful, and the place was comfortably warm. Magda sank gratefully into one of the padded armchair seats near the fire, and said, 'Oh, just tea, I think. I do so want a cup of tea!'

Copper ordered buttered scones and pastries, and said, robustly, 'Don't be a fathead! You've got to eat something. You look as if you're half-starved.'

'Do I?' Magda smiled. 'I'm sorry, Copper, but it's about myself that I want to talk.'

'Yes, I thought so,' Copper said.

'Oh. Why?'

Copper grinned lop-sidedly. 'I saw you the other day and you didn't see me. You looked awful. I wondered whether I'd stop and speak to you, then I felt rather a fool. You know, carrying on about one thing and another, and as usual I'm wrong and you're right.'

'What on earth are you talking about?'

189

Magda gasped.

The tea came then, and Copper applied herself to eating before she said anything in explanation. She made Magda eat, too, and when at last she got to the pastry stage, she slowed down a bit, and said:

'Oh, about that wretched Brand woman and everything. These last few months have been rotten. I was an ass to give up nursing. I can see it now. You said I was, and you were right. It isn't any fun at the Brand house—that cat sees to it that it isn't! I thought I'd get a bit of fun with Max, too, and I was furious when you went out with him. But it didn't make any difference. He liked you because you're serious and can talk about books and things. That's all. It wouldn't have mattered if he hadn't even met you—I wouldn't have got anywhere with him—I can see that, and I freely admit it.'

'Well, look, that's pretty sweeping. I didn't think I'd made it that clear. If I did, I didn't mean to,' Magda said, unhappily.

Copper grinned.

'I suppose I'm a pretty foul sort of person to have in the family. I just jump on everyone until I get my own way, and when I've got it, I don't want it any more, and then I want to make it up again and act as if nothing had happened. One of these days I'll get what's coming to me, I suppose.'

'You are an ass, Copper, the things you say,' Magda said, trying to laugh, but her face suddenly crumpling. She turned sharply away and covered her face with her hand. Copper stared, and was aware that her sister was crying, a very rare thing indeed.

'Here, I say, Mag, don't. Don't!' she said, putting an awkward hand on her sister's arm. 'Not here, for the love of Pete—we're in a tea-shop!'

Magda regained her control with an effort.

'Sorry. Didn't mean to be such an idiot. But that's how it is lately. I howl in corners by myself. Feel so ill and all that.'

'You *are* ill, you know. Aren't you?' Copper said.

Magda nodded, agreeing.

Copper pushed a cigarette over to her sister, and helped herself to one out of a crumpled packet.

'Come on,' she said. 'Out with it. More tea?'

Magda absently lit their cigarettes and drew hard on hers. Slowly, haltingly, she told Copper of the way her health had gradually broken down, and the way Mrs. Debenham had pounced on it, and made her see the family doctor. But she omitted the bit about Andrew, and her fainting the day she went to the farm with him.

'Oh, help! What are you going to do now?' Copper ejaculated, rolling her eyes to the ceiling in dismay.

'That's what I wanted to talk over with you. I can't think any more, Copper. I'm . . . I'm done.'

'Well, don't cry any more, for that'd be daft. We've got to think this out. How long d'you suppose you'll be laid up? Any idea?'

Magda nodded gloomily.

'About six months,' she muttered.

'Oh, if that doesn't take the biscuit for bad luck!'

'Well, I suppose the doctor could be wrong.'

'Oh, no. Don't start that—I couldn't bear it! That's what patients' relations say, but not us; you and I know better. Those blokes never over-estimate. Rather the reverse.'

'Yes, I know.'

'What a foul bit of luck you couldn't have staved it off a bit longer, say till Jim came back, then when we were married you could have come to my place and stayed.'

Copper said it with a trace of self-consciousness which would have amused

Magda under any other circumstances. But at the moment, all Magda could do was to stare at her sister in amazement. Of all crazy people, surely Copper was the worst!

'Copper! Are you going to marry that poor long-suffering young man after all?'

Copper shrugged.

'I suppose so. What else can I do? What else *is* there to do?'

Magda could think of any number of things, but didn't say so.

She said, instead, and choosing her words carefully: 'Copper, you're not just going to marry him because you're sick of working for Mrs. Brand?'

'No!' Copper said, indignantly, and then grinned a little shame-facedly, 'Well, not entirely. A bit of that, and a bit because Jim expects me to marry him, and because he'd be so fed up if I didn't, and that'd make me miserable. Then I suppose I've got used to the idea of marrying him. After all, you can't be engaged for eight years, and cast it all away like an old glove, though I do admit I tried to. But it didn't work. He wrote the most heartbreaking letters. (Thanks for slipping the last over to me, by the way!) He wants me to hang on a bit longer, because he thinks he's got something that'll not exactly make scientific

193

history, but will be quite important and probably make him.'

'And then?'

'Then he'll be coming back to this country. He doesn't say what for. But I suppose he means to marry me and take me with him to wherever he's going next. I don't care much where we are, so long as I can get out of the Brand house.'

'I'm so glad you're going to marry Jim after all. He's about the only man I know who'll be able to cope with you, Copper.'

'Thanks. Only from you I'd take that!'

'But even if you were going to be married to-morrow, I wouldn't come and stay with you. It wouldn't be fair or right, though thanks for the thought, all the same.'

'Oh, Jim wouldn't mind!' Copper said, extravagantly.

'Now look, Copper, Jim's put up with a lot, and whether you think up the idea of me coming to stay with you or any other daft idea, my advice to you is—don't! Live your lives alone, at least for a time, to get adjusted to each other. You owe it to Jim.'

'But what are *you* going to do?' Copper asked in some dismay.

'I don't know. That's what I wanted to talk over with you. I had rather hoped that you might remember someone whom I'd forgotten. Someone living in the country or by the sea, who'd take me as a sort of boarder. I've got a bit of money saved, and I think I could make do. But it'd have to be someone we knew, wouldn't it? I just couldn't go to strangers.'

'An old patient. That's an idea.'

Copper thought hard.

'Well, there's that old lady who lived in the Cotswolds, but you'd never stand her. She drove us crazy in hospital. She keeps you on the run all the time, and that wouldn't do. D'you remember she used to say that the young were put on this earth to wait on the old?'

Magda smiled at the memory.

'No, she wouldn't do, even if she'd take me.'

'She'd take you, all right! No, and besides her there's only Jane's cousin, who lives at Eastbourne, and she's crawling with children. Well, anyway, she's got two sets of twins and two others, and I think they're all boys!'

'Oh, no, that wouldn't do. I must go to a quiet place.'

'Well, what about our own rest home?'

Magda looked shocked.

'Copper, what, for six months?'

'No, I see what you mean. You couldn't do that. Well, I don't know. Maybe I'll think of something. Ask around the other girls when I go back to hospital.'

Magda, who had been gathering her gloves and bag, and starting to get up, sat down limply again.

'What did you say, Copper?'

Copper grinned.

'You heard me. I'm going back to the hospital. I've written and applied, and they're short-handed, and welcomed me with open arms.'

'But—but you left nursing!' Magda gasped. 'I thought you loathed it!'

'So did I. But you never know. You always said I'd jump out of the frying-pan into the fire, and I did. Only being me, I've got the chance to jump back again, and I'm taking it. At least they'll be the people I'm used to, and they won't cut my throat for two pins. Magda, you don't know what you missed, when you swapped appointments with me— at least you've got to thank your health for getting you out of that one!'

'Don't! Don't remind me about that awful thing we did, Copper. I'll never forget it or stop feeling ashamed of it. I only hope they don't find out when you go back to the hospital, that's all!'

Copper said nothing to that. Instead, she paid the bill for them both, swept aside Magda's protests and took her arm.

'Shut up, you old idiot! Let me pay the bill for once, to celebrate the end of our squabble. And we must do this again before you pack up your job, and before I go back to Town. I mean to take a week or two off, as a breather, between jobs. If I wasn't such a spendthrift, I'd give you some of what I've put by in this job, so you could start your rest somewhere,' she said, looking sideways at her sister, and hoping Magda wouldn't jump at the offer.

'It's all right, Copper. I wouldn't dream of taking your money, but thanks all the same,' Magda smiled.

'By the way, what does the Big Boss think of all this?' Copper said, keeping her fingers crossed and hoping Magda wouldn't get angry at the mention of Andrew Debenham.

'Oh, he doesn't know about it yet, and I don't suppose he'll care one way or the other,' Magda said, evasively.

'Oh,' Copper was disappointed. 'The rumour's going round that he was nuts over Mrs. Brand all the time, and that it's only a matter of time before he proposes to her.'

'Did Mrs. Brand start that rumour too?' Magda couldn't help saying, with a wry smile.

'I expect so,' Copper said, cheerfully.

'Well, I'm glad we're friends again,' Magda said, warmly. 'And this talk has helped me, although we haven't thought of any solution to my problem yet. It's helped me to be able to talk it out of my system to someone.'

'Well, let me know how you go on, won't you?' Copper said, wrinkling her forehead anxiously. She was beset with the feeling that she was being inadequate, and she had never liked that, although to assume responsibility of any kind had never been a popular move with her.

'Yes, I'll let you know,' Magda smiled, 'but we'd better not be seen together. You know what this district's like.'

'I think we've left it too late to bother about that old worry,' Copper grinned. 'Look who's in that whopping big car—or I'm a Dutchman!'

Magda swung round and stared with unbelieving eyes at a familiar black sedan parked at the kerb across the street. The owner had just got in, and was engaged in starting up the engine to go. Magda didn't know whether he'd seen them or not, but without a doubt it was the one person whom she didn't want to see the twins together—Andrew Debenham!

CHAPTER NINE

ONE day was so much like the next, where Mrs. Debenham was concerned, that even if Magda only went out to the village, she would question her closely about everything she had done, seen and heard, when she came back. To-day, on hearing that Magda had been farther afield for her afternoon off, Mrs. Debenham settled herself down for a nice chat about a town she hadn't seen for weeks and which seemed like years.

'Does the clock in the tower go yet?' she asked, wistfully, and when Magda agreed that it did indeed go, and now kept good time, Mrs. Debenham said, 'And what about that wool shop they were going to open—the new one by the Town Hall?'

'Oh! Oh, Mrs. Debenham, I'm so sorry, I forgot all about matching your wool. And I promised you, too!'

'Oh, that's a pity. What have you done with the little ball I gave you?'

Magda went and fetched it from her hand-bag. It was a lovely shade of pale lime green, with a thread of green silk running through it.

'Put it up against you, my dear. Against

your hair!' the old lady said. 'Yes. Yes, I thought so. It certainly becomes you, that colour.'

'I'll match it the very next time I go out,' Magda promised.

'No, that won't do. That'll be nearly three days ahead. You must go to-morrow, Magda.'

'What's the hurry?' Magda laughed. 'You've lots of other knitting jobs you can start on, and it's only a bed-jacket anyway, and you've loads of them.'

'It wasn't for me. It was intended for you, for a Christmas present. Now you're going so soon, I want to get it finished for you.'

Magda's face registered dismay.

'What's the matter? Don't you like it?' Mrs. Debenham, anxiously.

'Oh, yes, it's lovely, and that pattern's so complicated, I could never hope to make myself one like it.'

'That's what I thought. Then it's the colour you don't like!'

'No. No, honestly, I love it, but it just brought home to me the fact that I'm leaving here, and the reason for my going.'

'Yes, well, I want to talk to you very seriously about it, Magda. My doctor is very perturbed about you, and he tells me that it'll be some six months or more before you're fit again, and then only if you have a complete rest and get looked after properly. Now how do you propose to go about that?'

'Oh, well, of course, I am thinking of going somewhere by the sea for a week or two,' Magda said. 'I shall be all right.'

'No, child, that won't do. Come and sit by me here. I want to talk to you very particularly about something. Now, Magda, let us have no nonsense about this. You and I know in our hearts that I haven't long left.'

Magda didn't deny it, and she knew that Mrs. Debenham wouldn't want her to.

'Very well, then. I want you to pander to me and do what I wish, without argument or quibble. It's something very dear to me, and will give me a lot of pleasure to see it carried out. Will you do that?'

'I'll try,' Magda promised, her eyes misty.

'I've been wondering what I could do to compensate you for all you've given me, my dear. Not just superb nursing and comfort, nor companionship wholly, but something else. There's something about you, Magda, that serenity, that acceptance of life—I don't know quite what it is—but it's very pleasant to have around one. If I'd been going to get well again, I think I should have been selfish enough to try and keep you here with me for always, under some pretext or other. But however, that is not to be.'

She stared past Magda's shoulder, to the great windows, where the dying sun with its thin wintry light, seemed to be sucking swiftly all the life out of the scene, leaving only mist and dusk.

'My time is running out, and I want to leave you something, but I have a feeling that if I leave you money, it will go, not to you, but to the someone or something in your life that haunts you. There is something in your background that takes the best of you away, and denies you the right to happiness. Yes, I'm prying, and the old think they have a right to pry, even though confidences are slow in forthcoming.'

She smiled and waited, patting Magda's hand.

'I didn't know I gave that impression,' Magda said, slowly.

'Well, well, perhaps you'll tell me of your own free will. Meantime I've thought of a way to give you something for yourself. I'm arranging with my doctor to have you sent to a nursing home on the Downs, within sight of the sea, where you can have every comfort, and be kept there until you're really well, even if it's going to be longer than six months.

And there'll be something over for when you start your life again, so that you won't have to rush immediately back into nursing.'

'Oh, Mrs. Debenham!' Magda said, brokenly.

'Now, now, no tears, child! I'm too weak to stand the sight of tears without indulging myself, and that will be bad for me, as you know.'

'But I can't go away and leave you to be cared for by a stranger. Who will you have to look after you in my place? Someone from the hospital?'

'Ah, yes, that's the least pleasant part of it all. You know me so well, don't you? You know how I hate the thought of a stranger, however pleasant and efficient she may be?'

'Yes. Yes, I know.'

'I feel that I shall get a shock if I wake up and see a strange face bending over mine. And to hear a strange voice at night. . . . I'm allergic to new voices, and some are so brisk and un-alive, if you know what I mean.'

A strange face. Magda thought of some of her friends at the hospital, and how difficult they would find it to fit into this house, with no regular times off, and where meals—those very private sessions of hospital nurses, taken with a great deal of noise and conversation in their own hall—were just as likely to be demanded to be taken either by the patient's side for company, or in the chill dining-hall with Andrew Debenham at the other end of the table. That had happened several times before, whether by a whim, or a mistaken kindness, Magda didn't know. She only knew she had hated such meals, as indeed she had hated all the other unconventional incidents and innovations that had been thrust on her, and which not everyone could rise to with complete poise.

No, a stranger might not like it at all. But Mrs. Debenham might be made easy by a face not so unlike Magda's own.

'Would you be happy if your new nurse at least looked like me?' she breathed, playing with a mad idea and praying that it would work, and be acceptable to all parties.

'Is there anyone else who looks like you, child?' Mrs. Debenham asked, laughing a little.

Magda felt that something was driving her to do this, against all her better judgment, against every instinct within her. Mrs. Debenham would never forgive her for not speaking about this before, after all the opportunities she had given Magda for confidences, and yet it was the only way. It had to be done, Magda felt.

'So like me that I don't think you'll know the difference sometimes,' she assured the old lady gravely. 'And she's a good nurse,' she added loyally.

'No. You're teasing me, Magda.'

'No, I'm not. She's my twin sister.'

Mrs. Debenham was silent for a minute. Then she said in a low voice:

'A twin sister. A nurse. Where is this young woman now?'

'Quite near,' Magda said, unhappily. 'In fact, she's in Mrs. Brand's house.'

The old lady's face changed a little. Some of the friendliness went out of it, dying, like a light that was being carried away into the darkness. Magda felt chilled, and wretched, yet in no way sorry for what she had done. It was not a thing to regret. It was just a pity that it couldn't have been done before.

'Hadn't you better tell me all about it?' Mrs. Debenham said, lying back on her pillows and never taking her eyes off Magda's face.

'Yes. Yes, I want to,' Magda said, urgently. 'Believe me, I've wanted to tell you about her all along, but I couldn't There was a reason, a big reason, why I couldn't, and why both Copper and I have tried to keep her existence a secret. It wasn't easy, with her in the neighbourhood.'

'Yet Mrs. Brand knew about her? Obviously she would know!'

'She knew, yes,' Magda said, knitting her brows. 'It was more than we hoped for, that she'd keep the secret too. I don't see why she did, but we were very thankful.'

'And what was the big reason?'

Magda drew a deep breath. Now it had come to the telling, it wasn't easy to know where to begin.

'I want you to understand that outside of her being a good nurse, my sister Copper isn't like me in nature. She's fun-loving and joyous (that's the only word that describes her, I think!) but she's the unluckiest person alive. If there's trouble to be got into, she seems to land in it. But the trouble I've been trying to keep her out of since she's been with Mrs. Brand has been of my making.'

In restrained language, Magda tried to tell fairly and leaving nothing out, the switch the sisters practised, because of Magda's being unwell at the time. The start of this present illness.

'I can't ask you to understand what it's like, having fought—starved at times—to get a training as a nurse for both of us. Not just for one, but both of us,' she stressed, thinking back over those lean days. 'When we were probationers, entering the profession for the first time, there was no State aid. That came afterwards. We had to work for it.'

She couldn't say that Copper was a joyous spendthrift, and that what she spent, Magda went without to put the money back, so that Copper shouldn't have any excuse for flinging up her new profession on the excuse that there was no more money for studying or exams. All that, she glossed over, and hoped that Mrs. Debenham wouldn't notice. Explaining the exchange of appointments wasn't so difficult.

'When I told you about my father the other day, it was all true, except of course that I left out any mention of my sister. I was sorry to have to do that, but you will see that we had to keep the secret as long as possible, because it was a really awful thing to do, switching appointments. By all rights, Copper should have been here, nursing your nephew, and then you. Perhaps it would have been better, for then she wouldn't have had to leave you on account of her health.'

'And Mrs. Brand knew all this?'

'Yes. Copper told me she'd blurted it out and that Mrs. Brand didn't seem to mind, and agreed to keep quiet about it. It seemed incredible to me, but Copper said she was a—' Here Magda fumbled a little to find a more dignified expression than the one which Copper had used, but failed. 'My sister said Mrs. Brand was a sport, and that seemed to her an adequate explanation, but I confess it's always puzzled me.'

'Yes. I find it unconvincing, too,' Mrs. Debenham said, dryly. 'And does my nephew know about all this too?'

'No! Oh, no!' Magda was shocked at the idea. 'You won't tell him, will you?'

'And why not?'

'Well—' Magda spread beautiful and expressive hands. 'He's a governor of our hospital.'

'In other words, you want me to be a party to this piece of duplicity, too!'

Magda stared unhappily, and then shook her head. It all seemed to have taken a wrong turn. Perhaps after all, she should have left Mrs. Debenham to select a stranger to take her place, and to hope that the old lady would get used to her in time. As it was, she seemed to have antagonised her, and at the same time how could she be sure that Copper herself would take kindly to this new idea? It struck her, now, that that should have been the first thing she should have thought of. Asking

Copper if she was willing.

'No. Perhaps I'm asking too much,' Magda said. 'But after all these years of struggling, and now I've got to be the one to give it up—'

She blinked fiercely at the mist settling before her eyes.

'How will you give it up? You'll go back to nursing when you're well again, surely!'

Magda shook her head.

'It isn't easy to get back when you aren't fit, and I can't afford the time nor the money to get really first rate again. As things have turned out, even if you still wanted to give me that generous gift you spoke of not long ago, I couldn't accept it. It's funny, isn't it? You've wanted me to confide in you for so long, and I felt I couldn't. I came just now to you of my own free will, and told you everything, and— well—'

'But my dear Magda, I could forgive what I consider to be no more than a schoolgirl scrape, bad though it might be for discipline. I daresay you've both been punished enough by your own anxiety of being found out! But what I can't bring myself to stomach is what that girl has been doing all this time in Sylvia Brand's house. Or isn't she still there?'

Magda smiled sadly.

She wasn't going to be the one to say that

Copper had got sick of nursing and flung it up for the delights of a better paid and easier job in a private household. What she did mention, however, was the offer that was made to Copper.

'My sister and I seem to have that curious thing about us that makes people loath to let us go. Mrs. Brand asked Copper to stay on as her companion-help, or some such thing. Copper was expecting to give up nursing soon, anyway, because of her impending marriage.'

'And when is your marriage to happen? I have been waiting to hear about that, but apparently it isn't to be included in your confidences.'

'Marriage? Me? I'm not going to be married to anyone!' Magda gasped.

'Well, I've always thought my nephew a hot-headed fool, but I never imagined he'd get things so wrong as to believe that a girl was engaged to be married to some fellow in Africa, when the girl denies all mention of the idea.'

'That's my sister,' Magda said, in a small voice. 'You must think me very deceitful, but the fact is, I had a letter for Copper, from Jim. I was going to take it to her. You see Jim expected her to be here, so he wrote her care

211

of this address. I suppose Copper forgot to tell him she had exchanged jobs with me. She's like that. Mr. Debenham picked the letter up and saw my sister's name.'

'So you let him think that it was you! I don't think I like it. It *is* deceitful, Magda!'

'It wasn't entirely because of my sister,' Magda said.

They stared at each other, the old lady hurt, Magda in agony.

'Aren't confidences awful,' Magda murmured, at last. 'You start, and there's no stopping, till you've bared your whole heart. You can't leave off.'

'Please don't tell me anything you don't wish to,' the old lady said, rather stiffly.

'It doesn't matter,' Magda said hopelessly. 'I think you know, anyway. It's true. I love him. But I couldn't let him know that. So I made it appear that the letter was for me, and that I was waiting to marry Jim. It worked, you know.'

'Yes, it certainly worked,' Mrs. Debenham agreed, her voice softening, the hard unforgiving look leaving her face. 'My dear child, I always thought you were privately suffering, but I never realised just what you were going through. But why didn't you come and tell me sooner? I gave you so many opportunities, and

I might have helped you!'

'How could you?' Magda asked, bluntly. 'You warned me not to fall in love with your nephew, didn't you? How could I confide in you after that?'

'That was for your sake, not his,' his aunt said, softly.

'You didn't have to warn me about him,' Magda said, unaware of the warm, tender smile playing about the sad lines of her mouth. 'He's hurt me, as no other man could or would, and yet I don't think he meant to. It was her all the time—Elizabeth. She must have haunted him, through me. It was his bad luck that his nurse had to have her colouring, and it must have made his pain and endurance while in bed, ten thousand times worse. I would have hated it from the bottom of my soul, if I'd been him. I know how he felt.'

'And are you going away, and leaving him to that Brand woman?' Mrs. Debenham asked, softly.

'I don't think he'll marry anyone, any more than I shall. You can't live with one person and love the ghost of another. It's madness and torture and . . . oh, no,' she said, covering her eyes with a shaking hand, 'life's difficult enough as it is.'

'I think I must see my nephew and have a

talk to him,' Mrs. Debenham said, smiling a little.

'But I have your promise that you won't let him know,' Magda reminded her. 'All this was in confidence, remember.'

'Oh, I shouldn't tell him of anything you told me. I just want to find out his impressions. You see, my dear, after all this, I find it rather incredible that you should expect me to take your sister as my nurse. What will my nephew think, when he sees her? Do you think he won't know the difference?'

Magda nodded.

'And that's why I don't want you to tell him any of this. You see, it's happened before. He saw her once, at Mrs. Brand's, and thought she was me. That proves he doesn't . . . care at all for me. If he had, he would have known. So you see, when she comes here, if you consent to have her, he'll be as rude to her as to me, and no one will be any the wiser.'

'Won't your sister resent that very much?'

'Copper?' Magda smiled. 'Possibly. But I doubt it. She isn't. . . .' She had been going to say that Copper wasn't the caring sort, but didn't want that misconstrued. 'She isn't the worrying sort, nor the noticing sort. She might not even notice that your nephew was being rude to her.'

She straightened her shoulders, and shook her head.

'But somehow, Mrs. Debenham, dear Mrs. Debenham, I don't think you're going to have my sister here, even though I've told you everything. (Perhaps *because* I've told you everything). But it's been a relief to unload it all, and thank you for listening so patiently, and for not feeling too angry with me for concealing all this. Part of it wasn't my secret to tell.'

'Don't be so stupid, my dear,' Mrs. Debenham smiled. 'Nothing's changed. I want this Copper of yours to come and look after me, because it will be almost like having you here. I confess I'm intrigued, too, about the likeness, and the bond between you two. I want to hear more about it, and about you both. And I want—well, well, never mind.'

Magda didn't know whether she was relieved or sorry. Now that it was more or less fixed, she only hoped with all her heart that Copper would agree to come, and that if she did, she wouldn't get into any more scrapes, that she would look after her patient with gentleness and curb her own roaring high spirits, and that she wouldn't fall foul of Andrew Debenham, nor let him know that it wasn't

Magda still there. For certain he wouldn't like the exchange nor the close relationship between them. He would feel a fool and be suspicious and furious.

Furthermore, there was Mrs. Brand to consider. How would she take the whole thing? Suppose she wouldn't consent to it? Suppose she decided to tell Andrew the whole truth? And then Magda recalled that Andrew had been in the car so near to them both when they had been in town. Had he seen them? She couldn't tell. She hadn't seen him since.

She wandered downstairs later, after her duties were over for a while. She often felt at a loss to know what to do with herself in this house. She wanted to wander all over it, touching and loving it, poring over everything, but something about the place seemed to be trying to press her back, back to her own room at the top of the second staircase. Fancifully she told herself that it was the ghost of Elizabeth pointing out to her that she had no right to be in this house. Would Copper feel like that, too, and, worse still, if she consented to come here at all, would she take to her heels, protesting as she had done before, that these old houses gave her the willies?

Magda closed her eyes, and told herself not to be so foolish. Strains of music came from the music-room, the door of which was slightly ajar. Someone was softly playing the harp.

Intrigued in spite of herself, she went along and looked in through the crack. Andrew Debenham sat there with the great harp between his knees, and at the slight movement of the door, he looked up and saw her.

'Oh, come on in, don't stand there peeping!' he shouted, and the harp music came to a discordant standstill.

'Am I intruding?' she murmured, closing the door behind her.

'Of course you are! But now you're here, come on in. When are you leaving?'

She almost blurted out that she was going almost at once but realised in time that it was from Andrew that they were going to hide the fact that Copper was Magda's twin and was only deputising. Magda wondered as she stared into his dark accusing face, whether his aunt realised that in keeping this fact from her nephew she was laying herself open to the same deception that they were all taking part in—Copper, herself and even Sylvia Brand. Andrew would never forgive them, any of them!

'I don't know,' she said, slowly, again conscious of the fact that it was a half-truth. She wasn't really certain when she was going, but a half-truth would be as abhorrent to him as a whole untruth, she was sure.

'You're a sticker, aren't you?' he said, suddenly smiling, though it was a grim smile.

She found herself murmuring something platitudinous about having her patient's welfare to consider first, and hated herself for it.

'Sit down. Don't just stand there. Listen to this,' and he began playing on the harp again, softly, then increasing the volume and speed into a frightening burst of wild emotion and agitation.

When he finished, he stared at her, and said, 'Music affects you, too,' and there was surprise in his voice. 'Tears, eh? Tell me, you're engaged. What d'you think of this love business?'

He always left her speechless with his direct attacks. He saw this and laughed, a strange, mirthless laugh, not unmixed with bitterness.

'Come, don't tell me you're too shy to discuss such an embarrassing subject? I didn't know there were any shy nurses!'

'I believe we suffer most human emotions,' she said, stiffly.

'All right. I apologise. I deserved that,' and his voice was a little more friendly. 'You must think I'm all kinds of a boor. Well, so I am. I don't consider people's feelings, but that's because I've been so hurt myself. Ever been hurt, little Magda?'

'Yes, badly. Terribly,' she heard herself saying.

'This Jim?' he demanded.

'Oh, no. It doesn't follow that he is the one who hurt me. No, this man didn't even like me. In fact, I sometimes wondered if he ever really saw me.'

'He sounds a blighter!'

'Oh, no. You don't have to be necessarily bad to hurt someone. After all, you can't make the heart go where you want it to. That's why all this business about love being so wonderful, is so silly. It isn't wonderful, really, except in a terrible way. It's pain and hopelessness and disillusion.'

'Poor little devil, so you've suffered too,' he said. 'But at least you're being more sensible than I am. You are going to be married and forget the blighter!'

'Who says I'm going to be married!' Magda flashed, and then recalled that if he spoke to Copper, when she had taken Magda's place in his house, she would probably be wearing her discarded engagement ring. 'Oh, yes,' she murmured, 'Jim.'

'I've come to the conclusion,' he said,

leaning back and staring down to where Elizabeth's portrait still hung, 'that the best thing to ask in life is companionship. Does your Jim offer you that, Magda? Because if so, don't despise it.'

'I didn't say I minded being in love,' she said, quietly, 'and I didn't say I was looking for something to take its place. It's a painful experience, it's true, but I wouldn't have missed it for anything in the world. You don't live till you know it, even if it isn't returned.'

'Even if it isn't returned,' he repeated. 'And how do you know if it is love, Elizabeth?'

She gasped, and got to her feet. The scuffle her shoes made on the polished floor, hit the silence, and the echo came back from the harp. He got up too, and stared down into her wild dark eyes.

'What is it?' he muttered. He, too, was conscious of a coldness in the atmosphere.

'You said "Elizabeth",' she whispered, and left him staring after her as she fled.

CHAPTER TEN

MRS. DEBENHAM lost no time in arranging for Magda to go into the nursing-home. Magda was amused to see the old lady's zeal in getting rid of her nurse, while (Magda guessed) there was a flush of excitement about the whole thing and Mrs. Debenham didn't have time to consider what it would be like when Magda had gone.

'I don't want your nephew to know anything about it,' Magda kept insisting. 'It will be possible to keep it from him, won't it?'

Mrs. Debenham smiled.

'That isn't your worry, my dear, it's mine. I notice you don't seem unduly worried about my deceiving Andrew as you and your sister have done?'

'I'm sorry about that, but he does make such a fuss,' Magda said, ruefully. 'I do hope he doesn't talk to Copper. She *is* so tactless. She'll let everything out in no time if he does.'

'Have you found out yet whether the girl is willing to come?' Mrs. Debenham wanted to know.

'Yes,' Magda frowned. 'I was going to tell you. I telephoned her. She jumped at the idea.

221

She doesn't have to go back to the hos
just yet, and anyway, she'll probably ma
to get their consent to come here, so it w
all right.'

'Lucky for me that my nephew is on
board of the hospital, or else that interf
doctor of mine would have wanted to fi
up with a new nurse,' the old lady sm
grimly.

As it happened, Andrew wasn't there
Magda went away. Magda gathered that Mrs.
Debenham had talked him into going on a
business trip that should have been made
before.

'Just because he knows I'm ill, it doesn't
mean to say that everything should be at a
standstill,' she complained to Magda. 'He was
going on this trip when my silly heart first
started causing trouble, and now look how
long it's been put off. He could have gone
away and got the business done, and been
back again long ago. Besides,' she added, smiling a little, 'it gives me rather a gruesome
feeling of standing still, waiting . . . and I
don't like that.'

'Are you sure you didn't do this to get him
out of the way while Copper was installed?'
Magda said, with a smile playing about her
mouth.

222

'No, I didn't, but it's a very good idea I think, don't you?'

But Magda was glad that he was away. She didn't want to have to slip out of his life without a good-bye, but now that he had gone, she couldn't say good-bye if she wanted to, and it was easier. Easier, too, to pack and go, knowing that he wouldn't pop up suddenly, and look at her with those penetrating eyes of his, and make her self-confidence slip away, leaving her defenceless.

She quietly went about the business of her packing, knowing that at this moment, Copper was probably tackling Mrs. Brand about her promise to keep their secret.

'It's all so sudden,' Mrs. Brand was complaining, suspiciously. 'I think Andrew Debenham *ought* to know.'

'He won't be very interested, and anyway, his old aunt doesn't want him to know. He'd make a fuss on principle,' Copper said, bluntly.

'I thought you'd stay with me for always,' Mrs. Brand said, returning to the attack in a different way.

Copper shook her head.

'I'm expecting to be married in the next year, and anyway, Max is so very, very good that I feel redundant just to look at him.'

'I can't ask Max to run messages for me,' Mrs. Brand said, sharply, and apparently she was quite oblivious of how tactless she was being to Copper.

'Well, you don't really want me,' Copper reminded her, and Mrs. Brand was forced to admit it.

'I'm glad to see your sister has come to her senses,' she said, smiling at Copper in her particularly infuriating way. 'I think she ought to have gone sooner, myself.'

Copper flushed dully.

She didn't often get angry in Magda's defence, and at once the other woman saw she had made a mistake.

'She's ill,' Copper said, briefly.

'Oh, yes, of course, but it's fortuitous that her illness happened just now, isn't it? Don't think I'm against her. I'm not. I'm rather sorry for her. I mean, it's so silly to set your cap against a man like Andrew Debenham, when you're just an employee in the house, isn't it? He'd hardly look at her. Yet the servants don't like it. Have you heard how she gets on with the servants?'

Copper, who hadn't, but had had an inkling that something wasn't very comfortable about the set-up at Debenham Mount, looked dubious.

'You know, you're going in on a pretty sticky wicket, my girl,' Sylvia Brand smiled. 'I think it's awfully decent of you, myself, and conversely, I think it's not quite the thing of your sister to pitch you into that and not to warn you about it. After all, if you two still want to keep up this absurd secret about there being two of you, after all this time, just think what it means from your point of view.'

Copper made an effort to think, but thinking wasn't her strong point. She found it a bore. She just wanted to go storming into Debenham Mount to jolly the old lady back to health, conscious of her giving her sister a break and being very good-natured about the whole thing. Problematical things such as an undercurrent from the servants' quarters seemed to Copper to be looking for trouble rather unnecessarily. People always liked her, unless she got into one of her real patches of trouble and involved them, and then there was no question of an undercurrent. There was a mighty storm, and everyone knew just where they were.

'Oh, I think it'll be all right,' she said, easily.

Privately she thought it rather silly of Magda to be so honest with Mrs. Brand and to tell her what they were doing. All that was

225

really necessary was for Copper to tell Mrs. Brand that she was fed-up with the job and wanted to be released. She had said as much to Magda over the telephone.

Magda, however, had been adamant. Mrs. Brand might make difficulties over what she might consider as just a whim, whereas in telling her the truth, she could hardly make difficulties over such a major reason as Andrew's aunt's illness. Added to this was the fact that if they hadn't told her (and although it was no one's business which twin was nursing at the Mount, Magda felt that Mrs. Brand would feel it was her business since she had been the only one to know about their dangerous switching of jobs in the first place) Mrs. Brand with her colossal good luck, would have been sure to find out, and to be at once suspicious and mischievous.

'Well, if you want any help, don't forget me, will you? I don't like to see a girl pushed around. There's still that rumour, you know. Of course, we don't know what has been going on there. Mr. Debenham might very well have got tired of it himself, and Magda was glad to go. I don't know what you're going into, at all. Have you met Mrs. Debenham, by the way?'

Copper hadn't, and said so. One patient

was very much like another to her. They were all miserable, and looked for her jolly face. They all needed a lot of fetching and carrying, which she didn't mind. And if she were apt to forget things, there was always a doctor at hand.

'Well, I don't want to talk about her. She's ill, and may never be well again. But all I would say in passing is, I don't know how you'll find her, but I find her an extremely difficult old woman to get on with. Heaven knows, I've tried. I've gone out of my way to understand her, and to make her like me, but no! I've found it impossible. And you won't be able to leap out of that job light-heartedly, I warn you! I've heard that she may linger for years.'

Copper suddenly laughed, her own merry laugh.

'Oh, Mrs. Brand, thank you for warning me, but you don't know me! Mrs. Debenham herself may kick me out before long—flat on my ears, if I know myself and my record! She'll be jolly glad to get rid of me, and she'll welcome some strange nurse with open arms! Poor old Magda, she forgot that, when she was being so solicitous for her patient!'

Mrs. Brand frowned as Copper left her. Something had happened to reconcile the sisters and to heal the breach so that she couldn't open it again, and she couldn't imagine what it could possibly be. She had found, before this, that Copper was not proof against her little barbs, and that although the girls were twins, Copper was not by any means proofed against believing things of her sister, even against her will. But now it was different. Mrs. Brand could see that nothing she could say would put Copper against Magda again.

She was uneasy for the rest of the day, and not very good-tempered.

The weather was bad. She hated the winter months. Like a cat, she loved being in the warm, and her indolent nature helped that. But now it became increasingly necessary that she go out, over to Debenham Mount to see Andrew.

She was not clear about what she would do. Certainly she had no intention of giving the twins away—outright. But there were many little ways and means at her disposal that would help her to sound him as to how he felt about Magda and to make him wonder if it were still Magda in his house.

Sylvia Brand's lips creased into some semblance of a smile at the thought of what she could do, given half an hour with Andrew before she had to go and visit his tiresome relative. The thing about Andrew was that it was possible to have such fun with him without his being aware of it.

Magda, wearing her brown topcoat and little brown beret, went into Mrs. Debenham's room to say good-bye, just after lunch. Copper had been installed, expressed gloom at the interior of the Mount, and had promised to make the best of it.

Mrs. Debenham stared at Magda in her unfamiliar clothes and smiled.

'I ought to be feeling sorry you're going, my dear. I thought I'd be very upset. I don't know what's coming over me. But the fact is, I think I've been aware of your own bad health for a long time, and it's unsettled me. I've been conscious of a selfish feeling, of trying to close my eyes to it, because I didn't want to lose you.'

'I don't want to go, either,' Magda said, thickly. 'But there, we're both being stupid. At the end of the six months, I shall be fit as a fiddle again, and back here to see what's going on, and I shall find you well, and up and about again. (Going slowly, and taking it easy, of course!) And we shall both be inclined to think back on this time with a little embarrassment, because we both were so foolish.'

Mrs. Debenham stared at her for a moment. Then she said, 'I believe I wish that were true. But we both know it can't be. But you will come back, my dear, when I . . . when I go? I'd like you to. I think I'd like you to be here when my nephew. . . .' She broke off, and folded her lips tightly. 'You know, Andrew is just a boy underneath that brusque and at times rather unpleasant exterior of his. I know he will be feeling lost and unhappy when I'm gone. I'd like you to be here.'

Magda was surprised.

'He won't want *me*,' she said, gently.

'No?' Mrs. Debenham smiled. 'I wonder. I wonder if he'll know *whom* he wants. You know, my dear, I think I wish you were going to marry my Andrew. I know I shouldn't say that. If such a thing were to ever happen, you'd have a hard task in front of you. It isn't easy to assume the mantle of mistress of this house. Its traditions, alone, would weigh you down. And if folk found you weren't fitted for the job, you'd have such a bad time. Your sort suffer. The sensitive sort. No, perhaps I'm wrong.'

'If Andrew were just an ordinary man, would you, then? Would you think I could make him happy?'

Mrs. Debenham nodded, patting Magda's

hand.

'Yes, my dear. I think you could make him happy in those circumstances.'

'Then you don't think that the way the heart feels, is enough?'

Mrs. Debenham hesitated.

'I come from the generation that believes that love alone is not enough,' she said, at last. 'But my generation may well be wrong.'

Magda felt she had had enough. She got up to go, but Mrs. Debenham motioned her to stay.

'Your bed-jacket. I got it finished,' she said, with a slight smile. 'I stayed up a little later last night than I should, but it was a labour of love.'

Magda took the lovely garment, and touched it gently. It had huge bishop sleeves drawn up at the wrist with satin ribbons and edged with swansdown, and the swansdown edging ran all round the neck and down the fronts.

'It's too lovely to wear,' Magda said.

'I want you to wear it,' Mrs. Debenham said, firmly. 'You'll need something when you sit up in bed and have your breakfast. I shall think of you in it.'

'Breakfast in bed?' Magda murmured, wonderingly. 'What a funny thing! I don't remember when I had that last!'

'And you must open the envelope pinned inside it, when you first put the jacket on.'

'Envelope?' For the first time, Magda noticed the rustle of paper, and saw one of Mrs. Debenham's heavy deckle-edged square envelopes peeping out from inside the bed-jacket.

'Not now. Don't open it now,' Mrs. Debenham warned. 'It was intended for your Christmas present, but it may be more useful now. Just a little something, so that you don't feel you're without pocket-money. I know that even in these days nurses don't get over-paid, and I don't know what arrangements will be made for you from the hospital while you're ill.'

'Oh, Mrs. Debenham, you're so sweet to me,' Magda murmured.

'Will you write to me?' Mrs. Debenham asked. 'I shall look forward to hearing what sort of life goes on around you. You'll want to know how your sister is getting on, too, won't you?'

'I don't think you ought to tire yourself with writing, but I'll certainly write to you,' Magda promised. 'Tell me, what do you really think of Copper—apart from being surprised at how much alike we both are?'

'Isn't there an old story, or a parable, about identical jars, one being filled with water, and one with wine?' Mrs. Debenham said, obscurely, but hastened to say, in case she hurt Magda, 'However, your sister is very gay and cheerful, and I'm sure that's essential in a nurse.'

Magda said good-bye to Copper in a preoccupied way. Her whole thoughts were obsessed with the way old Mrs. Debenham had looked at her, when she at last left the old lady's bedroom. It was a yearning look, a look the old lady couldn't help, as if she had to stare and stare, because she would never see Magda again. Magda kept thinking, *I'm being morbid. She'll get well, these cases sometimes do.* But the doctor's words, and the old lady's unspoken conviction, weighed heavily. It was as if they knew, Magda and Mrs. Debenham, that they wouldn't see each other again, and up till that moment neither had been fully aware of how closely the relationship between them had knit together.

'Will you?' Copper was insisting.

'Will I what?' Magda asked, in bewilderment.

'Stamp this letter for Jim at the Post Office, and post it. You'll have heaps of time.'

'But I can't ask the station taxi to wait

while I fool around with letters, can I?'

'Oh, my dear,' Copper laughed, 'no common station cab for you. Your patient has ordered the car to take you. Your bags have already gone down. Now don't forget, will you?'

Magda promised she wouldn't, but had her doubts as to how the chauffeur would feel about it. The staff at the Mount were still a little distant in their manner to Magda, and she wondered how on earth the old lady expected her nephew to be kept in the dark about the two of them, when the servants knew. Or perhaps it was that Mrs. Debenham thought that it didn't matter all that much, and wasn't going to be involved in the deception at all. After all, Andrew Debenham would surely be too much interested in his coming engagement to Mrs. Brand to bother his head about what the nurses were up to.

Magda didn't see Mrs. Brand's car sweep into the drive. She missed her by seconds. Nor did Mrs. Brand have any idea that Magda had already gone. She was thinking of what she would say to Andrew, and what sort of approach to attempt. It all depended, she supposed, on how he looked.

She was told guardedly that Andrew was not in at the moment, and invited to cool her heels in the drawing-room, like any other un-privileged visitor. She hid her fury, and told Hobbs coolly that if Andrew weren't in, she would visit his aunt, and could find her own way up. She hoped that would put the dignified Hobbs in his place, and at the same time impress him with the fact that she was privileged and could wander about the house as she pleased.

She frowned as she went up the massive main staircase. The oak everywhere depressed her. Her own staircase was delicate and winding, wrought iron enamelled pale grey, and made for light and sunshine. She felt that the fat carved newel posts were reproaching her for her modern outlook and for her lack of background.

At the top she was confronted with the hideous uniform of St. Joseph's, and a pair of solemn dark eyes under the starched cap. She took it for granted that this was Magda, and was unreasonably angry that the girl was still here. She felt rather foolish, as if she had rushed over the minute she had thought Magda would be gone, and that the girl must be laughing at her, especially as Andrew was apparently out.

'You're leaving it rather late for your train, aren't you?' she asked, in her specially cool voice.

'Yes, ma'am,' was the meek rejoinder.

'Well, I'd better see your patient, I think, while she's alone. I understand she *is* alone?'

'Oh, yes, quite alone,' and Sylvia Brand was presented with a prim back and neatly tied apron strings.

As she walked along behind the nurse, Sylvia began to feel better. What had she to fear from this quiet young woman in the black wool stockings and flat dreary black shoes? Why, her manner was enough to put Andrew off! So very polite and calm and unexciting.

She smiled and knew just how she was going to attack Andrew when he at last arrived. Then, at the patient's door, the nurse turned, and as she opened it, she creased up her face in repressed laughter. The dark eyes danced with impudence and even the voice was different as she murmured:

'Fancy you not knowing, Mrs. Brand! I'm Copper!'

Her face was flushed as she sat down by Mrs. Debenham's bedside and tried to concentrate on what the old lady was saying. It struck her that she hadn't been so clever with the twins after all—or had she? She tried, while listening and making polite rejoinders

236

to Andrew's aunt—to think what it would do to Andrew, if he found out that this was not Magda at all. Would it irritate him, or intrigue him? If he were not inclined to look at Magda as a second Elizabeth, would he not do that in Copper's case? Copper was bubbling over with life, just like that other wretched woman. True, she was (or appeared to be) interested in some young man out in Africa, but what did that matter? Hadn't she been furious at the thought of her sister snaffling a rich husband? How would she react if Andrew Debenham were foolish enough to get interested in her?

'Mrs. Debenham, I came over right away because, to tell you the truth, I'm worried about those Rushton sisters,' she said, suddenly making up her mind to start the attack through Andrew's aunt.

Mrs. Debenham, who had been wondering what lay at the bottom of this sudden visit, and decided that Andrew hadn't bothered (or thought to) to tell Sylvia Brand of his intention to go away, said, politely, 'Oh? Why?'

'Why? Well, doesn't it fill you with panic, the thought of two people being so alike that you can't tell them apart?'

'No. I can tell them apart,' Mrs. Debenham said.

'Well, I can't think how you can! I've just mistaken Copper for Magda, but the little monkey was acting. Or didn't you know that she can impersonate her sister?'

Mrs. Debenham didn't, and frowned worriedly. She didn't know what had gone on between Andrew and Magda, and felt that it would be tragic if Copper impersonated her sister in a spirit of fun, to tease Andrew, and he mistook her for Magda. Andrew had never liked that sort of boisterous fun, and hated to be made to feel a fool. He would find out that Magda had deceived him, in the sense that she had not told him she had an identical twin, which would have prepared him for this sort of nonsense. And he would never forgive Magda, while Copper would go scot-free.

'Oh, well,' the old lady said, resolutely fighting down her fears and telling herself that she had got to keep calm until Andrew came back, 'it might not happen. You see, Magda has gone, and so has Andrew.'

There was a little silence.

'I mean, if Copper does impersonate her sister, there is no one here now to whom it will matter.'

Mrs. Brand thought quickly.

What Andrew's aunt said, had two implications. One, that Andrew was already interested in Magda, and the other that he, too, had gone away. With Magda? The question batted itself to and fro in her head, and she could find no way of asking Andrew's aunt, without betraying the fact that she knew nothing about it.

'Oh, yes, of course,' she murmured.

'You did know he had gone away, of course?' Mrs. Debenham murmured, wondering if she had said too much, and thinking with some astonishment that Magda's departure had upset her more than she would have believed possible.

'Oh, yes, of course!' Sylvia Brand lied.

'Yes, of course. And you know, then, how long he'll be away? He will have told you that too?'

'Yes,' Sylvia agreed, wondering frantically if that meant he would be gone a long time, and how she could possibly find out. Why hadn't he told her? What had happened to necessitate this sudden change of plans, and how was it he hadn't even telephoned her before he went?

'Then you will have come over specially to see me! How nice,' Mrs. Debenham said. 'I thought perhaps, just at first, you might have

239

come over to see Andrew, not knowing he had gone just yet.'

'Of course I came specially to see you,' Sylvia Brand said, thinking quickly. 'It's because I'm so perturbed. You see, I can't think why you took the other sister, except of course, that you wouldn't have heard—I suppose you did verify her record at the hospital?'

'No. No, I didn't. Magda told me her nursing was good, and of course, you engaged her—'

'Oh, no, I didn't! I engaged Magda, but it was the other girl who arrived. It so happened that I wasn't seriously ill, otherwise I might have been anxious. Oh, her nursing's all right, I suppose, but to be honest, I'd prefer her sister.'

'But you don't know what Magda's like,' Mrs. Debenham said, worriedly.

'Oh, yes, I do. She has a very good record,' Mrs. Brand asserted.

She didn't leave Mrs. Debenham until she was sure she had the old lady thoroughly anxious about what she had done, and more than ready to consult the doctor on a change of nurses, or at least a verification of Copper's nursing record.

As she went through the hall, Hobbs came to open the door for her.

240

'Oh,' she said, casually, 'I forgot to ask Mrs. Debenham when her nephew is expected back. Do you know?'

Hobbs did, but he had since checked up on his own belief that Mrs. Debenham didn't like this lady enough to give her *carte blanche* in wandering about the house and entering the old lady's bedroom without being announced. He couldn't forgive Mrs. Brand for giving him the wrong impression, and he was very jealous of his job and his discretion. He assumed the boot-face, and said:

'I couldn't say, I'm sure, madam,' which infuriated Sylvia Brand more than Copper's trick had done. Now she didn't know where Andrew had gone, or with whom, but strongly suspected that he had gone off with Magda. What was more, the servants now knew that she didn't know, and they were probably well aware of what had happened in the house.

But Magda herself was due for a surprise that afternoon and a not very pleasant one.

While she was in the Post Office, she heard someone speaking about the family at the Mount. There weren't many strangers in the district, and when one appeared, everyone stopped to look and listen. Magda heard the Post Mistress tell her that the Debenham family still lived there. Her husband, who had been serving Magda with her stamp for Jim at the time, looked up and joined in the conversation.

The person enquiring was a woman in her late thirties. Obviously wealthy, and looked much older than she was. She had, she said, come from the Far East, and had once known Andrew Debenham. Motoring through the district, she wondered if after all this long time, he was still there.

As in a dream, Magda heard the garrulous Post Mistress assuring the person that Andrew was still there, that his aunt lived with him and was ill, that there was as yet no Mrs. Debenham, and that the house and the grounds were pretty much the same as they had been ten, twenty, or even more years ago.

Magda went back to the car, and was driven off to the station, haunted by the fact that the woman in the Post Office was no stranger to her. Where had she seen that bold pair of blue eyes, set in that face that might once have been goodlooking but was now tanned and leathery by Eastern sunshine? Where had she seen that proud set of the head? She shook her head in bewilderment, for the woman, though not that old, had grizelled faded hair, almost grey. A most unattractive woman, yet a compelling woman,

242

a woman who might have been beautiful once. . . .

It wasn't until Magda was in the train and watching the landscape slip by, that landscape that had been her background for the better part of the year, that she realised how it was that the stranger had struck such a familiar chord. She realised it with a sense of shock, and sat back in the corner of her compartment shivering a little, and then she was crying. Crying with the sudden snapping of the tension, and with sheer relief. For now she no longer need feel haunted any more by that magnificent painting in Andrew's music-room, though she might well never see it again. For this unattractive stranger, whose once-glorious red hair was now bleached and greying by the force of the elements, could be no one else but Andrew's Elizabeth.

CHAPTER ELEVEN

MAGDA'S new life was a curious one for her. Back in the hospital atmosphere, of necessity different since the nursing home rules were so easy that it seemed to Magda almost comical, she found it impossible to believe that such a place as Debenham Mount existed.

She lay relaxed most of the day, looking out over the wintry sea, and let the ill feeling that had been gathering momentum, sweep over her to such an extent that a simple task like writing letters became too much for her to bother with.

Mrs. Debenham's letters, on the thick creamy paper with the familiar deckled edges, came and accumulated. Copper's missives were mainly on picture postcards of the village and district, but one Magda treasured because it was a picture of the Mount. The photograph had been taken at a curious angle, and was said (on the front, in white capitals,) to be one of the last of the old historical homes of the district.

Both Copper and Mrs. Debenham spoke of bitterly cold, damp weather, of roaring log fires, and of the preparations for Christmas.

Neither mentioned Andrew, nor any visit of the person whom Magda believed to be Elizabeth. Life, it seemed, was flowing as evenly at the Mount, as it had done when she was there. With the exception, perhaps, of Sylvia Brand's visit and Copper's trick on her—an incident which seemed to have passed off without another breath or whisper about it.

But neither Copper nor Mrs. Debenham had the power nor the fluent use of words to put on paper what passed between themselves. Neither could record for Magda the little undercurrents, the first piling of doubts, and the uncertainty which both nurse and patient had about the other.

Mrs. Debenham missed the *sure* feeling she had had when Magda was there. It came from Magda's meticulous timing of medicine and meals, and all the other little details in their daily routine. It came with Magda's touch, that comfortable, secure, yet impersonal touch with which Magda handled her patients. It came, too, from the spring within her, that love of nursing that all her patients sensed within a few minutes of her taking them over.

Copper had none of those things. She was a good nurse, but mechanical, uninspired. She knew all the rules, but gave nothing extra. It

245

was a job to do, and if her mind sometimes wandered elsewhere, there was a break between its wandering and her wrenching it back with a guilty sense, that the patient was conscious of and didn't like. Copper hadn't the trick of making the patient feel that there was nothing else in her mind, no desire in her heart, than the getting of her patient well again. And Magda had.

But Mrs. Debenham found herself smiling at Copper as the days went by. The girl had such an infectious gaiety, such a merry life, such an animal joyousness of life. She ought, the old lady felt, be out in the fresh air, just being alive, not being cooped up in a sickroom, with the infirm or the old. Not having to earn her living at all, but just being alive and enjoying it.

'Tell me, my dear, what was it like when you two were at home? Before you started nursing?'

Copper grimaced, and willingly sat down to talk about it. Copper did no knitting or needlework, nor did she do anything with her hands, as far as Mrs. Debenham could see.

'Pretty . . . well, you know. Magda and Daddie learning together, and me sloping off. Magda and Daddie talking together and me listening, bored, and then . . . well, sloping off. That's all I seemed to do.'

With her casual way of telling it, Copper disclosed a picture of a man and one of his daughters in a close bond of friendship, while the other daughter had nothing to offer anyone, beyond a liability, a duty to get her out of trouble.

Copper had been in trouble all her life, and told of her scrapes with a sense of fun, laughing at herself all the while, and being apparently quite unaware that she was rather selfish in getting into trouble at all. Indulging herself, and waiting for Magda to get her out of the mess. Indulging in lateness, slackness over duties, indulging herself in having fun outside the hospital, and relying all the time on the likeness of the twins, for her absence to be more or less unnoticed.

'I can't understand Magda. She never wanted anything for herself. She just never bothered to go to the pictures or dancing. Never bought herself anything pretty. Never wanted anything nice to eat. Never bothered about men friends.'

Copper didn't add that there was never much money, and what there was, she saw that she had, so that there was little left over for Magda to have. And yet, seeing all this, Mrs. Debenham couldn't find it in her heart to dislike Copper. As with so many other people, Copper was one of the cheeky ones and impressed them with her 'getting away with' so much, with utter charm and lovableness. No one could dislike her, though they knew that all the time (or most of it) she was wrong.

'And so Magda never had a beau?' Mrs. Debenham asked gently.

'No. Not as far as I know. Only Max, of course, if you can call him a beau. But I don't think Magda wants to get married. She'd die if she couldn't find someone sick to nurse. And she's like that with children and animals, only more so.'

They had many little talks, and all the time Mrs. Debenham was finding out more about the sisters, and managing to fall in with the new feeling that came with Copper's care of her. Somehow she managed to get her quota of medicine, even if she had to remind Copper of the time, and the doctor was in attendance more and more. She used to lie and wonder if she would see the Christmas she had longed for so much, and to wonder also if she would be feeling fit enough to enjoy it.

Andrew's business had taken him longer than he had at first thought. He wrote to his aunt, and once he had a long talk with her on the telephone, but discovered that it tired her so he didn't repeat the experiment. Once he spoke to Copper on the telephone, and asked her confidentially how his aunt was. Copper, never noted for her quick thinking, did as Magda had asked her to, and spoke as though it were Magda, merely repeating the doctor's last report, which gave no grounds for anxiety. Allowing for her superb mimicry and the distance between them over the wires, Andrew had no doubt about it being Magda, and put her distant tone down to the fact that he hadn't said good-bye to her.

He wondered, with a grim smile, what she would have thought of him, if she had known how bothered he had been that day. What would she have thought if she had known how he had vacillated between going to her and telling her about his going away, and how long he expected to be, and saying a good-bye that was more friendly than anything he had said to her yet? He put the thought away in irritation, embarrassment at himself, and felt glad that he had at last gone without saying a word. What was happening to him, he asked himself viciously, to start at this stage to behave like a complete fool? The girl had her own affair—in South Africa, it is true, but likely to be much nearer before long. What, then, was he thinking about her so much for?

Once he asked about Magda in one of his letters to his aunt. A casual enough enquiry, and one which she didn't answer. She felt that she couldn't, without practising the deception on him, and she didn't like it. She played for time, hoping he would be home soon, when she would help him to find out for himself, in a gentle manner, so that he wouldn't be angry with the twins. She felt convinced that if he knew that Magda was away somewhere, ill, he would go and see her, and perhaps in the talking over of the whole thing, he would not be so preoccupied with the fact that Copper existed and that he hadn't been told about her.

And because the normally astute Mrs. Debenham was hoping that such an unlikely event would occur, she realised that she must be very ill indeed. She did no more knitting these days, and thought it fitting that Magda's bed-jacket was the last thing she attempted.

She read quite a lot, because reading didn't take her energy. She didn't even have to hold a book, since it was balanced on her bed book-rest.

Copper came in one day and asked what she was reading, and looked at her curiously.

When Mrs. Debenham mentioned the Greek poets, and showed her the pile of books by the bedside, ranging from the Bible to Browning, with a good sprinkling of essays and letters, Copper's face had changed and she sat down suddenly.

'What is it, child?' Mrs. Debenham asked.

'Oh, nothing. Just being silly. Only it's like home, and the sort of stuff that Magda and Daddie used to wallow in.'

Mrs. Debenham was surprised.

'Magda must be very well read,' she murmured.

'Oh, she is. Daddie was a Professor. At least, he used to be before he ran to seed.'

'That's no way to talk about your father!'

'Well, it's true, and I never was one to mince words.'

'Does Magda know any foreign languages?'

Copper raised astonished brows.

'Oh, didn't she tell you? Six—or seven, I think. She used to read that stuff in the Greek, the same as you are. That's why it gave me such a jerk. I never managed much more than French, and indifferent French at that.'

'But why take up nursing? She might have been—' Mrs. Debenham mused, then broke off.

'It's all right,' Copper said cheerfully. 'Oh, I know Magda loves nursing, but it was also because of me. She wanted a roof over my head, and nursing's the only profession that provides that. She wanted to keep with me, too, and keep an eye on me. I know! I sometimes catch on to things without having to be hit on the head first with a blunt instrument.'

Mrs. Debenham found Copper's robust use of the slang of the day a little enervating, and longed at times for Magda's quiet restrained speech. But she had to admit that Copper toned up conversation, even if you couldn't feel up to taking part in it. And always, Copper brought from her a smile. A tender smile, as for a wilful yet lovable child.

Copper wrote none of this in her letters to Magda, but she did mention one day that a 'dowdy individual with a booming voice' called and asked to see Andrew. She happened to be passing through the hall at the time, and got a peep at the card left. It said, 'Mrs. Basil ffoulkes,' but it meant nothing to Magda, though the description might well have fitted the person in the Post Office. Anyone was dowdy, to Copper, who didn't wear absolutely youthful and up-to-the-minute clothes, and the booming voice was merely an exaggeration. Magda was certain

252

that Elizabeth had gone back to the Mount, and she lay back thankful yet apprehensive; apparently Mrs. Debenham knew nothing of the visit yet, but would she be allowed to remain in such ignorance? Magda didn't want the old lady's wonderful memories of Elizabeth destroyed. To be remembered in such a way was something that should be preserved, particularly as Mrs. Debenham hadn't much longer to live.

That letter was the last Copper wrote to her sister for the next communication she sent was a telegram.

Magda lay back in her rest-chair with her eyes closed, the telegram in a tightly screwed ball. It had been debated whether she should be allowed to have it, and when the effect was seen, there was some surprise. Magda had been pulling round much better in the last few days.

'A very old friend has died,' she gasped, at last. 'It was a shock. I want to go and see her.'

It needed a lot of persuasion for them to allow her to go, but as she was already about, and because it was the person who had arranged the financial details of her entry into the nursing home, she was allowed a few days, provided she didn't tire herself too much. A car was hired to take her all the way and she found herself thankful that there was no train journey.

It was a journey that she had promised to make, and yet didn't really want to undertake. She looked on Mrs. Debenham as her old friend rather than her old patient, and the thought that the old lady had died, and so soon after she herself had left the house, shocked her beyond words.

In such a medical case, it was difficult to assess just how long the patient had to expect. Mrs. Debenham herself had seemed to think that she wouldn't live much longer, and yet Magda recalled the eagerness with which the old lady had looked forward to the Debenham Christmas, as she called it, and must have thought that her life wouldn't end before that time. She wondered whether the old lady had sustained a shock, to hasten the end, but dismissed the thought. Copper would have mentioned it.

The car slid through the wintry scene, and brought Magda by way of the home farm. Up through the trees, now bare of their leaves, she could see the bluff where she had almost gone over that day, and remembered with that tortuous banging of the heart, Andrew's strong arms around her. She remembered, too, his reactions when he had gone down again for her letter, and his bitterness and embarrassment when he thought he had been making a fool of himself.

Well, Magda told herself, this was the end, she would have no more reason for coming back to Debenham Mount. Perhaps it was as well in many ways that it had happened like this, before that odious Mrs. Brand married Andrew and changed everything. Before Elizabeth could spoil anything. . . .

In some ways Elizabeth had been a greater menace than Sylvia Brand. Magda was sure that that unprepossessing woman in the Post Office would, before long, make herself known at the Mount, and take a dominant hand in the proceedings. If that were really, truly, the Elizabeth of the portrait, what would Andrew think when he met her again? And had Mrs. Debenham already seen her?

Magda hoped not. She found herself hoping feverishly that the old lady had been allowed to keep her treasured memories of that glamorous young woman Andrew had once loved, right to the last. They were things to treasure, bearing in mind the fact that a discerning old person such as Mrs. Debenham, could not see through the surface beauty, or perhaps didn't want to, but just derived a great deal of pleasure from remembering that beauty alone, and not bothering about what lay beneath.

Another car paused at the big gates, to allow Magda's to go through, and followed up the drive after hers. As she got out, slowly of necessity because the journey had tired her, Andrew got out of his car and hurried round to where she stood. He was white-faced, strained, and showed signs of hidden grief, as she had expected. But all this gave place to astonishment when he saw that she had been the person in the car, and had been wrapped under a rug.

'Magda! What on earth are you doing here? Why aren't you in the house?'

She shook her head weakly, and was conscious of a desire to burst into helpless tears.

'I've been ill. Away,' she said, watching his face all the time.

'But . . . the telegram, with the news. It was signed "Nurse Rushton".'

'That was from the nurse in charge of the case,' Magda said.

'Using your name?' he frowned, perplexed.

'It's her name also,' Magda said. 'Shall we go in?'

He didn't ask why she was there, but seemed to take it for granted that she should be there. He took her arm, but neither of them seemed aware of the little action.

And then the rest of the day seemed to pass in a dream for Magda. At some period of it, Copper and she were standing side by side, and Andrew was staring at both of them. Staring as if he couldn't believe his own eyes. Oddly, it was Copper who supplied the explanations. A restrained Copper, sadly jolted by the loss of a patient, and unhappy (as Magda had known she would be) in this house, which seemed so impregnated with the past, and the Debenham family, that Copper felt crushed. Here was no place for her lively nature. She had said to Magda, when the sisters had got together for the first time:

'Gosh, I can't stand it. It's like being in a church.'

After that first time of Andrew's knowing about the twins, and seeing them together, Magda saw very little of him. He shut himself up in the study, or in the great deserted drawing-room, for long periods. At other periods he was out and about, doing all the work that had become neglected while he had been away.

He never spoke of what he had been doing while he had been away, but once he spoke to her of his aunt and how much she had thought of the twins. It appeared that on her last day, the old lady had had a premonition that she wouldn't see Andrew again, and she had written him a letter, anxiously telling him about the twins, and begging him not to be angry with either of them. Characteristically she defended Magda, but showed that she had found a warm feeling for Copper, too, in the short time the girl had been there.

'You'll stay until after the funeral,' he suggested, and Magda agreed. They both knew that the old lady would have liked that.

It was such a strange feeling in the house now. Andrew went about white, silent and preoccupied. The servants seemed to be held in a sort of tension, and so did the tenants. As if they were all waiting.

It struck Magda that they felt that Andrew was holding back his own life while his aunt was ill, and that now she was no longer there, there would be changes. One of the changes they feared was the advent of Mrs. Brand, but one of the changes they seemed to have overlooked was the return of Elizabeth.

Copper reported it one day to Magda, without realising the implications of the visit.

'She's in the drawing-room taking tea with him,' Copper said. 'She's an awful woman. She's got a voice like a man! I heard him say "Elizabeth" as if he'd seen a ghost!'

'He has,' Magda agreed, and took Copper

to the music-room to look at the oil painting, but it had been taken down.

'That's funny,' Magda mused, and they both went back to Magda's room to have their tea.

'Well, who is she?' Copper asked.

'Did Mrs. Debenham ever mention Elizabeth to you?'

Copper considered the point.

'She was nutty over some girl who'd been engaged to his lordship in his wild youth,' she grinned. 'Come to think of it, that was the name. Elizabeth!'

'Well, that's the same one, only I think the tropics have played havoc with her complexion and hair. I didn't think you could get like that in ten years,' Magda said, staring ahead and picturing all the ways in which Mrs. Debenham remembered her. 'So she never came while Mrs. Debenham was—'

'No. I'm positive, or she would have told me,' Copper said. 'Besides, I was with her most of the time. She seemed to want someone with her, to talk to. She kept talking about you.'

'Did she?' Magda smiled tiredly. 'What about me?'

'Oh, just about how she thought of you, and everything. She seemed to be as fond of

259

you as if you were related to her. I don't think she liked me overmuch.'

'Has Mrs. Brand been here?'

'No. Just that day when she thought I was you. I say, the boy-friend didn't tell her he was going away!'

Magda frowned.

'Why can't you refer to him as "Andrew" or "Mr. Debenham," Copper? You're as facetious as you used to be, and I did think I'd got you out of that habit.'

'Well, all I can say is, if I look as bothered about it in saying "Andrew" as you do, then I think I'll leave that name alone.'

'Who says I get bothered?' Magda demanded, flushing.

'You do! You know, I believe you've got a crush on him after all! Perhaps Mrs. Brand wasn't far wrong!'

There was a tiny silence, and Copper realised she had been tactless again, though where she had slipped up she couldn't imagine.

'Sorry. Did I tread on your toes?' she said, amiably, but stared speculatively at her sister.

'If I look bothered about anything, it's because I feel so rotten. I wish I hadn't got to stay until . . . it was all over. I shall hate it. I would have just liked to take a peep at her, to sort of say good-bye, and then go. Quickly. I didn't even want to see Andrew Debenham again.'

'What will you do?' Copper demanded.

'Do? Go back to the nursing home, I suppose. She made me promise I'd stay there the six months. But it seems an awful waste of time. I'm not ill enough to be in bed all day but they make me stay there until almost lunch-time. Isn't it funny? We're so used to taking temperatures and bossing patients about, and it's so utterly beastly when you get it done to yourself. I shrivel up inside when a nurse bustles in with a thermometer.'

'What shall I do?' Copper ruminated.

'What do you want to do,' Magda asked, wondering what mad-hat scheme her sister had thought up now.

Copper shrugged.

'I've still got some leave due to me before I go back to the hospital. Or I needn't go back there. I was wondering if I could get an outside job to be near you.'

'I shall be all right,' Magda protested.

'Oh, I know that,' Copper said, airily, 'but I can't manage to keep out of trouble when you aren't around, so I thought it might be better to work near you.'

'Well, what will you do when you marry

Jim? I can't be near you then,' Magda laughed.

'Jim will take your place, of course. That's if I ever do marry him.'

'Oh, Copper, it isn't all off again, is it?' Magda cried in horror. 'You never stay put for two minutes.'

'It's none of my doing. Jim said he thought he'd stay out there just a bit longer. I don't believe he wants to come back to England at all.'

'If you're in love with him, you shouldn't mind where he wants to be, you should just be content to be with him,' Magda said, automatically, her mind with Andrew and the home farm. All the lands for miles around belonged to the Debenham family, and although some of it had been sold to meet taxation, and they had lost two or three farms, there were still a great many acres belonging to them. Wherever she might want to be, if she thought of Andrew at all, it was on this land. This cruel lovely countryside, with its treacherous dips like the one she nearly fell over, and its biting winds and fogs, and the toll the soil took out of those who worked it. Andrew was a hard-bitten farmer, and she loved him as such.

'How do you know when you're really in love?' Copper thrust, and sat waiting breathlessly, watching Magda.

'Oh, you know,' Magda said, still staring out of the window, and across the bare tree-tops to where the brown hills stretched away. Debenham lands. 'You know, because you aren't like you used to be, inside you. You were once free, and then you're suddenly bound to one person. You listen for his foot-steps, and your interests are his. He makes life for you, and when he isn't there, you feel lost, as if a limb is cut off. And when he is there,' she finished, softly, 'the world is a much more beautiful place than it ever was before.'

'So you *are* in love with him!' Copper said, with triumph.

Magda turned and stared into her sister's eyes.

'You can't leave anything alone, can you?' she said, in a low, intense voice. 'You never stop to ask yourself if a thing belongs to you before you touch it!'

'What have I done now?' Copper asked, aggrieved.

'It was all I had of him, just the memory, and the way I felt. I'll never have anything else. Yet you had to make me drag it out in the open, for the sake of your argument about Jim! Or was it that you wanted to trick me into admitting I loved him? Well, now you

263

know. I do. I love him with every ounce of my being, and nothing will ever come of it. Are you satisfied?'

'Don't be so rotten, Mag,' Copper pouted. 'I just wanted to know, so that I could help you!'

'Oh, no, don't do any such thing!' Magda cried, in a panic. 'Leave it alone. Forget all about it, but above all, don't meddle with it. I know what your help is like!'

On the day of the funeral, the house took on yet another unfamiliar aspect. It seemed filled with strangers. Distant relations of the Debenhams, friends and tenants, all who had had anything to do with the old lady, and knew and loved her. Magda and Copper wore their uniforms, and mingled with the backwash of the crowd. A cold, damp, dreary day, and for Magda, a very sad day. A day full of black clothes and genuine sadness for a very real loss, the tang of the raw air and the overwhelming scent of the flowers. . . .

She was glad when with nightfall the house seemed to fold in on itself; quiet, maddeningly, threateningly quiet.

Magda went in search of Andrew Debenham, to tell him of her arrangements, and to get Copper's release, and ran him to earth in the study.

She knocked three times, and finally looked in, expecting to find the room temporarily empty, though there was a band of light under the closed door. Andrew was sitting in a deep armchair by the roaring fire, his head in his hands.

'Oh, I'm sorry,' she murmured, and backed out.

'Who is it?'

'It's Magda Rushton.'

'Well, come along in, Magda,' he said, in a voice much less rough than his own. 'I have to make sure. I can't even tell your voices apart.'

'Can't you?' she asked, sadly, sitting facing him. She noticed with a smile that he still had that autocratic trick of motioning you to a chair, as if you were one of the servants.

'Well, what is it?' he frowned.

'I don't want to intrude, to-night of all nights, but you have to know that we're not staying here any longer, and I thought you might be too busy to be bothered to-morrow.'

'Going?'

'Yes.' She seemed surprised that he should question her.

'Oh, yes, of course. There's nothing more for either of you to do here now.'

He stared into the fire again. Magda had never seen him looking so haggard, so lost, before.

He said, suddenly, jerking the words out: 'To think that I was coming back the next day, anyway. To think I had to be away just at that time. I should never have gone.'

Magda shook her head.

'Don't feel like that,' she said, softly. 'Your aunt was so happy to think you had gone. She hated to feel that her illness was holding up any business you had to do.'

He looked sharply at her.

'It's true,' she assured him. 'I wouldn't say so if it weren't.'

'No,' he agreed, 'I don't believe you would. Tell me, what did you think of my aunt? As a person. And you don't have to be nice. I want you to be candid.'

Magda flushed.

'You won't like what I'm going to say. Why ask me? It can't mean a thing to you, what I think.'

'What do you know about that?' he said.

'Well, I think she was a good, kind, affectionate person, but I also think she gave the impression of being wise and discriminating, but that she wasn't, really.'

He shot his head up again, and looked angry. But he was fair enough to allow her that he had demanded the truth from her.

'How d'you mean?'

'I told you you wouldn't like this,' Magda repeated. 'I mean about the way your aunt felt about . . . your ex-fiancée.'

This time there was little anger in him. It was as if he were relieved that that was all that Magda had meant. He relaxed a little, and smiled faintly.

'Oh, about Elizabeth. Yes, I know. Tell me, you saw the painting. What did you think of her?'

'Yes, I didn't tell you at the time, did I?'

'I remember you were very careful and polite about that picture, and I couldn't get you to be candid. Well, I want you to be candid now.'

'I think at the time I was shocked. I saw the picture as the artist saw her. Under the beauty she was ruthless and cold. Typical to be pictured on a horse. A woman who'd ride rough-shod over you, and be charming and surprised afterwards.'

If she expected him to be furious with her, she was disappointed.

'Yes, I know. I got out of that affair pretty easily, only I didn't know it at the time. I was piqued. Hurt. Bitter too, I suppose. How dare anyone jilt a Debenham.' His face darkened. 'I still feel that. Ever been jilted?'

267

She shook her head.

'It's the rottenest feeling on this earth, I believe. And there my dear old aunt flopped badly. I needed her support but it was all for Elizabeth. "There must have been some good reason," Aunt Laura said, and kept saying, and I believe to the very last, she didn't know that Elizabeth walked out on me with intent.'

'That's true,' Magda said. 'I asked her, and she didn't know. Didn't want to know, I thought. Just regretted, with all her heart, the fact that you and your fiancée hadn't made a successful marriage.'

He nodded.

'Do you suppose my aunt was happy? You were with her more than any of us, and you must have known pretty well what she was thinking.'

Magda agreed.

'I think she was fairly happy, but she would have been happier, I believe, if you had been happily married to the girl who presented such delightful pictures in her memory, and of course, if there had been a family . . . forgive me, but your aunt did mention that. And you asked me.'

He nodded, in agreement.

'She said there ought to be heirs to the Debenham lands, but I think heirs to her merely meant Elizabeth's children.'

'Yes.' He was staring into the fire, and without looking up, he said, slowly, 'I saw Elizabeth the other day.'

'Yes,' Magda said.

'Had you seen her?'

'In the Post Office. I thought it might be her.'

'Weren't you surprised . . . at the change in her?'

'I think "surprised" is too mild a term.'

'And what did you feel about it?'

Magda said, 'I found myself praying that your aunt wouldn't ever see her. The very old and the sick can't take disillusionment as we can.'

'Disillusionment. Yes, that just about sums it up. And my aunt never saw her?'

'No. I was glad about that,' Magda murmured.

'Are you such a kind person, really,' he said, leaning forward, 'or is it just the nurse in you, talking?'

'I don't think I can follow all this analysing,' Magda frowned, feeling suddenly overwhelmingly tired and spent. 'I'm just me. The nurse and myself are all so mixed up, I can't sort them out. You asked me things, and I answered them truthfully and sincerely. Now, I

269

think I'd like to go to bed. I'd like to say good-bye now. I won't be seeing you to-morrow.'

'Why? Are you leaving at dawn or something? Where are you going?' he asked, in astonishment.

She couldn't say 'I can't see you because I couldn't bear it,' so she contented herself by murmuring, 'Oh, pretty early. We're going back to the coast.'

'You said something about being ill. My aunt spoke of it in her letter, but there was reams of it. I haven't had time to study it yet. You must see me to-morrow. There are things I want to discuss with you—about that letter, you know.'

'There's nothing to discuss,' Magda said. 'I've made up my mind. I feel that now your aunt isn't here, I can't take the gift she made, of those nursing-home fees. I'm leaving there just as soon as I can, and it won't be in six months' time.'

CHAPTER TWELVE

SHE fled to bed, and once between the sheets she tried to sort out in her mind what had made her make that curious statement. It hadn't been in her mind until that moment. Her old friend had made her promise to accept the fees as a gift, and she had agreed.

But somehow, now that Mrs. Debenham was gone, it looked different all round. Whose money was it that had paid her fees? Mrs. Debenham's own, or Andrew's? She had a strong feeling that whatever had happened before, now it struck Andrew as all being different, too, and Magda wanted to take nothing from him. Her independence was all she had left. Surely, surely, she could get well again after a few weeks' rest at the sea, but not six months'? She felt that it wouldn't seem so bad, persuading herself to accept a few more weeks' stay at the sea, and to feel that Mrs. Debenham had settled for it. But six months would be impossible.

Magda was up as early as she had said she would be, but arousing Copper was a different matter. It appeared, too, that Copper hadn't finished packing the night before. And so it was nearly lunch-time before they were ready to go.

'I can't understand you, Copper. It's awful to hang about in someone's house like this, when we've no business here any longer,' Magda fumed.

Copper was unrepentant. 'I was acting under orders,' she said, grinning.

'Whose orders?'

'Mr. Andrew Debenham's,' Copper said, again with that infuriating grin, as if there was something funny that Magda didn't know about.

'I would have been gone at eight this morning,' Magda said. 'I ordered a car—' she gasped. 'What happened about that? They made me promise I wouldn't go on a train!'

'I cancelled the order,' Copper said, blandly. And, as her sister got angrier, she said, 'Oh, keep your wool on, old dear! Mr. Debenham commanded that I keep you here by fair means or foul, until he got back this morning. He wanted to talk to you.'

'I know he did. That's why I didn't want to stop. Oh, Copper, how mean of you. Why on earth didn't I go without you?'

'Well, I thought the old gag about not being packed would work. Remember when we were kids, how you always threatened to go without me if I hadn't finished packing? But you never did.'

'Will you be good enough to go and hire a car for me?' Magda cried, in exasperation.

'Yes, I'll do that, because it's now eleven-thirty, and his lordship should be waiting for you in the study. At least, that's what he said. If he's let me down, after all this effort at keeping you chained to the dump, I'll die!'

Magda went very unwillingly to the library. Her unwillingness was written all over her, from the fact that her pale face (despite its marks of tiredness and illness), had mutiny stamped all over it, to the fact that her coat was buttoned up ready for the cold raw day outside, and that she was pulling her gloves on. Andrew Debenham noticed all these things, and smiled faintly.

'Magda, don't be so angry with me for getting my own way,' he began, in the disturbingly gentle voice he had used the day he took her to the home farm.

'But you always get it,' she accused, without thinking. Then, realising how she had spoken to him, she said, 'I didn't mean to be rude, but it's true, and you've used my sister against me this time.'

'Did she tell you that? Bad show,' and she saw he was smiling broadly now.

'Come and sit down by the fire,' he went on. 'You don't look very warm.'

She sat on the edge of the chair and stared into the fire for a minute. He was shocked to see, in the daylight, the hollows in her cheeks, and the dark shadows beneath her eyes. He blamed himself for not having noticed these things before. He had been so taken up with sorting out his own chaotic thoughts and putting off coming to that decision which must come, sooner or later—probably sooner. Sylvia Brand would not be put off so easily now, now that his aunt was no longer there.

'Magda, you and I have so much to talk over. Last night was hopeless. We were too tired, too spent. It was a wretched day. A day to put away and forget about. All those people, everything turned upside down . . . but now,' he said, drawing a deep breath, 'now we must have a lot of things thrashed out.'

'Must we?' Magda said, tiredly. 'Oh, why? I'm going. Copper's going. You'll never see us again, unless it's at St. Joseph's. Just let's say good-bye, and let it go at that.'

He looked rather taken aback.

'Is that the way you want it, Magda?'

It seemed to her that all he wanted was to finish up tidily, with no loose ends, knowing everything about them and all that had happened, so that he could put them in a pigeonhole to themselves, and mentally file them away as he was going to the day of the funeral. Andrew, she felt, was like that. She felt that perhaps, too, he had filed away the last sight he had had of Elizabeth. Another closed episode. Tidying up before he married Sylvia Brand, and started a new and entirely different life.

She found herself resenting it. She didn't want to say so. Her innate good breeding forbade that. But she felt that it would not be in bad taste to gently fend him off, prevent him from finding out all the things he wanted to, and to keep shielded from his idle curiosity the poor secret of her heart.

'Well, what is it we have to talk about?' she smiled.

He lifted helpless hands in a gesture unlike him.

'Well, after you'd left me last night, I went to bed, but I couldn't sleep. I put the light on again and studied my aunt's last letter she left for me. Poor old soul, she must have been feeling ill when she wrote it, the writing was hardly more than a scrawl in places. And yet I felt that there must be something of importance in it, for her to make so great an effort. I persevered, and the things she had to tell me, puzzled me in the light of what I know—or thought I knew—about you.'

'I don't think I understand,' Magda said.

'Well, I don't think you've deceived me, Magda. Like my aunt, I don't think it's in you to deceive me. And yet there are things that you and I have been led to believe, that don't tie up.'

'And you feel that they matter now?' she probed.

He frowned.

'I don't like to be in the dark about things, or people, whether they matter or not,' he complained.

Again that mental tidying up, she thought, rebelliously. He doesn't want anything else, but to have his mind tidied, so that he can forget us.

'I'll see if I can help you sort things out,' she said, not very willingly.

'Well, first of all, this twin business,' he said, sitting forward. 'I suppose it's fun for you two young women to keep a secret the fact that there are two of you, and I suppose you both get a kick out of letting people make fools of themselves in mistaking the separate identities. But frankly, I don't see where you both thought it would get you, with all this ferocious secrecy about which nurse had taken on which case. My aunt was most unhappy about having to keep the secret, and why Mrs. Brand joined in, or even consented to be a party to it, I can't imagine!'

'I didn't know it upset your aunt so much,' Magda said, levelly. 'I'm sorry about that. As to Mrs. Brand, I don't know why she agreed, either. I'm afraid my sister blurted the whole thing out. I thought it best to not mention it.'

'But why? Wasn't it rather dishonest?'

'Perhaps. But it meant a great deal to us, and it couldn't possibly matter to anyone else, as you say, which nurse was assigned to which job. So long, that is, as no one in authority found out.'

'Were you afraid of getting into a row, then?'

'Terrified,' Magda told him.

'Well, that's rubbish! All you both had to do was to apply for the switch in the first place, then all this nonsense need never had happened.'

Magda didn't answer for a moment, but as he waited and the silence grew, she made an effort to explain.

'You don't know what it's like, to be hanging on to a job,' she offered.

'But, my dear girl, you weren't in danger of

losing the job. If you did, you could have got an appointment elsewhere, a good nurse like you.'

She shook her head, and to her consternation, her eyes filled with those tiresome weak tears. She regained her control, and said, with an effort:

'I haven't told Copper, but the fact is, this tired feeling hasn't just come on. I've had it for months and months, and I've been haunted by the fear that if I got myself examined, I'd find that it wasn't just an illness such as, say, appendicitis, that didn't last long, and might happen to anyone. I was afraid I'd find it was something that . . . well, something that would prevent me from continuing a strenuous job like nursing. I can't do anything else.'

'But my aunt mentioned several foreign languages, and any number of things that you might have turned to account—' he began.

'With poor health?' she asked, with a smile, and shook her head. 'Besides, there was Copper. I had to stay in nursing with her, or she'd have left it, or got into trouble too often and . . . oh, I don't know.'

He watched her bend her head, and lay a tired head in one hand, resting the elbow on her knee. In such an attitude, she looked spent, beaten, unfit for fighting for herself any longer.

'But it didn't turn out like that,' he said, gently. 'They discovered you had a tired heart. Quite bad enough, but all you had to do was rest. Well, Magda, your next six months are taken care of. Now what have you got to worry about? After that, we'll see.'

She shook her head, decisively.

'I'm sorry, but I can't accept six months in idleness. I'm sure that a few weeks by the sea will do me good, and then I must work again.'

'Independence? Or something else?' he asked, a little of the friendliness vanishing.

She closed her lips tightly. She couldn't say that she wanted nothing from him in the way of money, since he could give her nothing else. And she was now convinced, from the way he spoke, that it was his money that had been paid, not his aunt's, or at least not hers entirely. She had probably asked Andrew to do it for her.

As if interpreting her thoughts, he said, 'Magda, it was my aunt's wish that you should accept this as a gift from her. It was her money, and she did it from the goodness of her heart, and from her deep affection for you. That affection she had for you impressed me deeply. I ask you to accept it, if only in memory of her. She wanted it so.'

Magda shifted uneasily, and slowly capitulated. 'All right, then, since you put it like that.'

'And if the fellow you're going to marry has anything to say about it, just refer him to me. By the way, does he know you're ill? And if so, what's he doing about it?'

'Did you aunt say in her letter that I was going to be married?'

He frowned across at her.

'She mentioned the matter at some length, but she seems to have got a bit muddled between the two of you. She seemed to think that it was your sister who was engaged to this chap in Africa, and not you at all.'

Magda smiled faintly, and was unaware that he misconstrued her smile. It struck her suddenly that Mrs. Debenham had done her best, with her last strength, to say to her nephew, not in so many words but there for him to see if he would—Magda is free, despite all she has said. But being Andrew, he couldn't see. His aunt wouldn't say it outright, because of her promise to Magda, but she had done her best to make him see it and failed. He thought—and how Mrs. Debenham would be furious, if she knew— that in those last few hours, she had felt too ill to sort it out, and made a cardinal mistake between the twins' identities.

'Poor Jim,' Magda murmured, thinking of how he, too, would be amazed and puzzled by all this, and probably vastly amused to think that anyone should consider him Magda's property. Magda, to Jim, was the ideal sister, the person to come to in trouble, but not the person to inflame his heart. To that role Copper was assigned, and had done the job successfully—more successfully than she knew. 'No, he doesn't know. Naturally,' Magda added, with truth, 'I haven't told him.'

'Um. So my aunt was wrong, then,' Andrew said, and his voice was full of the crushing disappointment he felt. It was obvious that he had hoped against hope that his aunt had been right. That it had been his mistake and not hers, and that Magda was not really the one who was engaged to be married. But then, he argued to himself, how could that be? Hadn't she as good as told him she was engaged, that day she had lost her letter and he had retrieved it for her?

'Well, that clears that up,' he said, and there was a change in his voice. 'When are you being married?'

'I don't know,' Magda said, suddenly tired

of the whole thing, 'and I think, if you don't mind, that I'd better go now.'

'It's nearly lunch-time. Take lunch with me, both of you,' he said, smiling cheerfully.

'Thank you, but I don't think—' Magda began, when the telephone on the desk suddenly shrilled.

'Excuse me,' Andrew said, and got up to answer it.

Magda wandered over to the window and looked out. The first week in December and snow was beginning to fall. Over the bare trees threatening clouds merged together to make a lowering grey ceiling, almost touching the tops of the branches. The hills merged into this ceiling, and all was a dark, menacing cloak that seemed to move forward and to stifle the Mount. The icy cold crept through cracks and crevices, and the muted pad-pad of the snowflakes came against the window-panes as if the weather had a mind to force its way in, to touch her. Magda shivered, and subconsciously took in the one-sided telephone conversation in the room behind her.

'But Sylvia, my dear, of course I can manage it,' Andrew was saying.

Sylvia Brand said, 'Somehow that doesn't sound convincing, darling. You sound just a teeny bit as if you were putting me off. I do so

282

want to talk to you about something—you've been away so long, and I don't seem to recall your telling me you were going.'

He scowled, but Magda couldn't see that. His back was to her. He said, trying not to sound quarrelsome on the telephone, while someone else was in the room:

'Sylvia, I've got loads to tell you, and this is the first chance—look, we'll fix up something. I can't talk now—'

He wasn't any good at subterfuge, and realised to his dismay that Sylvia considered she had scored a point. She became less querulous, but fastened on a time and place and forced him to agree. He put down the telephone and turned round to Magda's armchair, but she had gone.

There was the sound of a car driving off. It couldn't have been three minutes since he had made that devastating remark, to the effect that there was someone else in the room with him, and yet Magda had apparently made her escape. He called Hobbs, and learned that the car had been waiting at the door, as he himself had ordered some time ago. Copper had happened to be passing through the hall at the time, and Magda had come out of the study, and said to her, 'Copper, we're going. Don't argue with me. I'll tell you when we're away from here,' and they went at that moment.

Andrew muttered furiously beneath his breath, and went back to the study to think it over. Over and over again he went over his part of the telephone conversation, but could find nothing in the little he had said to offend her. To him it seemed horribly obvious to anyone that he had merely been putting off Sylvia Brand, and he was uncomfortably aware that Sylvia knew it, if Magda didn't. But why Magda should be so obtuse he couldn't say, unless after all she were really in love with that fellow, that Jim. And yet somehow he had the impression that although she had given him to understand that she was engaged to be married to him, she wasn't really in love with him. What was it she had said, that day when he had saved her life? She had been in love with some fellow, who hadn't even seen her, or been aware of her. Wasn't that it? And in the same breath she had also given him to understand that she couldn't therefore love Jim, but that Jim didn't mind.

Looking back, he was conscious that Magda had said none of these things in so many words, but had merely given him a series of impressions. Impressions. . . . Nothing to bite on to. He was still not sure about Magda, not sure where her heart lay, not sure of her future intentions, nor indeed of anything about her. Again he had that shattering sense of loss now that she had gone, and the only consolation he had was that he would know where she was, since his car had been ordered to take her all the way to her destination.

For Magda, there was no uncertainty. She sat in the back of the car with Copper, and there was a whiteness about her mouth that worried her sister. She lay back with her eyes closed, slow tears coursing down her face. Her hands were clenched, and shook slightly, and it was moments before she could speak.

When at last she did speak, it was to say in a voice little above a whisper:

'I've never been so humiliated in my life!'

Copper had difficulty in getting out of her what had happened, and when Magda recounted her impressions of that interview in the study, Copper looked blank and dismayed.

'But I thought—he gave me to understand—' she gasped.

Magda didn't wait to hear what her sister thought. She was sitting bolt upright, staring at the interior of the car and at the chauffeur's back behind the closed glass partition.

'Whose car is this? This isn't the one I

asked you to hire—it isn't a hired car!' Magda gasped, angrily.

Copper spread helpless hands.

'That's just it! Your fairy prince insisted on your going wherever you wanted to go, in the big car from the house. They just wouldn't let me hire a car. Talk about autocrats!'

'I don't know what's come over you, Copper. I ask you to make a simple telephone call for me, to hire a car, and you let everyone know what you're going to do so that they can alter your mind for you!' Magda said, scathingly, and picked up the speaking tube.

'Drop me at the station instead, will you—I've had a change of plans?'

At the sudden, unusual imperious note in her voice, the chauffeur found himself complying. After all, it was none of his business. He had been merely instructed to take the young ladies wherever they wanted to go, and the station seemed the place indicated.

He swerved to the right and took the station road in a blinding flurry of snow. Magda shivered.

'I think you're crazy,' Copper observed. 'You're due at the nursing-home in time for tea. Heaven knows what time you'll get there now, if you go by train.'

'I'm not going there,' Magda said.

'Not going there? Where are we going, then?'

'I'll tell you later, when we're alone,' Magda said, staring at the chauffeur's back.

'He can't hear a thing,' Copper said.

'Never mind. I'm taking no chances.'

He carried their luggage into the station, and asked if he could get their tickets, but Magda dismissed him. Only when they had found a more or less warm waiting-room, did Magda consent to show Copper the tickets.

'I just remembered someone—' she said, and her teeth were chattering too much for further speech.

'Oh, lord, I do hope you haven't caught a chill,' Copper said, worriedly. 'Here, sit by the fire. Let's see if I can stoke some life into it. Why on earth book to Wyverne Bay of all places?'

'Because it's in the opposite direction to the town where Andrew Debenham thinks we're going, and because we know the place. We've been there before,' Magda said. 'Remember old Mrs. Lennock, who kept that quiet little hotel where we spent Christmas when Daddie was alive? I thought we'd stay there the month. I've got enough money saved to cover both of us, then I'll go back to the hospital with you when you go.'

'Yes, if you're all right by then,' Copper said, doubtfully, and not at all loath to spend an unexpected holiday. 'Perhaps I'd better not spend the whole month with you. I'll go back after Christmas, eh, then you won't have to spend all your money.'

'No. Stay with me the month,' Magda said, with sudden firmness, and without quite knowing why she wanted Copper with her.

'Honestly, though, I do think you're crazy. You could have gone in the car all the way, and kept in the warmth. Look at you—you're simply shaking! Wish I had some brandy to give you.'

'I'll be all right,' Magda repeated. 'As to going all the way in the car, I might have done if you'd ordered one as I asked you. But in the Debenham car, no! I'm not accepting favours from Andrew Debenham, and I'm not going to make it easy for him to know where I am, either. I wanted to get free, and I have.'

'Well, I'm sure I don't know why, for I never saw a man before, who was so in love with a girl. I thought you were in love with him?'

Magda closed her eyes.

'Copper, once and for all, will you consider the matter closed? Whatever happens, I don't

288

want to hear his name again! Do you understand?'

Copper had the gravest misgivings about
the whole thing. When Magda dug her heels
in over something, there was nothing more to
be said. So it was that while Andrew Debenham was on long-distance that evening, talking to the nursing-home authorities, and
trying to sound convincing about not knowing where Magda had gone, Copper was
trying to steer her sister away from the particular abyss which her nurse's eyes told her
was fast approaching.

Magda lay on the bed in their small room at
the top of three flights of steep stairs, the only
room she could afford. Mrs. Lennock, they
discovered, was no longer there, and the present proprietress looked critically at the two
bright pink spots in Magda's cheeks, and
observed frostily that she hoped that there
wasn't going to be illness. It was bad for the
hotel.

As soon as they were alone, Copper took
her sister's temperature, and sat down with
shaking legs to think the matter over. Personally she thought it was the silliest thing for
Magda to have done, this mad careering away
from the nursing home at all. She ought never
to have come out, and she ought never to have

gone to the funeral. In fact, there were any number of things, culminating in that distinctly draughty and uncomfortable, slow and long train journey they had taken, which she considered that her sister was wrong to have even considered doing.

She was thrown back on her own resources for the first time for a long, long time, and she didn't like it. She was so used to Magda taking the lead, Magda making the important decisions, that she hardly knew where to turn. And yet she had for so long been complaining that she had not been allowed to stand on her own feet.

Magda stirred, without opening her eyes. She was murmuring something, almost inaudibly, and began to toss and turn. Copper knew all the signs, and while she bent an ear to catch what her sister was saying, she was subconsciously forming in her own mind her next actions.

'Andrew! Don't let Andrew know—' Magda was muttering. 'Andrew ... Andrew. . . .'

Copper quietly went out and got a doctor, and it was with a sigh of relief that she saw Magda settled into a hospital bed, in a long white ward with the old smells and sights and sounds, the familiar rustle of starched caps, and the reassuring quiet routine around them.

'It's good,' Copper whispered. 'She's safe, now. Safe.'

'How long have I got, before the crisis?' she demanded with professional interest, and when the doctor assured her that it wouldn't be just yet, she nodded firmly.

'Then I've time. There's something I've got to do,' Copper heard herself saying with unfamiliar firmness and responsibility in her voice.

She went and cancelled their room at the hotel, and took their things with her to a small room in a neat, clean house in a back street, for just about a third of the price. That done, she went to the station, but there her new-found firmness and responsibility deserted her.

Her knees felt wobbly, and she sat down on a seat and stared at the barrier, and floundered.

What was it she was going to do, this thing, this enormity for which Magda would never forgive her? And how did she know—what proof had she, Copper Rushton, that her own intuition about Andrew Debenham was right? Supposing she made this journey—this costly journey in both money and precious, precious time—and then found that Andrew was entertaining Sylvia Brand and had forgotten all about Magda and herself. And that meantime Magda had wanted her, asked for her, and she hadn't been there?

She could telephone Andrew. She played with the idea. There was a call-box, an enticingly empty call-box, just across the way, in the station-yard. But what could she say, when she got through?

'My sister caught a chill and they suspect pneumonia and she's dangerously ill,' she said to herself. And Andrew would say. 'Why didn't she go in the car, instead of footling about on trains?'

No, that wouldn't do. Again she tried. 'My sister is dangerously ill, and in hospital.' And Andrew would say, 'How is it that she isn't at the nursing-home? What made you two go to any other place when they were expecting Magda back at a certain time?'

No, again that wouldn't do. It might well be that he would be angry, for having been made a fool of. Or he might be specially angry at being disturbed, if he were dining with Mrs. Brand.

Worse still, he might be dining with Mrs. Brand at her house, and not at the Mount at all. Or if he were at the Mount, and had guests there, he might have given instructions not to be disturbed.

She sat, a forlorn figure, on a seat in the booking-hall, her scarf fallen back and her glorious red hair faintly flecked at the edge with snow. Her wide brown eyes had the misery of a lost child in their depths, and she didn't see the tall, brawny, tanned young man who strode through the barrier from the train just in, although she was staring straight at him.

He stopped in front of her, and the eagerness in his eyes was held in check by the faintest tinge of doubt.

'Copper or Magda? Fancy me not knowing my own girl!' he laughed.

She dragged her eyes back to focus on him, and she stared up at him as though she were having an elaborate trick played on her.

At last, with a little hoarse cry, she staggered to her feet.

'Jim! Jim, oh, Jim, *Jim!* It isn't—it *can't* be—' she cried, and launched herself into his arms.

'Copper, my girl! There isn't any doubt about your voices, thank heaven,' he said, thickly, burying his face in her rich red curls. 'Oh, my dear, my dear, what a dance you've led me! And what a dance I shall be led for the

293

rest of my life, I can see!'

'Oh, Jim, let me look at you! Jim, when did you arrive—how did you know I'd be here? What are you doing here? Jim, say something, *say* something!'

'Here, hold hard,' he said, and there was a warning note in his voice. He had always said that Copper was the one of the two of them, most prone to hysteria. 'I'm here because I used my head, and because I'm lucky. Lucky in that you two are so dashed spectacular that you couldn't hope to slip by without anyone noticing you. But I must say I didn't expect to find you waiting on the station for me.'

'Oh, Jim, I'm in such awful trouble,' Copper said, and to her own dismay, she was suddenly crying. Sobbing wildly against him. 'Jim, a nurse isn't supposed to cry, but every-thing's on top of me, and I just don't know what to do!'

'Hush, not here, my dear. Wait, I'll call a cab,' he said, and when he had got her inside its quiet, dark interior, he went on, 'Now, where can we go and talk? Where's your hotel?'

'I cancelled the reservation and got a room,' she sobbed.

'That sounds like the sort of thing my Copper would do,' he said, with a grim smile.

'It was to save money,' Copper wailed, and out tumbled the tangled, tragic little story.

'Poor Magda,' he murmured. 'Where is she now, did you say?'

She told him where the hospital was, and when its ugly, red brick exterior loomed before them, Copper knew with certainty that it was going to be all right. Jim was there. Jim would arrange everything.

'I'm no good without Magda,' she whispered.

'I don't think Magda has been very wise, despite that great heart of hers,' Jim said, tenderly, sitting in the over-heated hospital waiting-room. 'I think she ought to have let you fend for yourself more. But there, who'd want to alter the kind people of the world?'

'I'm not kind, am I, Jim?' she said, ruefully.

He smiled tenderly at her.

'You jilt me when you feel like it, and you take me back again when you're bored. But you're all right,' he assured her, squeezing her cold little hand.

It was Jim who found another hotel, and got them both fixed up, and installed Copper in her room with instructions to go to bed, and get some rest. He would telephone her if anything happened, or if she was wanted. He

295

went back to the hospital and waited.

Copper lay in bed in the darkness, feeling that a weight had been taken off her shoulders. She could imagine Jim, as he had told her the story, arriving in England after flying from Africa as a special surprise, and finding that neither of the twins were at the houses where they were supposed to be. How like Jim to woo the distant Hobbs enough to hear that the car had that day left the twins at the station, and how like Jim to quietly go to the station and find someone who remembered issuing their tickets.

She tried to imagine what she would have done in similar circumstances. From Jim, it all sounded so simple, so sweetly reasonable. As had his way of dealing with her problem to-night. 'Don't telephone Mr. Debenham yet,' he counselled.

'But Jim,' she had said, urgently, 'supposing anything happened—'

'It won't,' he said, firmly. 'You heard what the doctor said. You know as a nurse that the worst doesn't always happen if these things are taken in time. Besides, how do you know that it will matter a row of beans to this fellow?'

'But Jim, I'm sure—' Copper began.

'Honey, you've given me a very boggled

story. As I see it, the fellow employed the pair of you. He's rich, and hard to get. He's keeping company with a wealthy woman, a neighbour and old friend. He made Magda pretty wild by something he said to-day, and he didn't seem much put out when she walked out on him. Now, my dear child, that doesn't sound like a romance to me. I advise you to wait, and see what Magda has to say.'

'But I know what she'll say, Jim. She'll break my neck if I let him know where she is or what's happened, but that's only because she's so darned proud. She doesn't want him to know she's in love with him.'

'Then if that's so, I think you should do as you know she wants.'

'But she's been calling for him,' Copper said, having the last word.

When the crisis came, they both stayed at the hospital, waiting. The silent corridors, and the soft footfalls of nurses and doctors, lulled Copper into the old sense of being at home. She leaned against Jim, and tried to keep awake.

'No sense in us both keeping awake, pet,' Jim said, 'you just lie back against me, and have a nap. I'll wake you if they want us.'

Copper closed her eyes, then snapped them open again.

'Jim, Magda always used to take my watch. Did you know that I'm such a rotten nurse, I could never keep awake?'

'Some people need more sleep than others,' he soothed.

'Some people are more selfish than others,' she said. 'Jim, there's something I ought to do. I know it, in my heart, and I'm just putting it off because it's unpleasant.'

'What is it, my dear?'

'I ought to let Andrew Debenham *know*, and leave it to him to make up his mind if he wants to do anything.'

There was a tight little silence, then Jim said:

'I wasn't going to tell you, but I let him know, and nothing happened.'

'Wha—at?' Copper wriggled round in his arms and looked up into his rugged, dark face. 'When, Jim?'

'The day after I came down. You were so distressed, and I didn't want you bothered any more. He wasn't there, so I left a message. To ring the hotel. One of us was there all the time, so it would have been all right. That was two days ago, and . . . we haven't had a word from him.'

She met his eyes with distress.

'Oh, Jim. Magda's still asking for him. I

don't think she'll get well if he doesn't come.'

'There just isn't anything we can do,' he told her.

CHAPTER THIRTEEN

SYLVIA BRAND sensed the difference in the atmosphere of Debenham Mount, the first time she went after the funeral. She couldn't place what the difference was, but the old lady's influence had been strong, and now it wasn't there and everyone missed it.

She played her cards more carefully. Without intruding she dropped in and did the flowers, or telephoned Andrew about the local arrangements for Christmas. All things which in no way made him feel she was making an excuse to see him. He kicked around, moody, bored, strangely at a loss. It wasn't like him, and one day at tea in the study, she spoke to him of it.

'I suppose what's wrong with me most is the lack of preparations for Christmas. They died with my aunt.'

'But you could have the Debenham Christmas, the same as you used to, Andrew,' Sylvia urged.

He shook his head.

'I've no taste for it. And who would arrange it, anyway? It wants a woman here, and there isn't anyone to replace my aunt.'

'No—one?' she murmured, smiling at him.

He missed the smile. He was staring into the fire, remembering, for no reason at all, Magda, that last day, and how ill she had looked. For a thousand times he had asked himself how it was he hadn't noticed it before. For a thousand times he asked himself how it was that all the months she had been under this roof, he had been preoccupied with other things, and had told himself that he not only wouldn't care if she went but that he wanted her to go. Now that she had gone, there was such an aching sense of loss that it was at times unbearable. This was one of the times.

It ought to have been Magda, sitting there in the intimacy of the study, pouring tea for him. He wondered how it was that tea had been brought in here. He hadn't ordered it. The only person who had ever shared this particular intimacy with him had been Elizabeth, and at a later date, his aunt. The two women who had meant most in his life.

Sometimes, he found himself wanting to be desperately alone, and at those times he was shocked to find that he had Sylvia with him. There was no active dislike in him for Sylvia, and at times he was considerably cheered up in her company, but there were too many times when he found that he didn't want her at all, and this was one of them.

The snow was five inches thick. She had laughed about her car getting stuck on the way, but it hadn't prevented her from coming to the Mount, none the less.

'Don't leave it too late before you get back,' he murmured, thinking of how awful it would be if he had to ask her to stay the night, and play host to her at dinner and all the evening.

'Don't fuss, Andrew,' she laughed. 'There's been snow before, and I've been caught out in it before!'

It was relief that he got a telephone message from the farm, wanting his help. He explained to Sylvia, with great care, how it was that he had to go, and hoped that she would get back home at the same time. He felt inhospitable and mean, but he couldn't help it. He wanted, more and more, these days, to be alone.

'But Andrew, what if one of those stupid animals *has* been buried in a drift? Can't one of the others get it out?'

'If you were a farmer's wife, you'd know better than to ask such a question, my dear,' he said, lightly. 'To a stock-breeder, every animal is precious, and no animal is one man's work to get out of a drift.'

The cold, clean air cut him, and he

wondered, for yet another time, what Magda was doing, and where she was. He made up his mind to contact the nursing home again when he got back, if Sylvia had gone. He frowned. Sylvia's being there so much certainly hampered him in trying to trace Magda.

He recalled the conversation the night before, when she had asked casually if he had heard anything more about her.

'You know, Andrew, you are so foolish. Can't you see that it was her way of telling you that she knew she'd failed to get what she wanted, and that since you weren't interested, there was nothing else for her? Rather an uncouth way of doing it, but there—she isn't like us!'

To say that about the gentle Magda was almost tantamount to Sylvia's saying it about himself, it was so untrue and so unfair. He felt as if Sylvia had slapped his own face. And yet he felt that in all honesty Sylvia meant it for the best. She didn't know Magda as he did, and probably judged all nurses and in fact all other good-looking women by the same standards. He had found that Sylvia wasn't very kind towards other women, and until he met Magda, he hadn't minded very much. He hadn't known much kindness in women. Elizabeth had always reminded him of a beautiful prize cat with claws only lightly sheathed.

Only his aunt was kind, his aunt and Magda. Those two he now held as exceptions, and forgave Sylvia for what he considered was a general trait.

It was while he was out struggling with half a dozen other men with poles against the treachery of the soft snow in the drift, that the telephone call came from Jim.

Hobbs took it. He explained that the master was out, but that if the name and number were left, he would leave them on the master's desk.

Sylvia went to the door of the study and looked out. Because of her aspirations to be mistress of Debenham Mount, she was interested in all telephone conversations and callers. Hobbs, however, disapproved of her, and somehow managed to forestall her, so that she was rarely able to gather much from his side of the conversation.

She hesitated, then picked up the study extension. Hobbs was spelling out the name, an unfamiliar one to Sylvia. James Kinmere. Hobbs then asked, in his meticulous way, with what reference was the call. After the slightest hesitation, Jim, at the other end, unwillingly admitted that it was about Nurse Magda Rushton. He merely added the number where he could be telephoned, and rang off.

Sylvia replaced the receiver, and was lighting a cigarette when Hobbs passed the study door.

'Was that an urgent call, Hobbs?' she wanted to know.

He said no, he didn't think it was. It would do when the master came back.

'Well, it might be better if you left that message on his desk rather than on the pad. Mr. Debenham doesn't always bother to look at the hall phone, you know, and he might be waiting for that call.'

Hobbs was about to remark stiffly that he would see that the master got the message personally, when he was reminded of a number of little things that had happened recently, which suggested that the master was treating Mrs. Brand as if she were already one of the family. Finally, he gave her the written message, and watched her prop it up on the blotter.

'There,' she said, with that kittenish air that Hobbs found so irritating. 'Now he's sure to see it the minute he arrives.'

But Andrew didn't get it as soon as he

arrived. He never received it. Sylvia read it, considered it, decided that it would be better for Andrew—and incidentally for herself—if he forgot all about Nurse Magda Rushton. Having settled the point satisfactorily for herself, she rolled the message up into a small ball and dropped it into the waste paper basket.

She had no qualms about Hobbs asking Andrew if he had got the message. Hobbs wouldn't do that, for such an enquiry would be casting a doubt on one of the house visitors, the most frequent visitor at that, and he wouldn't even ask Andrew if he were to obtain the number for him, because Hobbs would have no means of knowing whether it was a call that Andrew would make, even if he got the message. No, she smiled to herself, she was safe, and she was also doing the right and wisest thing.

Andrew came back late that night, tired and cold, and thinking of the day he had taken Magda to the farm. She had loved the place so much, he recalled. He wondered what she would say if she could see it now. Blanketed by several inches of snow, silent as a churchyard, and intensely beautiful under a sky inky black and peppered with hard white stars. He remembered her in his arms, and felt again the warmth of her, and her mouth—as she lay back against him unconscious—her mouth, sweet and crumpled as a child's in sleep. Her eyes had had long dark brown lashes, curling upwards slightly at the tips, and even though she had looked ill at the time, she had managed to stay beautiful. A still, almost magic beauty that wasn't apparent at first, but grew on you until you ached for it—and the aching only came after she had gone.

He realised with a shock that she had been in his house a matter of months, the best part of the year, in fact. She had become part of the general scheme of things, and he was missing her more than he had thought possible.

She had a way of intruding into his thoughts lately, and he found himself thinking, on this particular night, of the way she did things without speaking, where another woman would have chattered. He recalled one particular night of pain, when it seemed that the whole of his leg, from the toe-tip to the top of the thigh, ached with a thousand throbs, and he felt he couldn't bear it. Magda had quietly materialised from somewhere, felt his forehead, took his pulse, and gave him an injection to quiet him. There was no fuss, nothing beyond a rustle of her uniform, and a fleeting smile (an intensely kind smile, he recalled), and then she had gone. But he had drifted off to a comfortable sleep, with a cessation of the pain and the memory of that smile.

There was another occasion when he had been perfectly foul to her. Blindly, unreasoningly angry about some small thing, and he had let fly at her with all the bitterness and the brevity of tongue which people found such an objectionable feature in him. He had continued in this way because it seemed to him that for all the notice she took, he might have been dumb. And then, when he had finished, she had had occasion to meet his eye, before she left him, and he was shocked at the deep hurt in her face, as if he had struck her.

It wasn't feasible at this stage, that he could have behaved like that to anyone like Magda. The other nurses who had looked after him from time to time, in all those accident-cases of his, had either irritated him or given him cause in some way or other, to wish they weren't there. He admitted to himself that there was no reason for his boorishness to them. His dear old aunt was right. He had no right to give way to a display of ill manners to these people. But to Magda, who was so utterly kind and good and sweet-tempered, it was beyond all things that he should have behaved in such a way.

Perhaps because he was tired, and still grief-stricken over his aunt's death, he sat by the failing log fire, and tried to send himself back to the time when Magda had first come to the house. He closed his eyes, and strove to *feel* what he had felt then. He was shocked to the core with the result, and horrified and amazed that he hadn't realised the truth before. Not only pain had he felt then, but a shaken feeling that left him spent, whenever she was about. He found his hand shaking now, as he recalled her nearness when she had lifted him in bed to rearrange his pillows, and he saw now why he had so resented the intimacy of the whole thing. The washings and the feedings and all the things she had to do for him as for a child. He was in love with her, and must have been in love with her from the first moment he saw her.

Perhaps some left-over pain from that first affair had been dragged into it because of her hair, and all that she reminded him of. This had soured the thing from the start, but he could have altered all that before it got too far, by a little clear thinking, if he had liked.

There were so many little things he remembered her for. The dogs had loved her, and his aunt had doted on her. She was so thoughtful in the little things, and he realised now that she had gone, that many things he had taken for granted had been done by her, and not his own staff, as he had supposed.

He let it all sweep over him, in one vast, all-enveloping wave, until he came to that day at the farm, and that wretched letter. And it was in that moment that the thing that had been teasing him for so long, eluding him, suddenly straightened itself out. Fitted into place like the last difficult piece of a jig-saw puzzle. The letter. It had been addressed to Copper Rushton. *Copper*.

He sat up suddenly, as he saw everything. It had not been Magda's letter at all. As his aunt had been so meticulous, so determined, in pointing out to him in that last painful epistle of hers to him, Magda was unattached. It was Copper who was engaged to be married. But why Magda should let him think that it was she who was attached to some man in Africa, who was apparently not in the least interested in her, but in her sister, defeated him.

Suddenly he wanted to see Magda. He knew he must find her, before he did anything else. Late as it was, he got into touch with his hospital, and found someone with whom he could discuss her. But they knew nothing. They did know, however, that Copper, the twin sister, had applied to come back on to the nursing staff, and that she had intimated that she would be resuming her duties in three or four weeks' time. No, they had no idea where she was at the moment, but had as a forwarding address that of her last appointment, with Mrs. Brand.

Back to Sylvia. He worried round the fact that to let Sylvia into this meant endless argument, and would probably gain him nothing. Certainly not at this hour of the night.

He abandoned it until the next day, then telephoned Sylvia and asked if she knew where Copper was. She sounded delicately surprised that he should want to know where she was, and recommended him to try the post office, in case she had left a forwarding address.

'Didn't she leave one with you?' he demanded.

'Andrew, darling, don't bark at me,' she complained. 'Of course she did!'

'Then what was it?'

'If you shout, I shall hang up,' she warned him. 'The address she left with me was your address, of course. She worked for you last,' and with that sweet reminder came the string of questions he had been dreading. Why did he want to know? Of what interest was

311

Copper to him now? And so on.

'You forget she's supposed to be on the nursing staff of my hospital,' he reminded Sylvia.

'No, darling. You're dreadfully out of date. She left St. Joseph's months ago.'

'But she appears to have renewed her appointment and they don't know where she is,' he told her.

'But why should they worry one of the governors about the address of a mere nurse?' she asked.

He winced. Magda was, after all, a 'mere nurse'. How Sylvia rubbed it in.

'They're not worrying me. I want to know,' he said.

There was the tiniest pause, then Sylvia said, in a small, clear voice:

'But why, Andrew?'

Something snapped inside him. He had a revulsion of feeling for Sylvia that appalled him. This was the woman he had been half-inclined to marry, for how long? Her possessiveness had never worried him before, but had, in fact, rather amused him. It gave him something to do, parry-and-thrust all the time, that staved off the sugar sweetness of those occasions when he spent time with Sylvia. Now it was a nuisance, and something worse. It was something to be afraid of, in the years to come, if he were so mad as to marry her.

'Oh, not now, Sylvia. I'm sorry, my dear, but I'm in a terrible hurry. See you later,' and he hung up on her.

Next, he applied to the nursing home. It was not a successful long distance call, but in the end he found out what he wanted. That they had heard nothing, knew nothing, and were considerably put out that a patient who was in there for six months should apply so strenuously to be allowed out for two or three days and then vanish, with no word. Andrew put down the telephone, frustrated.

Sylvia, on the other hand, was more than frustrated. She was frightened.

She telephoned through to Max and told him to cancel all her appointments for that day, then rang for her personal maid and insisted on having a special facial at that moment. Then she put on her newest dress and hat, a pale dove grey that enormously became her, and the dark fur coat that had impressed Magda so much. She looked very nice, and she knew it. She could do no more, other than remove the anxious look in her eyes, and that she would do when she saw Andrew, she promised herself.

She had difficulty in persuading the chauffeur to take the car out. Some of the lanes, he said, were impassable.

'Then drive me back into the town and back to the Mount by the main road,' she snapped.

Nevertheless, it was a longer journey than she had anticipated, and when she arrived at the Mount, it was to find that Andrew had gone out somewhere.

She said she would wait, and sat tenaciously in the drawing-room, shivering with cold. Hobbs hurriedly had the fire lit, but the great room was still cold when after what seemed hours, Andrew came in.

He stared a little at her. She fancied that there was a fleeting look of pleasure which fled as she looked up. She imagined that coming into the room and seeing a woman sitting there, he had at once expected it to be someone else. She couldn't tell why she should think that, and imagined that it was because her mind was taken up with the thought of Magda Rushton. Firmly she decided to put the girl out of her thoughts.

'Andrew!' she said, getting up and going to him.

He came in and thoughtfully closed the door. She put her hands on his shoulders and

314

looked up at him. There was a drift of perfume, a teasing scent she always wore, and he registered the thought that it now meant nothing to him, where not so long ago he had found that he liked it, even if he had not been able to summon up any more definite feeling about it. He registered, too, the fact that she looked nice, but that fact, also, left him unmoved.

'Andrew, say something,' she said, smiling uncertainly

'Why have you come, Sylvia? It's an appalling day to come out. Is anything wrong?'

'Wrong? What a curious thing to say,' she said, with misgiving. 'Andrew, I had to talk to you, and you hung up on me.'

He sighed a little.

'Oh, Sylvia, my dear—' He made a helpless gesture with his hands. 'What on earth could you have to say, to do this? It can wait, can't it? I'm cold and tired, and to tell you the honest truth, I don't want to talk about anything just now.'

If she needed any confirmation that something had gone wrong, after that disastrous telephone call, then this was it. But being Sylvia, she couldn't take it without a fight.

'Be an angel and ring for tea. I'd love a cup and I expect you would, too. I promise not to be a nuisance,' she smiled, sauntering over to the fireplace and warming herself at the now blazing fire. 'Hobbs was nicer to me than you are—see what a lovely fire he got going.'

He stared morosely at her, and rang the bell for tea.

'Funny,' she said, making conversation, and fighting down the desperate sensation of failing more and more every minute, 'how long these great rooms take to get warmed up.'

'Yes,' he said, taking an interest in the conversation at last. 'I'm used to it, and I wouldn't have it changed. But I suppose you want your hot-house atmosphere and central heating for the rest of your life.'

'How well you know me, Andrew,' she said, in a low voice. 'You know, I never thought you'd consent to have the Mount centrally heated.'

He nodded, grimly.

'And you were right, Sylvia. I never will. Open fireplaces for me, even if I freeze.'

She felt her face going blank.

'But you just said—'

He took her cold hands in his.

'I just said, my dear, that whereas you'd always want your central heating, the Mount will never be changed.'

316

She felt her face dropping. It was curious, this sensation of her facial muscles, as if the frozen feeling inside her were spreading outwards. He watched it, too, and saw, fascinated, that she looked ageing when she couldn't get her own way, and when she forgot to smile gaily.

'Then you . . . don't love me, Andrew?' she asked, with a break in her voice.

He turned away. Odd, he thought, how he'd hurt Magda without turning a hair, and yet he couldn't bear to see the havoc he was causing in Sylvia's life. He supposed it was because Magda had built up such an impregnable façade and it tantalised him to the extent of driving him to try and break it down. Sylvia, on the other hand, had no façade to protect her. She was so sure of getting her own way that she was utterly defenceless when someone stood up to her, as he was suddenly doing.

'Sylvia, I once told you (and you will remember it well), that if I wanted to marry you, I wouldn't court you, but I would just ask you outright. I hope you saw in that what I intended you to see—that I would pay you the compliment of straight talking without frills. The frills of courtship are not for you, and certainly not for me. Now I want to pay the same compliment to you, and to tell you that at this last moment I've found that a marriage between us would be a mistake, and that being the case, I wouldn't dream of landing you into it.'

'Andrew, but that would be the risk I would take.'

'And I also, if I allowed it to happen,' he said, with a little twisted smile. 'I mean that if anyone were going to be hurt, the odds were that I would be hurt just as much as you—if not more.'

She didn't follow the drift of that—or didn't want to.

She pouted at him, and her blue eyes filled with easy tears.

'Andrew, you're being beastly, and I don't understand. What have I done? You've been leading me to expect marriage, right up till this last few days, and now suddenly—what's happened?'

'Oh, Sylvia, don't be ridiculous,' he said, tiring of the conversation.

His boredom terrified and angered her. It had always done so.

'You've fallen for someone else,' she accused. 'I know—it's that ghastly nurse person! So she did it after all!'

He whirled round on her, closing her

mouth with his fingers, and holding her in a vice-like grip while he spoke.

'Sylvia, I beg of you—don't spoil this meeting of ours by saying a word about anyone else. I beg of you!'

The tea came in, and she broke free. They watched in silence as Hobbs wheeled the trolley and having set it in position, mended the fire leisurely.

When he went out, Sylvia started again, pouring tea and talking quickly and decisively.

'I warned you, Andrew, all along. She set out to get you, and it seems she's taken you in. Oh, how could you be such a fool! A little nobody like that, to be mistress of a place like this!'

'Sylvia!' Andrew said, warningly.

'I know what it is,' she rushed on. 'It's just because she's so like Elizabeth, isn't it? If I'd had red hair, it would have been me, instead, wouldn't it? Oh, what a fool I've been—I could just have got my hair dyed—'

'Sylvia!' he shouted. 'Don't! Don't dare talk like that about the two women who meant so much to me—'

It was out. Magda coupled with Elizabeth. In that moment, Sylvia saw that she had lost everything, and nothing could do anything to

319

change him—nothing could do any good, and at the same time, nothing could do any harm, now, it seemed. Magda had achieved the coveted prize, the rousing in Andrew Debenham that look, that special look in his eyes, that had been there for Elizabeth, but never for herself.

'As to her being mistress of this place,' Andrew said, in a quieter voice, 'if she would consent to that, if she would only consent to that, no one would be more pleased and proud than I. At least, she loved the place.'

'And so do I,' Sylvia averred, automatically.

He shook his head.

'No, my dear. I accepted, long ago, the thought that if I ever married you, I should have all my work cut out to keep your interfering little paws off the Mount. That was understood. You've been itching to change the place since you first saw it.'

They drank their tea in silence. A curious sort of anti-climax had taken the place of that little scene that had promised to be a first-rate row if he had let it.

'Well,' Sylvia said, at last, with her final barb poised with deadly aim, 'I still don't know which of the ghastly twins managed to ensnare you, Andrew. You were asking on the telephone about Copper!'

His face set in the cold lines which Magda knew so well, and his voice, when he spoke, made Sylvia think of chips of ice.

'I merely wanted to know where she was, in order to trace Magda. I suppose it isn't just possible that you have any idea where they went, have you, Sylvia?'

She smiled.

'No, but if I had, it isn't likely that I'd tell you, Andrew. For your own sake.'

'Magda was ill. She'd only just come from a nursing home, and she didn't go back there. She's got to be found!'

'Nursing home? How could she afford that?' Sylvia said, with narrowed eyes.

'She couldn't, of course. My aunt arranged it before she died. It was her wish. She thought a lot of Magda. Didn't you know about that, Sylvia?'

'No, I didn't know about that,' Sylvia said, with clenched teeth. She felt as though the last door had closed against her. Mrs. Debenham had been her enemy in life, and in death she hadn't relinquished her advantage in the fight.

Sylvia got up.

'Funny, I made a journey to the town and back, in order to get here, I wanted to see you so much, Andrew. You don't know how much you mean to me, yet, do you?'

He had had enough of the argument.

'Then, Sylvia,' he said, ignoring the last sentence, 'you'd better go right away, before dark, or you'll never get home.'

'I'm going now,' she said, lightly. 'And when, later on, you've realised your folly, and want to come back to me, I'll be waiting. You and I are selfish and hard, and eminently suited to each other. We've known each other for years and never quarrelled, and we never will. And that's something. It's spice, compared with the sugar your little nurse person is offering you. Think it over, my boy.'

Magda, too, was thinking about Sylvia at that moment.

Jim and Copper were on each side of her bed, and they had something on their minds, and the first thought that leapt into Magda's tired brain was that Sylvia and Copper had been in touch with each other, and that Sylvia had been unpleasant. Although what Sylvia could do to be unpleasant to her now, was difficult to imagine. Sylvia, and Andrew Debenham and the Mount, seemed terribly far away.

'Magda, you're not *trying* to get well,' Copper said, piercing Magda's thoughts in the way she had.

'What are you worrying about?' Magda smiled. 'I'm out of the pneumonia stage, and all I've got to do is recuperate. And you haven't any expenses on my account. Or have you?' she asked, in sudden alarm.

'Oh, no,' Copper said, hurriedly.

'Where are you two staying?' Magda frowned, remembering suddenly that it was in a hotel that she had collapsed.

'In a smaller hotel,' Jim said, firmly, blinking a little behind his horn-rimmed glasses in his earnestness. 'And the expense doesn't matter. You see, although Copper's been so rude about my discoveries, the one I've made is bringing me in quite a bit of money. Oh,' he said, as astonishment chased itself across Magda's pale, thin face, 'I don't pretend I'm wealthy, you know, but comfortable. Pretty comfortably off, in fact.'

'I'm glad, Jim. So very glad,' Magda smiled. 'Is it any use asking what you've discovered, or is it terribly technical?'

'Oh, well, you see, about three miles above the Tropic of Ca—' he began, eagerly, and then broke off with a smile. 'No, it's too technical. In layman's language, it's a sort of weed that produces a rare drug—Well, doesn't sound very exciting, but it is in the scientific

323

world, I suppose.'

Copper said, impatiently, 'Never mind that, Jim. Magda will want to know about our wedding.' Turning to Magda, she said, 'We can't get married till you're well enough to give me away. You're all I've got by way of family.'

Magda at once looked distressed.

'Oh, darling, I'm trying so hard to get well, but I'm so tired.'

Jim broke in, 'Now, don't you worry, Magda. The thing is, we're thinking of going back to Africa, and we want you to come with us, and you must be strong enough to travel.'

Magda shook her head, biting her lips hard, her dark eyes glistening with unshed tears.

'You're sweet, both of you, and I appreciate it all, but I don't want to go abroad. I couldn't. I want to stay in this country.'

'Oh, but why?' Copper, ever tactless, demanded. 'You've got nothing to stay here for now.'

Jim frowned at her, but she said it before she noticed his look. Magda looked wounded, and closed her eyes.

'Have I said something?' Copper asked.

'No, darling,' Magda murmured. 'You're right, of course. I've nothing to stay here for now.'

'Then why don't you come with us?' Copper urged.

'No. I want to stay here,' Magda whispered. 'In England. I'll go on nursing. Where I'll be needed. I must be needed.'

'But I need you,' Copper wailed.

'Listen, Copper,' Magda said. 'Why don't you two go off quietly and get married, without me? No, listen first! I want it that way. I'd love to be there, but it'll be ages before I'm well enough. I feel that, in my heart. I don't want to keep you two waiting. You've waited so long. Eight years is too long. Go off and get married, at least, even if you won't sail till I'm up and about. Do that, for me, will you?'

Copper hesitated, and at last she and Jim agreed, and Magda seemed more rested.

The hospital was uncomfortably full, and one day when Copper and Jim came in with the other visitors, Magda seemed more restless than usual.

'I've had a talk with the doctor,' she told them, 'and he tells me that I've still got to get in that six months' rest, if not more. The pneumonia pulled me down even lower, and it'll be months and months before I'm really fit.'

Copper's dismay was only too apparent,

though Jim managed characteristically to mask his feelings.

'So I want you two to listen to me, because I've got a proposition to make. You remember the nursing home and that arrangement?'

Copper gasped in relief.

'Oh, yes, you could go back there!' she cried.

'Wait a minute,' Magda begged. 'First of all, has anyone cancelled the arrangement?'

Copper and Jim exchanged glances.

'I don't think so,' they said.

'Does . . . does Andrew Debenham know where I am?' Magda said, stumbling, as always, over his name.

Copper flushed, and said nothing. It was Jim who gave the denial.

Magda nodded, at once pleased and disappointed.

'Well, if you can guarantee that he won't know I've gone back, I'll go back to the nursing home, and I want you two to sail at once. Before I get too used to seeing you both around,' she smiled, but there was a break in her voice.

Jim acted for them. It was he who got on to the nursing home, and having ascertained that Mr. Debenham had not yet cancelled the arrangement, he asked if Magda could now come back for her rest cure, merely explaining briefly that she had had one more visit to make before she returned, and it was during that visit that she had contracted pneumonia and been whisked off to a nearby hospital. She was, he told them, now well enough to be removed.

Magda was satisfied, but insisted that they book their sailing and show her the tickets before she consented to make the journey.

'You're sure they won't tell Mr. Debenham?' she pressed, anxiously.

'I don't suppose they'll be that interested,' Jim grinned cheerfully. He was immensely pleased with what he called his own astuteness, although he had misgivings about Andrew's being pleased, since Andrew had seemingly not bothered to answer their telephone call. But it was worth a trial.

They installed Magda in the nursing home two days before Christmas, and brought her their gifts and had a little impromptu party at her bedside.

It was a day full of emotions for her, for when she had been there last, old Mrs. Debenham had been alive, and there was still a possibility of seeing Andrew again.

'Copper, there's something I want to ask you, before you go away,' Magda said, urgently, while Jim was talking to a nurse. 'Something I haven't asked you before, but I want to know, and please be honest with me.'

They had only a few minutes left before they were due to go, and Copper wondered with misgivings what Magda was going to spring on her.

'All right. Fire away.'

'When I was ill, terribly ill, who was by my bed? You and Jim? Or was the man . . . the doctor?'

Copper, despite her usual blundering methods and lack of perspicacity, recognised that Magda was really asking if it had been Andrew who had been there that night when she had been calling for him. She struggled for a moment, knowing that the answer was no, and that it had been Jim. But even Copper realised that Magda wouldn't thank Jim for impersonating Andrew for her, much as she liked her new brother-in-law.

'It was . . . the doctor,' she managed, not meeting her sister's eyes.

'I see,' Magda whispered, and when Copper looked up, she was frightened at the grey shade in her sister's face.

Magda brightened, however, before they said good-bye, and neither Copper nor Jim knew what it cost her.

"'Bye, Mrs. Kinmere,' Magda smiled. 'Be a good wife, and lean on Jim as you've leaned on me. Look after her, Jim. She's a brat, but she's very dear to me.'

And when they had gone, the tremendous truth flashed over her, almost stunning her. For years and years she'd been weighed down by the responsibility of looking after Copper, and now Copper had gone. Suddenly. Just like that, in a matter of weeks. And her loneliness was a new kind of loneliness, the loneliness of the sick, in a white bed in a room kept for sickness, with the knowledge that there is no one left belonging. *Belonging*.

Magda let go of her last defences, and relaxed, lying there crying heart-brokenly, one arm flung across her eyes. Outside, small voices piped a Christmas carol, and further down the street a brass band was playing a different Christmas tune. Both mocked her, and so did the soft pad-pad sounds of the snow on the windows.

A hand, cold but firm, closed over her free one. She looked up, through tear-drenched eyes, and saw a man, in a dark overcoat.

'Jim! Oh, Jim, it's unlucky to come back,' she said, brokenly. And then she recognised the man.

'*Andrew!*' she whispered.

He said something incoherent, about the nursing home people ringing him up to say that he'd like to know of a return of one of their patients, and then, on this incredible day, the still more unexpected happened. His voice broke, and he was on his knees by the bedside, his face buried in her glorious hair.

Some time later, a nurse knocked, and came in, propping the door wide, for two porters to bring in an enormous Christmas tree in a tub. Boxes of decorations came in, and a lot of gaily wrapped parcels. Magda stared, but surprise no longer lay in her face. She looked dazed.

'What's that for?' she asked.

'Mr. Debenham says we're to come back presently and dress the tree for you, and doctor says you may have a little Christmas party in here if you promise to keep calm.'

She watched them go, laughing and merry, and turned back to Andrew.

'You've been hearing about the Debenham Christmas,' he managed. 'We can't have it at the Mount, so I've brought a little sample of it for you here.'

She couldn't take her eyes off his face. The tenderness that had been there for Sylvia Brand and for his aunt, was as nothing to this new, deep feeling that began in his eyes, and deepened in his smile, that lovely tender smile that she had never even seen before.

'Magda,' he whispered. 'Aunt Laura was wiser than I. She wanted this, but I was too stupid to read all that she intended I should read in that last letter of hers.'

'I don't understand,' she whispered.

'Magda, my dearest dear, you said something to me once, while you were nursing me. Do you remember? You said that in spite of everything, you'd stay with me as long as I needed you. Was that a promise?'

She nodded, smiling a little at the recollection.

'Then will you marry me? You see,' he said, his voice uncertain, and not like the voice of the old arrogant Andrew at all, 'I shall need you always. In fact, for ever.'